Parthian Stranger 5 Belarus

STEWART N. JOHNSON

Order this book online at www.trafford.com
or email orders@trafford.com

Most Trafford titles are also available at major online book retailers.

Printed in the United States of America.

ISBN: 978-1-4907-4105-5 (sc)
ISBN: 978-1-4907-4107-9 (hc)
ISBN: 978-1-4907-4106-2 (e)

Library of Congress Control Number: 2014911858

Trafford rev. 07/15/2014

www.trafford.com

North America & international
toll-free: 1 888 232 4444 (USA & Canada)
fax: 812 355 4082

ACKNOWLEDGEMENT

I want to thank Breanna B. Gibson, for allowing me to
be creative, and believing in my work, this was the most
difficult book to date to complete, thanks for being there.
For my wife, Penny, her computer skills, make
this book possible, she also did the cover,
nice drawing, thanks for all that you do.

CONTENTS

Chapter 1   Reorder of wives..1

Chapter 2   "Jack needs a helper, anyone?".......................20

Chapter 3   Let's find Keisha and make new friends 43

Chapter 4   Assembly to Belarus......................................55

Chapter 5   Special call for help 78

Chapter 6   Operation super cell blow up..........................94

Chapter 7   Rescue Victoria, Russian style......................107

Chapter 8   King of Belarus and Spies 131

Chapter 9   A day out on the back 400..............................145

Chapter 10 Flash backs 163

Chapter 11 Midnight games 187

Chapter 12 King's Review 213

Chapter 13 Meeting of the Spies......................................229

CH 1

Reorder of wives

Jack awoke to the buzzing of noise from his open window, he reached up to close it, to silence, looking around at both Sara and on the other side was Tia, he was in the middle of this new trio, much to Sara's liking, the two girls were virtually inseparable.

Down in the kitchen, a new regime was in place, to the once out of place Maria Ingles is the new house mother, as she care for Samantha's baby Sam, and Chelsea, Sara's child, while she waits the fate of her four other children, which actually only affects one. The police are still trying to find her estrange husband. Maria cooks incredible meals and has lots of cooked foods available, all the time. She has organized the kitchen, her story to Jack was, if her sister could take her responsibility, then she was off the hook, and would see her husband once again, however, once Henry Troussant the monarch of the family found out that Enzo Bonn and Jack Cash were the same, his next goal was to unite his family with US's next great spy. Jack could marry as many women as he liked. Henry knew immediately, that one of them was going to be his eldest daughter, sparing no cost to her already sizable family, his actions, took her away, from the husband. Her husband has since not been seen or heard from, her children, are in hiding and have since panicked all because she chooses not to marry

1

Jack. Maria was a disgrace; she was dumped in a dumpster as her Papa told her she was dead to him. For Jack, it meant for Maria a new husband and new demands, her and him did a good session together, she got through with it, in over three hours, and afterwards was ready for more, afterwards, she said, "It was the best lovemaking she ever received, and at forty she said, "I'll have four more children." That's why she is the happiest woman in the house, in the compound. Next up are the two tall long haired brunettes, both Christina and Cara, spent the weekend with Jack as he made love to them both a good twenty hours, afterwards they sat down with Jack to talk about their future, as Jack asked, "If you could be anything you want, as this life has to offer, what would it be and why?"

Cara spoke first, "Right here in your bed for the rest of my life, but if I had a chance to get a hobby while you're away, I'd like to attend Medical school?"

"Really, that's what Sara's family has been trying to get her to do."

"Well you can't force someone to go to school, No; I would do it, purely on saving your life."

"How so, what do you mean?" asked Jack.

"Take for instance, how many times have you been in the hospital?"

"Several, I guess?"

"Well that's not common, so I want to be by your bedside to serve you your final days."

"That's touching", said Jack.

"It's the truth, I was raised a Roman catholic school girl, and I was a virgin when you came along, but for all that time I spent learning and praying, the one factor for all of this was a man would come into my life and in one night completely change it forever as I know it now, and that guy is you Jack Cash, so you have me, as you will for the rest of my life, because I doubt an event like that will ever come along again, and besides I made a promise to myself, when that man who ever laid with me, then that was the man for me, regardless if you listen to Tia, yes it was our decision, to allow you to do what you did, but the sheer act was monumental in anything I was ever aware of." As she adds, "I knew I needed to be part of that, and that was like a pipe was pushed through, I took it easily and will so for the rest of my life, but it was all that and much more."

Jack thought about it and said,"Alright I want you to go back to school?"

She shook her head and said, "No, what for?"

"Well you said you wanted to go to medical school."

"New Orleans University has no medical school, I was going there for general studies, as it pertained to the church, and I was going to become a nun."

"Oh, I guess I did change your course."

"Yes, now it's on a path for you, so if you know a good medical school, see if you could get me there."

"Any preferences?"

"I have none; I'm at whatever you choose."

Jack checked his phone, and only one name was the best, John's Hopkins, it had a wait list and you had strict credentials, as Jack made a call to Lisa, who made a call to her boss, and at that very same night Jack had his answer, he told her, she was thrilled, and due to time constraints, and the fact she had no family, as she was an orphan, Jack and Cara, married at the garden in the courtyard, and that night, was all for her, they consummated it and then some. For the threesome, it was actually her sister Christina, who married Jack later that night, as she told him a similar story, of how they grew up in an orphanage, and that they were destined to become nun's, but after the encounter with Jack, she told him she wanted to be a researcher, scientist, and so it was set up for her to go to M.I.T., after Jack and Christina consummated their wedding and then some, the two were ready to embark on a new adventure. The next day they were off, to school. I drove them to the airport, and that was the last we have heard from them, although they both call Jack every night to tell him that they love him. Next up is Daphne Nicoletti, she and Enzo Bonn were an item for awhile, her family didn't like that he was a cop, that liked the mob life, and the mob life wanted more of him, but as anyone, he was expendable, and for that fact Daphne has fallen off the map, so much so she took a quick marriage, on December 6th, she was a troubled girl, but knew one thing, she had found the man she wanted to be with for the rest of her life, and for Jack that meant he had a sure thing anytime and anywhere, but she knew the mob life, and boundaries, she took up where Samantha left off, and took over the fishing business, and Mark works directly for her, it was a vacuum of cash, the fishing charters, she works with Tia, the two are passionate about the business, even considering building a second boat, life is good. Daphne has dedicated herself to Jack and the family, and even took the name of Enzo, for a last name. She is a regular at the table, She and Maria Ingles lay with Jack, one night and it flip flops back and forth, between Us and them, to share Jack, mixed in with the two nannies, Jen and Monica the six of Us equally.

Next up was baby Isabella, who just turned 19, she was the love creature Jack was longing for, a virgin, till Jack took her, and then it was over, she married Jack, in the morning of the 7th of December, and spent the rest of the day in bed and then a week to recover, she went back to NOLA, and is trying to calm the family down with a June wedding, Randy is her bodyguard, is at her side.

Next up was Lindsay Wagner, a young blonde hair, blue eyed, she had med sized breasts, her long hair touched them, she was a virgin, when Jack plowed her, into loving and easily consent to marriage, just because of that one act, she too professed her love, and she had advantages, the best schools, and no one she could connect with, she was technically rich, she came from a big family, on December 8th, she became number 12, or 11 who's counting, we also found out that once Jack decides to marry, he has six months to do it. For most of the girls that were well loved and respected, they chose a private agreement with Jack, and a big wedding later. Next up was Samantha White, another Blonde haired, Blue eyed, Model, same thing no solid prospects, and a superb girl, extreme athletic, super in the class, as a senior she was going to be an Attorney, after she graduates, it was on to LSU, which Jack signed off with it, she let alone took Jack all night, only one other girl was able to do that, it was Melanie, she and India stuck around to the very last day, India married, December 10th, and took Jack half a day, and hit the jackpot, she found out she was pregnant, as she rested the whole next week, to discover the changes were made, she went back to school with a body guard, Brad Thomas. Then last to leave was Melanie, she was the gopher, she went back and forth from the dock to the house, she loved the house on the hill, and like the others she came from money, but the money she grew up with wasn't this lavish house, a boat, jet skies, a helicopter, and all of her new found friends, all insatiable like her, she too was into the fish charter business, but was now a certified travel agent, and took an office in the boat house, in June after she graduates, it will become a full time occupation, she had a long drawn out ceremony, but after that it was three days straight, before they got it out of their systems. She just left yesterday, now it's the four of us, I mean the six of us. Sara stopped writing in her journal and put it away.

Jack was in Quantico this week, finishing up the new HQ for the spy academy.

Jack stood at the door it was Monday morning, the construction workers were still going at it, he closed the door, to silence, went by to see Erica Meyers hard at work, to plop down in a chair by her for Jack to say, "So how about after this meeting you and I fool around?"

"I'd love to honey, I have no time, I wish I could get Claire Montfork back, now look at what I need to go through today, I received a call from a woman, who is the wife of Florida State Senator, Jim Huggins, saying that their daughter Keisha was taken last night, from her dorm room, at Jacksonville state, and would like to know if you could find her and get her back?"

"Sure what's the urgency? Wait what about all I needed to do up here?" said Jack.

"Well it can wait, She, the mother is at the university now, and no one has last seen her since late last night, and no one is talking to her, here is some Intel for you," as she slid the folder over to him.

Jack opens the folder to see the lovely photo of Keisha, and the fact that she is a world class basketball player, she has missed her morning's practice, early CID reports indicate no foul play, and search of her room, revealed no sexual activity, also in the folder was a sheet that read, "Redneck bikers, is a criminal element that has terrorized Jacksonville for the last twenty years?"

"What's this?" said Jack fluttering the piece of paper in the air."

"I don't know I thought it would be a lead?" said Erica.

"Nice try, if it were them they would have made some noise and why do they need a coed, there are plenty of women available for that, this has a sole person behind this, either a classmate or..."

They both look up at the time, to see it was past the time for the scheduled meeting, as she said, "Figure it out yourself, but be safe." And got up, and motioned for Jack to follow.

Jack followed her into the room, as everyone rose, for her to say, "Please sit down, I need to make this brief, for most of you know who I am, and what I do here, but in the next month all that will change, because the person we support, Jack Cash has been chosen to go to the United Nations, to be part of the International Spy program, working solely for the International council, what that means for you, is one the Strike team needs to be on the ready for the flight out in two weeks, then during that stay for three weeks, as for you, the admin group, we have another task at hand, were forging on with the academy, as approved by the President of the United States, as our budget has been approved and ratified, but allow me the honor to present to you our leader, Mister Jack Cash. Jack heard the applause, to see Lisa in the back ground, he smiled at her, to stand at the podium, to say, "Thank you for that warm reception, I know some of you and others I'd like to get to know as well, the future is a funny thing, just awhile back I was just a bounty hunter, to now the title of International Super Spy, the word has been tossed around a bit, but never stuck with me, I'd like to thank each of you for your dedication to helping me get better, to realize my own dreams and to help me accomplish them, the goal of the academy is to churn out more like me, both men and women, our first class is in two months, so keep up the good work and see you soon."

They all stood and clapped as Jack and Erica exited, back into her office, he sat while she faxed the form in, to turn to toss another pamphlet at him to say, "All you need to do is check the boxes, in addition, Brian and Jim have included one of their own. "I need this back as soon as possible, thanks" she said, as Lisa enters and closes the door, to say, "Alright where do you want all of your cases?"

"She is talking about the", he paused as Lisa looked at him, to say, "Let's go outside and talk". They leave, to see Tami, who greets them with a folder to say, "Some more requests, this time local, in Washington."

Lisa hands hers to Jack, who collects them both up, for Tami to say, "No, one is for you and the other is yours, as sent over by Ramon."

"Right I got you, Jack hands the other file to her, to say, "Coordinate the cases with Tami."

"Will do, see you soon", said a smiling Lisa.

Jack opens his folder to see it was a dead agent, shot in the back, he was an FBI agent and to go see Doctor Elizabeth Snyder, chief Medical officer, and coroner, in Washington D.C."

Jack folds it up, to go back, in to see Erica, to pick up his pamphlet, to hear her say, "Take a look at this budget forms, for twenty three base organizations, and their budgets, in addition is the salary forms for all personnel, it is based on time in your service and status, it equivalent to a rank in the officers corps, for some it's a promotion and for others it's a pay decrease."

"I don't want that, find out from Lisa what they make, and then pay them that" said Jack.

"That's what I did, and their gonna to be making a lot more, what I meant was the working pool of people, called floaters?"

"It's really nothing for you to worry about, pay them a flat fee "said Jack. He was ready to go.

"I'll do that, I sure wish Claire was here to help me" hinting at him, he had none of it, to say, "No worries, I'll go follow this lead up, then off to Florida, can you have the plane ready for me and the team assembled, except Mike he still is on a month's leave?"

"Yes, he is gone on leave, I'll send the strike team down there with you?" said Erica.

"What is the status on Dana and Julie or Blythe or Dylan or Roxy?"

"Well I don't know about any Dana or Julie, Blythe is still at training and will be ready for your trip to Geneva, and Dylan is working for Lisa, and Roxy was the floater that made it through, she is yours all yours" exclaimed Erica.

"Great, in addition to her what or how about you find me Bridgett Owens, and Tiffany Bordeaux, they mentioned to me that they were from Quantico and see if they could help out."

Jack leaves her office with his hands full; to see Tami for him to say, "Continuing collecting information and send it down to me, whose cart is that?" asked Jack, looking through the clear window, and pointing.

"It's yours if you want it?" said Tami, smiling at him.

"Have you seen Trixie?"

"Yeah, I think she is getting ready for this trip to Florida."

Jack was on the move, outside, he took off in the cart, past the obstacle course that was using cranes to set the logs in place. Jack continued up the hill to the hangers, to see someone motioning for him to park inside, as Brian was standing watching the prop plane trying to pick up his car, the Charger, it fluttered and was spinning as Jack stands next to him, to say, "Why don't you have wings that protrude out, and a tail, to give it a glide path, to say, "Hey Brian, can I use the Mercedes?"

"Yep, it's in the other hanger", Jack took to the outside, to the other hanger, went inside, found the car, got in, fired it up, and off he went, past Brian, and down the hill, left through the Marines part of the base, to slow to see female officers all over the place, to think, "How an bout we sponsor an event for those girls, call it Global Games", thinks Jack as he exited the base, and into the flow of traffic, he hit the N and the license plate showed, he hit the button till diplomatic ones came up, then off on to the freeway.

Jack took his exit, and doubled back, to the chief's medical officers office, and parked, he got out, to say, "Lock and secure." Jack went inside, to a door that had a metal and object detector, he walked right through, as the guard said, "Go ahead."

Jack went to the main offices to see a young lady, to say, "Can I see Doctor Snyder please?"

An old man appeared to say, "How can I help you son?"

"Sir, I was looking for Doctor Elizabeth Snyder."

"That's my daughter, she is room 1-B, I'd wear a mask it's pretty brutal, in there."

Jack takes it and puts it on, and enters, to hear a woman speaking so passionately about her autopsy, that mesmerized Jack, as he entered, to the table, that had blood everywhere, to a woman of good and petite size, with her face covered in a mask, goggles and a visor, he could see her eyes were alive and on fire, from her passions she displayed for her, to say, "So sir, can you step off to the right or left, your blocking my light."

"You mean move my head" said Jack.

"That too, so what brings you down here?"

"To find out what happen to this man?"

"From the initial looks he fell into a vat of lye, now if he was pushed or dove in himself, I won't know till later, I can tell you his organs are all gunked up, with a real bad drug habit."

"Sorry to hear that" said Jack.

"So am I, he must have been about fifty."

"What did you say?" asked Jack.

"He was fifty", Jack looked at his file to see that it was in fact for Lisa and not his, his was a twenty three year old female, her mother reported her as missing."

Jack said, "I guess I was wrong for bothering you."

"It wasn't a bother, if you have a moment, I could sure use a coffee, buy me one?"

"Sure" said Jack as he followed her out to the laundry area, as she removed her visor, then her goggles, then her mask, then her gloves, as she pulled the rubber band out of her hair, to let it flow in one big motion, and for the first time, he got to see this real beautiful girl, with stunning blue eyes and magnificent blonde hair, to the incredible smile on her face, he was enamored by her, he actually stuttered, till he said, "Alright" for some reason, he discarded the mask, to follow her to the cafeteria, and once inside, Jack bought a large coffee black for her, and a coffee, with lemon wedges for his, to follow her to a seat next to her.

"What, is it with you", she said looking at him.

"Nothing" he said coyly back at her.

"Well the moment I saw you, you just kind of inspired me."

"Really because the moment I saw you it was your sweet scent" said Jack, flirting with her.

"Of blood", she said.

"Maybe I like that smell, especially on a lovely woman like yourself." As Jack pulled his phone, and dialed Lisa up, as he smiled at Elizabeth to hear, "There you are, we got our cases mixed up, I have your file do you have mine?"

"Yes "he said and added, when I see you I'll give it back to you, Lisa looked it over to say "Have you met this Doctor Snyder?"

"Yes I did, the guy is in waiting for you, are you coming here, to get it?" said Jack.

"Yes I could come now?" said Lisa.

"Great, I'll leave it in the main office." For a smiling Elizabeth to say, "Who was that?"

"Oh, one of my colleagues, she will come here, well listen, this was fun, I Imagine she will be here soon to bother you, so it was nice to meet you."

"Wait, where are you going in such a hurry, do you want my number?"

"Sure, what is it?" he says.

She gives him her cell number, to say, "What is yours, you know for a late night talk on the phone?"

"How late is late" asked Jack.

"Well you can call me anytime" she said, to add, "So what is your number?"

Jack thought about it, as he spun his phone numbers around to the least used number, he gave it to her, as she got up, Jack felt her arms, as he took her in his arms he kissed her on the lips, it lingered till he heard a man's voice, say "Doctor Snyder. There is a lady here to see you." Said her father, sternly.

"I told her, I thought you were in the cafeteria."

Jack broke the kiss to leave her to see Lisa, for Jack to say, "Another missing person case?"

"Yeah, I think so; were you just kissing this doctor?"

"Yep, and thanks for interrupting me, it was worth it", said Jack leaving.

"So you're the famous Doctor Elizabeth Snyder, how long have you known Jack?" asks Lisa.

"Oh we just met" she said with a smile, to add, "What did you say his name was?"

"Jack Cash."

"I've heard that name before."

"You might of; he was the one who helped the President get re-elected."

"Oh yeah, he was the one who rescued all those women."

"That's right, and that is where he was going to find another to release from captive" said Lisa.

"He could rescue me anytime he wants."

Jack was at the steps to the police station when at the side of the curb was a woman, who was crying, so Jack went to her, to say, "Is everything all right with you Ma'am?"

"Yes sir, I'm just so happy, that my daughter has been found."

"Really how so" inquired Jack.

"Her name is Tiffany Seltzer, she was in Puerto Rico, and was found, today?"

Jack looked at his folder to see her name, and went the other direction, around the building to his car, to see a gang of young black men on the opposite corner, harassing another young woman, he didn't even think and walked across the street to say, "Hey leave that woman alone?", a tall black man pulled out a gun and shot Jack in the heart, as Jack came on faster, as he gave them a flying kick, to the group, as some of the police officers, began to watch as Jack was defending the young woman's honor, as he kicked the knees out, and fighting with his hands, as three ran off, Jack pulled his weapon, and shot one in the leg, as he went further into the projects, more men came out with guns as they began to shoot at him, he held his position, to say, "I know my next project is to come back here and have some fun, he pulled out a zip tie, to cinch up the shot boy, as he picked up the gun, and went back to see eight others laid out as the police force, surrounded Jack, for him to zip tie the rest of them up, he pulled his phone to call Lisa."

She was busy listening to Doctor Snyder, when her phone rang, she saw it was Jack, she ignored him and she put it away, thinking he wanted the dear old Doctor for himself, only to hear, "There is something going on outside." Said her father.

The men were screaming, "Were, going to sue your ass, mother, fucker, you die white boy."

"You first," as Jack put the gun to the fearless kids head and pulled the trigger. The young man slumped down, as all stopped in their tracks; silence was heard, for Jack to say,

"My name is Jack Cash, International Bounty Hunter, I have the authority to kill anyone I choose on sight, for any reason, make no bones about this, I am leaving for now, but when I get back here, you had better be out of here."

A single sniper round whizzed by, as Jack absorbed it, turned and held his neck with his hand and went down to the ground, for Jack to say, missile, and the car responded as a missile shot off and moments later a huge explosion was heard.

Lisa and Elizabeth, went out to the street, to see the carnage Jack had created, as he lay on the street, as Lisa called in her support team, a van came moments later to pick up the prisoners, while all this occurred, Elizabeth helped Jack in, as the bullet missed his jugular by mere inches, to go through clothing and lodge in his shoulder, Elizabeth, helped Jack onto a table, to say, "Let me cut that off of you, why would you risk your life like that, I just met you and you went off to do that of a foolish thing, sure we all get harassed by them."

Jim and Brian and the strike team was in a panic mode as they heard a sniper round took out the Super Agent, and it was Erica screaming orders at them to get up in the air and get the strike team there, Jim loaded everyone, including doctors on board, and the plane was ready and ramp lifted, and taxied, and then flew off in the air.

Meanwhile, Lisa was at Jack's side, just as another SWAT group was called in to secure the area, as both Elizabeth and Lisa, pulled off his blood soaked jacket, and all across Washington DC was experiencing storm clouds as police from all over converged on that location, and started going door to door, clearing out and arresting all those who had a gun, under the police chief's orders. Meanwhile while working on Jack, they came to a point that the holster strap would not move as both of them got shocked.

Elizabeth just looked at Lisa, to say, "Who is this guy, is He real?"

Lisa dials up Brian, he answers to hear, her say, and "He is electrified."

"Calm down, the gun is sensing something, hold him still, I will be on the ground, to deactivate the gun, right now the gun senses fear, and will electrify his body. There must be something in the bullet round to have caused this, to keep him stable, were there in five minutes" said Brian, as he closed up the phone to say, "Looks like I need to jump?"

"Alright, I want you and Casey only, and then we need to get him out of there?" said Jim.

"Then let's pick up the car too" said Brian.

"This is way too dangerous for that" said Jim.

"Look if it fails, we will cut loose and it will parachute down, it's now or never?"

"You know he is right" said Bill Bilson, the other pilot.

"Shut up" Jim snapped back, as he too was in a panic mode, to add, "Alright, you have to get him into the driver's seat, as he followed him to the back of the aircraft as the others hooked up Brian, as Casey said, "I'll drop five seconds behind you in case."

"You got one in the back and one up front" said Bauer, as Morris lowered the ramp to start the count, "Three, two, one, and jump", out went Brian, head down, hands to his side he was going supersonic, his mind was on Jack, as his beeper went off, he pulled the chute, it opened, he guided it down, on a path above the power lines, to his other beacon, he landed, on his feet, pulling up the parachute, he unbuckled, to begin running as Casey, landed right after him, Casey collected the parachute, Brian ran into the building, as people parted, Elizabeth stood, back with Lisa, as Brian pulled out these gloves and a white box, he slid the gloves on, to touch the live gun, and set it in the box, to say, "Alright doctor, he is all yours, let's get this cleaned up, as Brian held up a vial, ready, as she undid his holster, and his shirt, she asked Brian, "Can I cut away his t-shirt?" asked a panicked Doctor.

"No just pull it off" as Brian moved in to assist.

Lisa held Jack's head as Brian pulled off his shirt to see the still live projectile."

"Wait, clear back, this is still a live round" he pulled out a visor, and another pair of gloves, and a can of liquid nitrogen, from his bag and with some forceps, he instructed Elizabeth to pull it out, as he froze it, he tapped on it and instantly it froze it as Elizabeth pulled it out, he placed it into a titanium test tube, to say, swab that for poisons, she did as she was told, while Brian's phone was ringing he said, "Lisa can you call Jim to say, "What our status is, and to circle around a bit longer, we got a poison here, that is quickly spreading, down his arm, wait I think the watch is drawing it all out, he watched as the green colored condition, at the top of his neck, moved as a group to his triceps, over and down his bicep, around his elbow, and just like that it was gone, then a digital reading came up to what the compounds were, and what he needed, as Brian called out to Elizabeth, on what to bring, she injected it into his blood stream, he was still out of it, as Brian called Casey on the phone to come in and pick him up."

Casey came in, picked up the lifeless Jack to throw him over his shoulder, and he carried him out, to the car, as another dilemma is found them. Meanwhile, caught on live feed was the whole thing via his camera to the President of the United States, that he, the President of our United States, sent Marine One over there.

Casey set Jack down, to step back as officers from all over were ready to lend a hand, as Jack was woken up by a capsule of smelling salts, and Brian broke open. Jack knelt up, to rest on the bumper, to speak, "Open up the doors and trunk", Brian kept Jack steady as Casey gathered the parachutes, and placed them in the back only to see the duffle bag, Jack rose to the cheering of those around him, minus his t-shirt, he wore his outer shirt, he stumbled a bit, to the driver's door, as the littler Brian, slid into the back, with his pack, and Jack's other clothing.

Jack was in the driver's seat, as Casey got in, the passenger seat, for Jack to say, "Close all doors, and trunk."

Jack was in and out of it as Casey said, "Let's go."

Jack was in and said, "Sleep" and down went Casey.

"Jack stay with me, command the balloon", said Brian, from the cramped back seat, as he was somewhat laid out, as Jack was out, it released anyway, where they were parked, for Brian to say, "Start, and back up", then Brian got on the phone, to hear were on approach, the plane is listening to the car, and in that moment, both Elizabeth and Lisa watched as that silver car was hoisted into the air, and off it went like it was flying, for Elizabeth to say, "Someday I'm going to marry that man?"

"Wait in line honey, the line is long and getting longer by the moment "said a woman standing by them.

The car kept an upright position the whole way, as the strong magnet, pulled them together, a ground plate was lifted up, and Jim went to his remote as everyone celebrated the test, while the strike team celebrated, Jim reached down through a hole, deactivated the ejection seat, and released the passenger, side roof, as it slid away, to see Casey, the strike team, pulled him up and out, then next was Jack, and he was lifted up, and the team carried him into his room, where the finest doctors worked, as their approach was back to Quantico, the main runway open, the pilot Bill Bilson landed the aircraft, taxied, into the hanger, as an ambulance was ready, the men then carried Jack out, an into the ambulance, escorted by Erica, Tami and Trixie, to the hospital, moments later they were there, off loading him, and into the ER where samples were taken, and Erica summoned Brian to come there, he carried the round, that held the poison, that Jim was there when the awaken Jack was asked to remove, the watch, as all the alert teams were put on hold as the watch came off, Jim caught the pin, to keep it secure, inside was a vial of poison, that Jim milked out, into a jar, then flushed the rest, and added another attractant, as he secured it, he came back to see Jack was resting, having been sewn up, Jim closed the curtain, to see Trixie was with him, he went to the other side, to his left hand to say, "Buddy how are you feeling, said Jim, as he moved away, to allow a little man in, and then to fasten on a new watch, activate it, and leave. Jim to say, "Where is your shirt?"

"I guess it's soiled" said Jack.

"Never mind that, let's put it on," said Jim as Trixie helps Jack get it on, with Jims help, he buttons it up for him, to say, "We have a new and updated outfit for you, when you're ready."

Erica comes in to say, "We just got word, that the round that hit you was a practice shot, and that you were a random target, we found plans for an assassination attack on the President, the missile you fired, took out thirty five terrorist, and we have uncovered their plans, and who was their roots, the President would like to know, when you're ready to go after them?"

Jack looks at her loopy to say in as slurred voice, "Where they at?"

"Minsk, Belarus, there is one of the places you can go into, only when you're ready?"

"Jim, come here" he motions to him to duck down to say, "Get the plane ready, I need a vacation, to Florida."

"Where too sir?"

"Jacksonville, Florida."

"Have Brian, get me those weapons to bring along, wake me tomorrow morning….", Jack was out, as Trixie stood up, to lower the head portion down, she and Jim covered him up, and Trixie said, "Don't worry, when he awakens again, I'll give you a call, can you turn out the lights?"

Jack awoke in the middle of the night, which woke up Trixie who was still holding one of his hands, to say, "Can I have a drink?"

Trixie offered her water bottle to him, he felt better, to say, "Get me out of here?"

"Wait let me call Jim to add, "He should be ready." as Trixie dialed Jim up and just like that Jim was there, the two took a side of Jack, and took the elevator down, to the basement, through a door, the short walk past Samantha's old room, and up the stairs, to the elevator, to the top floor, they got out, and down the stairs to the hanger, where the strike team was. They instantly took over, Morris and Bauer, to help Jack into the plane and into his room, the ramp went up as Brian and Jim took the plane out, and got the clearance to go, and just like that the plane was gone on their new destination. The plane landed in Jacksonville, the teams were disbursed, and all were waiting for Jack to wake up.

Jack awoke sore, alone and still tired, as he sat up with his head against the pillows, he pulled out his phone, to dial up Jim, who answered; Jack said "Do you have anything for energy, I just feel sluggish, yet my mind is ready to go."

"Yes sir, a shot of B-12, also may have it in pill form; I'll be in, in a moment, with breakfast."

Jack looked at all the missed call from all ten lines, bunch of diplomatic stuff, like some agents are already there, and hope to hear what our preferences are, as Jack flashed over to one by Elizabeth, who said, "Jack it was a pleasure meeting you, if at that time you told me your that Super Spy I would have let you sleep with me, anyway, I look forward to hearing from you, bye."

Jack hit the save button, the more and more, he played with this phone a whole new world was available to him, as he typed in Women, then Jacksonville, and only two girls came up, one a housewife on the ocean, her name is Tina Andrews and the other a young coed, named Barbie, for her bleached blonde hair, and amazing rack, she goes to southeast junior college, on the south part of Jacksonville. He placed them in favorites under Elizabeth's name, and set the phone aside as the door opened, it was Jim, solely, who carried in the tray, to say "I warmed up this tray, I hope you like it, and a cup of coffee, with a lemon, as he hands the tray to Jack, he takes out this weird looking syringe, and stabs him with it, then gives him two capsules to say, "Take as you need extra energy, their laced with a little speed, so be careful on how many you take, you could get addicted on them, they are very powerful."

"Then how many do you suggest?"

"Maybe two more max."

"Just give me two more, "as Jim hands him a dark vial, to say, "That's what I thought you would say?"

"Is Trixie around, or Tami?"

"Nah, they went into Jacksonville, one to the college, and the other to the local paper, it's just you, Me and Brian, Mark and the strike team, is following up on leads, Erica and Lisa sent us, and Mitzi said to send her, her wishes."

"Have Brian and Mark pick up two local agents."

"Go ahead I'm listening" said Jim with a smile, to hear their names and their numbers" as he left and closed the door.

CH 2

"Jack needs a helper, anyone?"

J ack thought, "He is such a nice guy, very considerate."

Back in the flight cabin, Jim closed the door, to lock it, as he hit a switch, and several screens appeared, in his mind he knew this was wrong, but it was by the order of Lisa, and confirmed by Erica, Lisa inner spy was showing off, just how vicious she was, spy club has fourteen agents in the area, mostly men, and the two, they said, both women are the ones Mark and Brian are going to pick up. "Yeah Jack, were way ahead of you, even though the sleeping pills I gave you should keep you asleep, that too was against my better judgment, what have I done I'm ashamed."

Jim closed down the screens, to unlock and open the door, he goes out, to the cargo bay, to see the Mercedes was gone, and then knocked and went into see Jack was gone.

"Oh shit" he said.

Jack felt awful, as he placed his phone in the dash, to take him to the girl Keisha, dorm room, Jack felt the urge to sleep, but as soon as the watch, identified what it was, it absorbed the tranquilizer, he was feeling better, enough so, as the car drove it herself, it parked out front of this three story dorm hall, where people quickly converged on, this shiny new expensive car, to see an old guy, Jack emerge, to hear "Ah, he is someone's dad", and the group broke up.

Jack had Keisha's picture in hand, as he went to the locked door, he knocked, then a voice from behind him said "What do you need Mister?"

Jack turned to see a very nice young girl for which he said, "I was looking for Keisha Huggins, do you know if she is in there?"

"What are you her father?"

"Nope just a friend of the family, her father asked me to come by, and take her out to dinner and give her money if she needs it?"

"Alright I'll let you in, she swiped her card, and the door opened, to hear, from inside, who is there and what do you want?"

"I was looking for Keisha Huggins is she in there?"

"No, I think she is on the third floor", Jack closed the door, shrugged his shoulders to say, "I guess she is on the third floor, she followed him in, for Jack to say "Is this a coed dorm?"

"Yeah, ever since those attack, it is a boy girl arrangement."

"In the same room" said Jack.

"No silly, girls together in even numbered rooms and boys in odd number rooms, although most have classes, now?"

"What about you?" asked Jack?

"Well I don't feel so hot, so I came here to puke", Jack went past her, as she went in the bathroom for Jack, to hear, "What a creep."

Jack took each room, the scent of drugs was evident, as he found the first even number, and knocked, no answer, so he went to the other side, and knocked, no answer, so he went to another room, when he heard, "Mister were you knocking on my door?"

Jack turned to see this stunning brunette, with a cute smile, and innocent eyes, as Jack came closer, to say, "Yes, I'm sorry to bother you, but I'm looking for Keisha Huggins, do you know where I can find her?" said Jack innocently.

"Can you come in for a moment, as you can see I'm all wet, just out of the shower?" with her hair up in a towel, and a towel barely around her body. Jack said, "I can stay out here and wait."

"No you can't, if security catches you then you will be in trouble, so come on in."

Jack followed her in, and stood at the door, as he closed it, for her to say, "Allow me to put some clothes on, have a seat."

Jack watched as she went through her drawers to find the clothes she needed, and went into the bathroom, he sat on a bed, looking at the wall when he heard, "There is some energy drinks in the fridge, go ahead and have one. Jack thought, "Yeah, I need that, I'm worn out, so he got up and went to the tiny fridge, bent over to open the small door, he saw the energy drink, to hear, "Toss me one please."Jack looked over to see the door was open and she had just pulled up her panties. Jack pulls two out and turns to see she was just standing in her bra and panties, to toss it to her, she cracks it open, and slams it down, Jack turned his head away from her, to hear, "Don't be bashful, it would be just like me in a bikini, so what the big deal, go ahead and drink it up, can I ask you a question?"

"Sure."

"How long have you known Keisha?"

"Oh, not long, I really know her father, Jim."

"Really she doesn't talk about him much, what does he do?"

"I believe he is a Senator from this state of Florida?"

"Really, wow, she is a daughter of a state senator, so what do you do?"

"I'm just a business man; you know investments here and there."

"Really, if you don't mind, can you look at me while you talk, don't worry I'm partly dressed."

Jack turns to crack the container, and takes a sip, to see her she has two pairs of jeans in her hands to say, "Which one do you think goes with this top?"

Jack looked at both, to say, "Neither."

"That's what I thought too, what do you suggest then?"

"A white tank top and green shorts" said Jack thinking of Sara.

"Oh my god, your right I love that outfit, as she came to him, as he backed off, as she pulled her top off, to find a white tank top, and slid on some khaki shorts, as Jack finished the drink, he felt like he was on cloud nine, his desire was to have two or three, as she said, "What about shoes?", to add, "Flats or running shoes?"

"Flats" said Jack.

"Yes your right, as she comes up to him to give him a hug, to say, "Sorry, I just feel like we have this amazing connection, so did you want to go out and get some lunch, wait I need to take a shot."

Jack thought, maybe this was his time to make a break for the door, or ask for another energy drink, so he said, "Do you mind if I have another energy drink?"

"No, help yourself."

Jack didn't care about anything else, as he knelt down, opened the fridge door, and began to pop the tops, and consume three more, empty, he threw them away, when he went for another to hear, "Hold on, those are expensive, and besides my roommate will kill me."

"I'm sorry", said Jack as he pulled out his wallet, to pull out a hundred, to set on the fridge, as she saw, "Oh my god, your giving her a hundred dollar bill, for what?"

"Can I have the rest of the energy drinks?"

"Sure, that will feed her for an entire month, what could I do for you, for say that amount?"

As Jack takes the rest, and sticks them into his pocket, the four, to say, "Have a seat, and provide me some information, and I will compensate you well."

"Really, sure" she said as she sat across from him and takes a syringe and injects herself, to show him a smile.

"First off, tell me what you know about Keisha?"

"How much will you pay me, can I see the cash?' she asks honestly.

Jack pulls out his stack of five thousand dollars from inside his Jacket not to show her his badge, to pull all of it out and with the other hand he puts the badge away, to gather the money to put it out, for her to say, "Looks like ten thousand dollars, as he spun the hundreds."

"Wow, how much will you give me?"

"Depends on the information" said Jack.

"Can I touch that?"

"Sure", said Jack as he tossed it to her, she caught it to say, "What can I do to earn all this, I could call my girlfriends over and we could have a party, you know that's what we do from time to time?"

"What is that, what you do?"

"You know sex parties, we charge guys to screw us and we have tuition money for a semester."

"Is that what you really do?" asks Jack.

"No, not me, but some of my friends do", she says as she hands the money back to him, in a down and out way."

"Listen how about I give you five hundred dollars, can you tell me who her friends are, and…"

"I will do one even better, I'll show you around, her friends won't talk to you, but they will talk with me, what do you say, is it a deal Mister?"

"Sure" said Jack, for her response was, "What is your name, my name is Austin."

"Names Jack" he tries to shake her hand and she went in for a hug, to say, "That's how we do it in Wisconsin."

"So Austin, what is your major?"

"Well I'm a sophomore, and I'd like to be a neurosurgeon some day, but all in all that is five hundred thousand dollars, can you help me?"

"Where's your dad at?"

"Well he is a doctor, and so is my mother, kind of runs in the family, so we're seeing how this school works."

"Where in Wisconsin?"

"A place called Madison?"

"Why didn't you go to the University of Wisconsin?"

"Lack of serious funds, roughly 100,000 thousand a year, and down here is 26, 000, so my parents decided down here."

"Was it truly them or was it you?"

"Your right again, I was at Wisconsin U, but I transferred this year, after coming down here for spring break."

"What to get away from the parents?"

"Mainly my ex, who can't seem to keep his hands off of me." Jack decided to change the subject, as it was all too clear, the same thing was happening to her that happened to Sara.

"Well let's go and find this Keisha, led the way."

Jack held the door open for her, as several coed's saw her and Jack and began to giggle, then laugh, as Austin went down the hall, to the second to last door, knocked a weird pattern, the door opened, and she went in, to have the door close, then it opened and a tall red haired girl, said, "Come on in, my name is Gia, I hope it isn't too messy."

Jack walked in on a slumber party two girls each occupied the beds, dressed in lingerie, some very exposing, as Jack felt he was rising, to hear, "Have a seat Mister" said one.

As Gia and Austin went into the bathroom, to hear, "So you're looking for Keisha?"

"Well I'm her better friends than most, my name is Carly, who wore the most revealing outfit of all, as Jack could see everything, she added, "How long have you been seeing Austin, she says your from Wisconsin, that's cool, she is a lucky girl."

Jack looked at her weirdly, to say, "When was the last time you saw her?"

"She has basketball practice twice a day, and I saw her last night, around nine, she said she was getting harassed by some guy, named Brian,"

"Brian Owens "said another.

"Yeah, that's what he does, he did that to me, for the longest time, he is harmless" said Jill.

"Yeah, till your boyfriend put him on the ground" said Carly

"What does that mean? "Asked Jack.

"Well what we're saying is he likes to go and hide in our rooms, then at night, he attacks us, individually, that's why we all sleep together, if your know what I mean" she said with a wink.

"Have you reported this to the authorities" asked Jack.

"They don't care, just last month a girl was gang raped and not one guy is behind bars and she is in an institution now."

"Really" said astonished Jack.

"And for some of us, we have tasers, we carry mace, several of us have taken self defense courses, but that doesn't help either."

"Your making it sound like there are others?"

"Well in fact there are, several of these perverts running around, but that isn't the worst of them, almost monthly a gang of bikers come to the school, to do recruiting, you know their looking for sexual partners, of those girls, we never see them come back." said Carly, yawning, and exposing her breasts.

"Yeah, but they go after the un-noticeable ones, not Keisha, she was recruited to play basketball here, they tend to keep on the down low" said Jill.

"Do any of you know where this biker gang hangs out?"

"Sure we all do, but you would be stirring up a hornets' nest" said Jill, looking surprised.

"I'd take my chances; can anyone of you show me where it's at?"

"Austin can, she knows just like us, besides she has the hots for you" said another.

"Leave him alone" said Austin emerging from the bathroom, with smiles on their faces, to add, "Did you get the info you were seeking?"

"That and much more" said Jack.

"Is there any place in particular you want to go?"

"Well they said you could show me where the biker gang hangs out?"

"Sure for some more money" as she was at the door, as the others said, "Did she say for money?"

"Nah, she is too proper to demand that, she has strict morals."

The door closed for Jack and Austin, as she said, "I've been thinking, Gia says it isn't fair, that I get all the money, so she will come over later, and service you as will I."

"Doubtful, you're like a baby, still, nah, show me where this place is at?" she led Jack out of the dorms, down the stairs to say, "My car is this way" as she points to a beat up Toyota, four door.

"I'm driving my car" said Jack, pointing the other way.

"Alright, that's what I like to hear" she caught up with him, as he held the door open, as she stepped out to see the only car out front, to exclaim, "This is your car, a Mercedes?"

"Yep", said Jack looking up at the windows that had many faces, looking down at him and as she was going crazy as she came to him, to say, "Let make love out front in front of all these people" as she was gesturing something to them all, with her hands, Jack said "Open, the doors opened for him to say, "Come on Austin, let's go."

"Hold on Jack, I'm savoring my status here."

The car fired up and she quickly got in, as the door shut itself, for her to say, "You don't realize what you have done for me," she said as she relaxes on the seat.

"Wait, calm down, let's get a focus here."

She looked down at him as she was pulling her shorts and underwear down.

Jack was trying to stop her from doing it, to say, "Why he thought, if that is what she wants to do, let her do it."

"No, now sit down your acting like a spoiled brat", Jack said as it came out, and she wasn't happy, her shorts and underwear at her ankles her armed crossed, she was sulking, realizing he made her mad, he said, "Alright one kiss."

She went from unhappy to literally excited as she turned and stuck her butt in the air, her lips were all over his, her tongue plunged to great depths, all the while, her free hand was trying to get him hard, finally after putting on a show, a police horn went off, and it all ended, as she pulled up her shorts, as the police officer tapped on his window, it went down, to say, "Drivers license and registration."

Jack thought about it, and he knew he had neither, so he said "Listen officer, I'm here to pick up my friends daughter, I'm down from Wisconsin,"

"That's not the plates I saw."

"You sure, check again."

Jack spun the correct plate, from his diplomatic plate, the officer saw it to write it down, then he went to his car and called it in, it came back, Jack Cash Investment banker."

He came to the window to say, "Can I see you're I D and Drivers license, Jack pulled the wallet and the police officer saw the badge, and its Presidential seal, to say, "Sorry to have bothered you, sir, carry on."

The officer went back to his car, to see his screen that said, "Do not interfere, Government operative, do not detain."

He sped past Jack, for Jack to see the eager, Austin, saying, "Can you buy me lunch?"

"Sure where too?"

"I know a biker bar that serves good hamburgers."

"So then that it shall be" said Jack as he kept an eye on her and the road, for her to say, "Do you have any tunes in here?"

Jack said display music", and the dash board lit up to show a screen.

For her to say, "You have a video screen, does it play while you drive", she was touching the screen, and nothing was happening, for Jack to say, "What kind of music do you like?"

"Hip hop", she said as a video of a hot artist appeared."

"Cool, all you have to do is say a command?"

"Well I think it was meant for me."

"Did you have this car customed made just for you?"

"Yep, it's all mine" said Jack as he drove to the GPS of two possible locations, knowing he didn't need her any longer, but there was something amusing to keep her around "Jack thought.

"No, take the next left, Jack slowed, to allow others to past, then he got in the left hand lane, while she was watching the music videos, in surround sound, at just the right level, she was dancing in her seat, moving her hands, as he drove the car, Sara released all the controls to him, as he got out on a country road, she said, "Slow down, it's on the left."

Jack slowed the car, to see a place up front, next to the bikes, and parked. They both looked up to see the sign said, "Reserved for the Manager."

They got out of the car, and up the stairs they went Jack saw the line of bikes looked like ten deep, and pulled out his phone, to text to Mark and Brian, and went through saloon type of doors, to see a rough bunch, heavy smoke filled the place, nudity was visible and all the bikers were on the pool tables, playing. Austin said,

"We like to sit over here, this is our section."

Jack helped her with her seat, then sat down, to see a hot waitress approach them, to say, "You're not from around here, what will you have?"

"The max burger and fries and a pop", said Austin.

"I'll have the same, but instead of pop, I'll have coffee black, with a lemon wedge" said Jack.

"Alrighty folks" she said, as she went to talk with the mean looking dude, from behind the bar, Jack watched as he called on to the others, Jack had a picture ready, to show when Austin said, "What do you have there, ah it's a picture of Keisha, how about I give you one of me?"

Jack pulled out his phone, and snapped one of her as she smiled at him, to say, "Someone is here to speak with you", she pointed at the big dude, with her finger."

Jack looked at him to say, "Have you seen this girl?"

"Here is your coffee, miss pretty, he was laughing at Jack, as Jack asked him again, "Have you seen this girl?"

"Yeah, her head was bobbing on my rod last night."

Jack kicked him in the inside of his knee, to a crack sound and the guy went down, as he began to scream, "He broke my fucking leg."

"Serves you right" said the waitress, "Right boys, carry this trash out, we don't want any trouble mister, me and my old man run a respectful place, he happened to be one of the Rednecks."

"Who's that? Are they important?" asked Jack as she sets the two plates down.

"Well actually, they run the women and drugs up north, but down here its open ground, they have been trying for years to take our place, but we just have to get them out of here, and that was the first step in doing that, this is on the house, thanks."

"Wow, you are one tough guy, Jack Cash" she said proudly.

The waitress stopped in her tracks to turn around to say, "Mister is you the famous Jack Cash from Mobile?"

"Yep" said Jack proudly.

She turned a shade of white, as she told her old man, as word got around, people started to clear out of the place, slowly, as the waitress came back to their table to say, "About the girl, you're looking for, it wasn't the Rednecks, that took her, and lord knows they have in the past, she came in here last night, with some weird looking fellow, tall lanky, and smelled of marijuana, heavy you know, listen I want to say thank you for taking out the Rico family, they were squeezing us for thousands per month, and now it stopped all of a sudden, and now were finally making a solid profit, as are our friends, if you ever need any back up ever just call my old man, Scott and we will be there like white on rice", she sees Austin come back from the bathroom, to say, "Would you care for any pie, the key lime is to die for?"

"Sure, that sounds good" said Jack, who sees Mark and this tall woman with him, Jack motions to Mark, to the bar, order something, and then to the bathroom?"

Jack waits, and then says, "I need to use the restroom."

"Alright honey, I'll be here waiting for you" said Austin, enjoying the burger and fries, as Jack past Mark, and into the bathroom, he did his business, to wash up, then sees Mark to say,

"I need you to drop off your contact, and go up north to a bike location called the Rednecks?"

"That is a biker group, there all over this place, Tina told me that they have a reservation up north, and no one is allowed on their reservation, they have been terrorizing Jacksonville for over twenty years."

"Really, Can you call Erica and have her research that, and if we can, that is my next place I'm going to hit, see ya."

Jack waited, for Mark to leave the restroom, then he left, to past by the bar, everyone just looked at him as Jack looked at him back who looked over at two bigger guys at the door, one held onto Austin by the arm for which she said, "Your hurting me."

"Shut up", the other spoke, to see Jack to say, "Someone told me your parking in my parking space?"

"Not anymore it's not yours, it's mine now" said Jack confidently, walking towards them to hear, "You and what army?"

"Me, myself and I, that are who, what and why, now let the girl go."

The smart one pulled his gun to point it at Jack, just as the saloon doors open, to hear, "Put it down Billy", said a meaner looking dude, pushes them away to say, "Evidently this man has some money, much more than you have, so if he wants to park next to the door then let him, we came here to get a beer."

Jack puts his hand up to say, "Not anymore, you're not or anyone with the Redneck's vests in here."

"Some would say that's discrimination."

"No, that is our right to refuse any customer as we so choose, as a right granted to us by the constitution, the same one that provides you the land upon you live, freely and with having to pay taxes?"

"Who are you their attorney?"

"Nope, a hired bounty hunter, ready to blast you and all your thieving kind to kingdom come, now, you have twenty four hours, to gather all your people, and go back to your reservation."

"Or what?"

"Or I will arrest each of you, and turn you over to the UN teams."

A single shot rang out, the bullet hit Jack in the heart., it stuck right there, as it was all quiet, then in a flash, as the three, and two others were caught off guard, Jack pulled his knife, and in a leaping jump kick, connected, with Billy, knee, to pop it sending him down, and a sucker punch, to his partner grasping for air, away went his, knife, for his weapon, which he had pointed at his forehead, for Jack, to say, "I heard from the grapevine that you like to kidnap young women for slaves, and you import drugs and disburse them around town, and lastly you terrorize this community, not anymore, on your knees, your under arrest" said Jack as the leader went to his knees.

"Now, all of your hands interlaced above your head", said Jack as he put his knife away, to hear, "You're not getting away with this we have thousands that will arrive to bail us out?"

Jack zip ties the three and the two inside, he also has help from Tommy the bar owner, as Jack calls up Lisa, moments later a van pulls up, as the leader Marcus pleads, "Listen I will cut you in on this whole operation?"

Jack knelt down to say, "You must of thought, that someday, this day would come, better now than later, because I spared your life, others I imagine would seek vengeance on what you guys do, so I have only one question for you?"

"Go fuck yourself" spit Marcus at Jack, to see men in blue suits, hop out, Jack raises his hand, to see that they halted, their movement towards them, for Jack to hear, "Who are you, are you with the FBI, we have them in our pocket, NSA."

"Shut up, now I want to know, I'm looking for a young girl named Keisha Huggins?"

"Nope never saw her, is this is what this is all about?"

"Basically it was at first, and then your man shot at an International Bounty Hunter, with the power to arrest and detain, anyone I see fit, for any reason?"

Marcus looked up at him somber to say, "I'm sorry."

"Yes you will be, for where you're going, has no court of laws, no appeal process, what I can suggest is that you cooperate to your fullest and you may be lucky and live, bye, bye" said Jack. Jack watches them being carted off, as another bigger truck arrives, to load up all the bikes onto the wrecker, and just like that everyone was gone except one lone individual, Lisa, who took Jack aside to say, "Update on that terrorist cell, in Belarus, the entire police force is on board, with trying to assist us in that capture, and is awaiting your arrival, as the UN clearance is approved, for you to go in, so what are your plans now?"

"How long before you get information out of Marcus?" asked Jack.

"Well, I have a local interrogator and one from Washington D C." said Lisa.

"One more thing, who's idea, was it to drug me, yours or Erica?"

"I don't know what you're talking about, holding back her lie."

"Well I want to find who has Keisha, and every minute, I'm talking to you, I could be."

"I got cha, go, who's the girl?"

"Just some coed I picked up along the way, can't seem to get rid of?"

"Hand her over to me?"

"Nah, that's alright, she will be fine, as he begins to leave, and he turns to say, "Hey how much involvement can I have with your spy club?"

"All of it why? What do you have in mine?"

"Oh I have a reservation, I need searching, which could take me all week?"

"I'm on it; shall we wait, or go right in?"

"You're the boss; you do what you think you would like to do."

"No I'm not the boss, you are, were working under your authority."

"Thanks' I just wish, I could see what you're doing?"

"I can make that happen, that easy, I'll have a film crew with several camera, and patch it to your phone, you know you have video on that phone you know?"

"Know, I didn't, but thanks, I'll check it out" said Jack walking over to his car to see Austin waiting, and Tom and his wife, she was tearful, to say, "Thank you, your always welcome."

Tom said, "We mean it, we can gather our friends to help you."

"No thanks, but I got this under control, I'm going to look for this Brian Owens, and see what is up with him, honestly I think the bikers are harmless, they just needed to be told more often, No than yes."

"Open" said Jack as the car responds, Austin slides in, as Jack gets in, to see her smiling at him to say, "I know all about you Mister Jack Cash."

"Who told you?"

"Why Connie the waitress, said you took down the mob, yourself."

"Ssh, let's keep it our secret" said Jack as he backed out, to put his phone into the dash, to say, "Take me to Brian Owens, a senior at Jacksonville state university."

"He is probably in school now?" said Austin.

"Ssh, let Sara tell me herself."

"Who is Sara?"

"She is my wife."

"You're married, oh I don't like this at all, and I thought you and I could hook up."

"Did you want me to take you back to your dorm room?"

"Yes, that is what I want" she said with her arms crossed and sulking.

"Sure you don't want to help me out and find Brian?"

"Oowe, no, you're grossing me out."

"So before, you wanted to have sex with me, now I'm grossing you out, to tell you the truth I have fourteen wives."

"Now your a pilgrim, I'd have you stop and let me out, but there is something exciting about you, and I know I can trust you, you seem like a gentleman."

"Thanks' Austin, coming from you that seems like a compliment."

The small blip on the GPS screen was small, but the dot was getting closer, as was he to dropping her off, one more turn, the straightaway, Jack pulled to a stop, to have her door unlock, for him to say "Good... bye" the door closed as she was at her building and he drove off.

Austin got to her floor, to see a flood of people, yelling and screaming, and then she saw her friends, who whisked her into a room, to say, "Oh My God, you were there?"

"What are you talking about?" asked Austin.

"You were with him, the famous Bounty Hunter, and what was it like?"

"What are you guys talking about?"

One girl clicked on the news, to hear, "That's right, John, it is true, The International Bounty Hunter, Jack Cash, is in town to clean it up, first up was the gang, of Rednecks, that have terrorized, Jacksonville for years, is seen here walking to a escort van, discovering huge sums of drugs, to include, Marijuana, cocaine, and heroin, just to name a few, in addition, several young girls working on the reservation, and some coed, were seen here, trapped for months, and in one warehouse alone millions upon millions of dollars, worth of goods stolen, and then lastly shallow graves of agents discovered, once thought just missing.

Austin sat on the bed, thinking "Oh how I have wronged him?"

"What are you talking about" asked her friend.

Meanwhile as Jack drove, he began to hear this ring tone, of music that kept going off, as he closed in on his target, he slowed and parked, as it went off again, he reached down to pull up a phone, he looked at it to show it said, "You missed five calls", then it returned to show it was Austin's phone", "Great," thought Jack, to think does he go back or move on this, it rang again, so he answered it, to say, "Yes" as Jack heard giggling in the background, then a stern voice said, "We know who you are, and we us girls want to see you, Mister Jack Cash", in the background, he could hear them tell Austin to take the phone, finally she said, "I'm sorry Jack, they made me do it, it wasn't like the first time I lost my phone."

Jack looks at the building to say, "Well you could come down here and pick it up and maybe I could make it up to you."

"Alright, maybe I jumped the gun, and thought that something would happen?"

"It still may" said Jack.

"Really, you're not mad at me?"

"No, not at all."

"So where are you at and I'll come to you this time?"

Jack looks at his GPS to say, "I'm parked in the middle of the falconer building, just down", to hear some rushing, he hears another voice say, "Hi, this is Gia, again, so what have you and my friend been up too?"

"Oh not much" says Jack hearing some more rustling, and then as if they were running, then a car starts, as one of them says, "Hi, remember me, my name was Carly, what do you think about Austin?"

Jack is looking at his watch, and down at this pink phone to think about what to say to this young girl, so he says, "Oh I think she is dandy?"

"Where are you going to take her tonight for dinner?"

Jack looks at a map of Jacksonville, to see the highest to lowest priced restaurants, to say, "I believe if she will allow me, I'd like to take her dress shopping, then to the Hilton head on the beach."

Jack pulled the phone away from his ear to hear the shriek, the girl let out, and several more Oh, my Gods, he knew it was time to get moving along, so he said, "Look I need to go?", the phone was silent, but still on, as a small car came around the corner, to see four girls all yelling and screaming, they parked next to his car, Austin got out to hear encouragement from the others, Jack put down his window, to allow her to see him, he hands her, her phone, she takes it only to hold onto his hand to say, "Look I was wrong and over reacted, can we start again?"

Jack was thinking about it as her hand felt so super soft, for her being anxious was getting to be a bad thing, because her girlfriends were egging her on, to go, so Jack said, "How about you do something for me, and earn that money we discussed?"

"Right, here, you want to do it right here?"

"No not that, button up your blouse, listen which one of your girlfriends knows this dude named Brian?"

She turns to look at them, all the while still holding onto his hand, she turns to say, "It would have to be Carly, She or Jill, would have to be, it."

"Excellent, what do you think it would take, for either to participate, in this operation?"

"Oh believe me; they all would do anything you asked?"

"Then see if they would go up there and lure him down here, and I'll do the rest."

"That's the least I can do for you?" said Austin, finally releasing Jack hand, to watch as she told them, all three exited, scantily clad, outfits, all three walked over then, Austin slid in next to Jack, to say, "I'm sorry, and yes I will allow you to take me out, married or not, I'll let you fuck me anyway?"

"That's good to know, but were on a mission, so let's focus on this and when we find Keisha, then we will go out?"

"Fair enough" said Austin.

Jill led, Carly as the two argued, who would do what and how they would do anything, that allowed Gia, the tall red headed to take the lead, she knocked on his door, as the other two, waited behind her, to see the door open slowly, to hear a guy say, "What is it?"

"Hi, is Jim around we were going to ask him if he and some of his friends would like to come to our dorm room, and party with us lonely girls?"

"Jim's not here" he said, for Jill to hear Brian's voice to say, "Brian, Brian Owens is that you?"

The door, closed then opened a little bigger, for Jill, to step to the door, wearing a see through bra, she said Brian it is you, listen I want to apologize for my ex-Neanderthal boyfriend."

Jill sees the dirt bag, which was half naked and only wearing underwear, showing her how happy he was to see her, to say, "You're wearing almost nothing?"

"I could take it off if you like, are you going to let us in?"

"Sure for you, but not her, she is the schools gossip girl, looking at an even more nude, Carly."

"What about me Brian, you know me" said Gia.

"Sure come in Gia, but you stay out there" he said to Carly.

"Come on be nice to her Brian" said Jill, she has feelings" said Jill.

"Well alright, under one condition."

"What's that Brian" said Jill.

"That she gets naked" as he pointed at Carly.

They all look at Carly who shrugs her shoulder and say, "Yeah, what the hell."

"You know it isn't like you haven't seen any of us naked before, aren't you the one who has that spy hole in the women's shower" said Gia.

"So what is the point? I'm waiting, strip" he said with a smile on his face, roughly enjoying himself, meanwhile back at the car, Jack says, "What is taking them so long?"

"What do you mean?" asked Austin.

"Just that, I'll I wanted them to do was bring him back down here."

"Oh, I thought you meant entertain him?"

"Why would I say that, Jack shakes his head at her, as she rubs his shoulder to hear, her say, "Later I could give you a really good back rub if you know what I mean?"

"Sure, let's go before it's too late", said Jack on the move, and she ran to keep up, to the elevator, for Jack to say, "Listen we get to the door, you knock and get one of your friends to open the door, then stand aside, as they came to the third floor, they got off, to see a vending machine, to look in his wallet, he turned to say, "Do have a few bucks?"

She looked disappointed, to hand him four dollars, he inserted it into the register, and out came an energy drink, he loaded the next two bills in to have finished the first, when out came a second, he popped its top to hear, "Are you coming my friends are with that psycho?"

Jack drank the next one down, to let off a burp, pretty loud.

"Sss he will hear you."

"Calm down Nancy Drew, I'll be right behind you."

"The least you could have done was offered me a drink, you know those things are very addictive."

They get to the door, Austin knocks, as Gia stood by the door, while Carly was on one arm, nude and Jill was on the other, kissing on him, as Jack could hear "No," real loud.

"Calm down, it only our friend Austin, who is with us."

"Go ahead let her in."

Jack motioned for her to go in and he will follow her, Gia opened the door, Austin went in followed by Jack into a sauna of a room, he quickly could smell blood, literally, to hear, "Ah, Austin, why don't you take off your clothes and we can have a threesome, as Jack stepped out with his gun drawn as the girls both fled away from him to hear, "Yeah, I knew this was a dream, which girl is yours?"

"All four of them."

"What, what is going on here, who are you, and where is your warrant, I never invited you in?"

"Girls behind me, alright get up, and get dressed, no wait, Gia, go in and find Mister Owens some pants and a sweater and shoes", as Jack has his gun trained on him, moments later he heard a scream, and she came back out horrified, her face white as a sheet.

Jack says, "Whoa wait a minute, Brian hands on your head, interlock your fingers, Jack holsters his weapon, to pull a zip tie, and did his wrists, then he said, "On your stomach" only to zip tie his ankles, as he did that he thought what if it were me, I'd need a razor blade to cut through, or a laser, on the watch, to say, "Stay here and watch over Brian, as he made his way in, to the last bedroom, and on the big bed, was a naked woman, similar to Gia, in size, her throat had been cut, but the blood was fresh, over in the closet he saw a man, naked under some clothes, he checked his pulse, he was dead, and went to the woman, and felt her pulse, it was weak, but she was alive, he thought about dialing 9-1-1, but remembered what that was like, so he went to the door, and closed it a bit, to dial up Lisa she answered, to say, "I got a situation here, one down, and one bleeding out, send help", Jack hung up on her, to dial up Doctor Snyder, it rang, for awhile, then he tried her work number, to hear Washington Metro Coroner's office?"

"Yes, can I speak with Elizabeth, it's an emergency?"

"Wait a moment I will page her" moments later, she answered by saying, "Its Doctor Snyder, how may I help you?"

"This is Jack; I have a situation and need your help?"

"Are you alright, I was just so worried?"

"Listen, everything is alright, except I have no energy, anyway, a woman's neck has been cut, from what looks like a sexual encounter gone wrong."

She asks him to see where the blood is coming from.

"It looks like its pretty superficial, horizontal to the vocal chords."

"We see that all the time, find a t-shirt, and cut it in half, on to and then apply to the wound, but once you do, you have to hold it there till help arrives, are you in Washington?"

"Nah, I'm in Jacksonville?"

"As in Florida?"

"Yep, I m looking for an abducted woman, what do you think about submerging her in an ice water bath?"

"Absolutely, and you called me first?"

"Sure you're my doctor now, look I'll call you later I got to go."

Jack put his phone away, to yell, "Gia, come here" she was at the door to say, "Yes, is it safe to come in?"

"Yes, but before you do, I need you and the girls to go and get as much ice as you can, now."

Jack went into the bathroom, and put a plug in the tub and ran the water cold, then went back to pick up the woman, then carried her to the tub, he set her in, then, went around to a drawer, to find a clean t-shirt, he ripped in half, rolling it up, he went to her head, and tied a tourniquet around her neck. Then he shut off the water, to go back into the bedroom, to take the covers and threw it over the bed, only to hear the girls coming in one by one, each with one five gallon bucket of Ice.

"Come on in, and pour it in the bathtub, she is breathing and still alive, can you girls stay with her, while Austin and I find Keisha."

They all watched as the tub overfilled, Gia went to her head, as Jill and Carly said, "She could stay here till help arrives, but we could go with you" said Jill smiling at him, Jack was finding it hard to say no to her, she was un like any girl he had ever seen before, his mind was racing to say, "Alright but you need to get some clothes on, find some shirts and pants to wear its getting cold out there."

They went into the next room, as Jack past by to see them getting un dressed, he made it to the living room, to see Brian still on the floor, Jack turned him over, to say, "Two choices, help us out or I leave you here?"

"What do you mean?"

"Take us to where you live, off campus, and I'll let you live, if not you can stay here?"

"Oh Jack look what I found" said Jill, who was topless, coming out to the living room, to hand him his wallet."

"Thanks, go get dressed, so if you found his wallet bring his pants will you?"

A knock at the door, signaled the end was coming soon, he opened it to see a young girl, who said, "Am I too early for auditions?"

"For what", asked Jack?"

"To be a model, Brian told me I could make five hundred dollars."

"Nah, right now isn't a good time, how about next week, this day, you'll meet with Gia at the Hankers building say around three?"

"Alright thanks" she said as she left, Jack saw the reinforcement were coming, to include SWAT from the local police, to yell back, we need to go, "Here, as Jack cuts Brian's ankle ties, on went the pants, then he zipped him up, then put on his socks and shoes, and the others, did nothing as Jack pulled the sweatshirt over his neck and down, then lifted him up, and they were on the move, instead of the way they came, they took the east side stairs, Jack had his car move, to that location, to mutter, "All door open, and trunk, Jack tossed Brian in the trunk, as Austin and Carly fit into the back well, as Jill took the front seat, and off they went, Jack hands her the wallet to say, "There may be more of these guys, what is the address, I'll punch it in, listen I know if you don't want to get involved, I'll understand?"

Jill places her hand on his arm to say, "Count us in, we all love an adventure."

"Alright then, let's go."

CH 3

Let's find Keisha and make new friends

Jack drove slowly, down an old gravel road, thinking a trap could be anywhere, the GPS was going haywire, from some radio signal, no reception what so ever, he thought he could be rolling into a trap, he drove over a cattle fence, then open fields on both sides as day turned into night, on his mind was the lack of useable agents, not to mention his team, Mike was somewhere, Mitzi, was in the hospital, Trixie was on an airplane and Mark and Brian, the armorer, who knows, Jack continued to drive on, to hear that the girls were very quiet and probably in fear, then Jack saw where he was going, as old crosses, and headstones, littered one side, in the center was a house mason building that smoke was burning off, and then as the smoke came clear, he shut off all outside vents, he drove through it, to park and say, "Wait in the car."

Jack got out, to say, sleep, and secure."

Jack went around to where all the smoke was and went in, to see some old guy stoking a fire, on the furnace, only to feel a gun in his back, to hear, "Pop's we got a live one."

Jack moved forward, with his hands up to see the guy wearing chaps with a graying hair and clean shaven say, "Do you know what we do to trespassers?"

"No" said Jack.

"We kill them."

"Step on up here and make it easy on us, so that we can push you in to the vat of molten steel?"

"Clever, is that where your son is going?"

"What did you say?"

"I said, is this is where your son Brian is going?"

"How do you know him?"

"I know about the whole family that is why I'm here to see if you would surrender to me and release the girl?"

"What girl?"

"You know a tall girls basketball player, named Keisha Huggins?"

"Sorry friend we don't know any girl, of that name."

"If it's real young, our son takes care of them."

"Now step up here so that you can jump freely."

Jack turns to take the gun away from the slightly younger woman, to hold onto it" to hear, "Hold on Mister, people come out here all the time to commit suicide, so we changed from incinerator to molten steel, it works faster."

"I'm not here to die, not yet, you're both under arrest?"

"For what, this is our lively hood, we ain't done anything wrong."

"True, but your friend there put a gun to the back of a government official, which constitutes a felony, punishable to life in prison."

"Whoa wait" said Pops, as the smiling woman, was in near hysterics, and crying on the floor, Jack held the gun on Pops to say, "Come down from there, and we will talk this out."

Jack jumped to the ground to zip tie the woman's hands behind her back, as a shovel aimed at his head, grazed him, an angry Jack was all over Pop's giving the oversized guy several rib crushing punches, that subdued him, rolling him over the zip tied him, then his ankles, he went over to the woman and had to kneel on his legs keeping her from kicking him, to zip her up, then used another, to tie the two together, he did the same, as he placed his knee in Pop's back, to pull the three zip ties together to finally make it.

Jack was on the move towards the house, he took the steps, to the old wooden door, and it opened with a creaking noise, an eerie feeling overcame him, one that made it worse when his phone went off, he answered it, to say, "What is it?"

"Were on the reservation, and your right, there is a fracture of those who allowed the Rednecks to camp out on their reservation, all in all there are fifty four families living in poor conditions."

"Can you take them all to a local hospital for care and a check up, and to some hotel, I'll pay for it, and continue to survey the grounds I think you're going to find something you're not going to be happy about", and adds "I see the conditions and they are poor, alright keep me informed" said Jack.

Jack sat in a chair in the kitchen, and next call was to Tami, his assistant, she answered he said, "I need you to find the architect that did our work, and coordinate with Robert Bradley, the builder, to get over here, and then he heard something, a voice calling out, faintly he hear, "Johnny is that you?"

To add, "Next contact Commander Ted Johnson and have his whole base come over from Tampa to clean up."

Whose, was the sound of the meat cleaver narrowing missing his arm and head as he dove off the chair he ended his call to see this blind woman wielding a instrument meant for death, she swung to say, "You're not my, Johnny Duval, he loves me who are you, speak up or I will kill you and that young girl he has."

"Hold on," said Jack with his hands up as she deflected off of everything, using a two handed motion, in a pattern of a eight, he was safe for the moment but the wood table was splintering, as she was calling out to her mom, and Pops, Jack thought, "What a dysfunctional family, to hear the new weapon, a cast iron skillet, hitting a refrigerator, as he sensed she was tiring, and moving away, Jack rested and let his guard down, to dial up Lisa and say, "Holy Shit."

Two blood thirsty dogs were at his feet barking and biting as Jack kicked them to keep at bay, thinking what could he use to calm them down, his options were fading fast, this decision would have to be now, then the front door opened to hear, Carly say, "Jack are you in there I need to use the bathroom?"

In that moment he knew what he needed to do, one shot each, each dog was dead as it fell short of Carly, they were wounded, Jack scrambled up, to hear the banshee scream, and come at him with the cleaver, he said, to Carly, "Go back into the car you'll be safe."

Jack closed the door, to avoid the swings, then he grabbed her fragile arm and with his force he broke it into two, she slumped to the ground crying, to hear in between sobs, "It was you, that killed my dogs, it was you that killed my mom, it was you that killed my Pop's, are you going to kill me too?"

"No, I'm here for the young girl" said Jack seeing the girl was next to one of the dogs that was whimpering, while the other was letting off a harrowing yelp, till Jack shot that one, to say, "Sorry miss I had no choice, help is on the way, hold tight", Jack was on the move, as he took a left turn down into a faintly lit basement, to really see a psycho lived there, dolls were everywhere, big ones little ones even life sized ones, or is that human, on a dresser mantle piece was a snap shot of what looked like a girl and a boy, he tore off the back holder, to read, "Mary and her boyfriend the late Johnny Duval, he took the picture with him, as he sensed he was on the right trail, knowing his trunk was full of Brian, he dials up Mark, who answers to say, "What's your location?"

"Oh about five miles south of your location, we have found a clue that some guy, who is weird, only comes out at night, to shop, and lure woman, another girl went missing, just an hour ago?" said Mark.

"Go ahead continue on that, have you seen or heard from Brian?"

"He told me, that he felt uncomfortable with all this, and he went to go back to the plane."

"Fair enough, keep me informed, I'll be here a while longer." said Jack as he slid his phone closed to see the Calvary was coming at him, as he stood by his car, as Lisa and her crew exit, for which Jack points to the smelter, and Lisa meets up with him to say, "We did it your way and not one causality, the Rednecks went peacefully, and the natives, were all placed on buses to all area hospitals, for care, some five hundred plus was accounted for, what is your plan now?"

"I'm going to survey their land, and if need be build brand new houses, a new school, hospital and clinic?"

"What about Belarus?"

"Any new word yet?" asks Jack, as he adds, "Open trunk", it automatically open to hear, "What is going on here, I have rights?"

"Sure you do, tell me about Johnny Duval?"

"I don't know what you're talking about" as he tried to poke his head out, to see where he is at, only to hear, "We have bones, cut up" said an agent running to them, to stop, catch his breath, to say, "Ma'am, you have to see it, there must be over a thousand skulls and counting."

Just as a puke green sedan drove up, it stopped a mean looking man got out to say, "Which one of you is Jack Cash?"

Everyone pointed to Jack and Lisa by his car, as he came to them, he said politely, "Mister Cash, I'm Clarance Morey, your interrogator, where are they at and what info do you need?"

"Well the captive is here in my trunk, but he says he has rights?"

"Aw horse shit, the only right he has is to live, that is unless you want him dead, and I can do that too?"

"It's your prerogative, he is useless to me now, unless I find out, where and who this Johnny Duval really is", said Jack as he and Lisa stepped aside to see two big burly men, carefully, lifted the struggling man out only to see he had wet himself, for the man named Clarance to say, "I believe he made a mess in your trunk." The guy struggled up the stairs and into the house.

Jack and Lisa both look at the huge wet spot in the trunk, to hear her say, "Jim won't like that."

"I wouldn't worry about it too much, as you can see the carpet comes right out, besides I think I'm going to ask him to reconfigure the trunk, for some padding, as you can see I use it to haul around my prisoners" said Jack.

"I can see that, but also see the front is for all your cuties" and adds, "How is it you're attractive to so many young girls to you?"

"It's a talent really" said Jack as Lisa walks off, to have Jack continue speaking he hears behind him his name to turn to see Clarance.

"He is singing like a canary, your man says the guy you're looking for is his brother, and lives, off of cedar point road, within the Mohaupt reservation."

"Is the guy still alive?"

"Oh yeah, you wouldn't believe it, we took him in and he saw his beloved pit bull dead and flipped out, so I used that, against him, and he talked, you know that dog is huge, I couldn't imagine any bullet killing it, well it's all on you now, you don't mind if we follow you?"

"What about your prisoner?" asked Jack?

"Oh he is a little incapacitated if you know what I mean?"

"Well then let's go" said Jack, to say, "Close trunk", Jack got in to see the girls all were awake, and each were smiling at him, as Jill said, "Sorry, we must of all been tired to help you, I see were at the cemetery, you know this is where the kids go to commit suicide?"

"Interesting so you know about it, that info could have been helpful earlier?"

"Again sorry" said Jill.

Jack started the car, back out and drove out, past all the people, back on the gravel road, he came down to the crossing and in front of him was the reservation, he took a left, he pulled up his display screen to hit the S and the tire traction spikes were deployed, now the drive was smooth, and in a controlled manner, up the road, to a gate. That said, "Property of the Mohaupt reservation, keep out."

Jack stopped the car to get out, he went over, to the huge lock, and pulled out his pick kit, put in the file, and pick and found the lock arm and it unclick, he put the tools away, to unlock the chain, he wrapped it around the post, and swung, the gate open, as he got back in to hear, "Did you have a key?" asked Jill.

"Yes I did" said Jack, as he drove forward, to a T in the road, a sign on the right said, "Beware flood plain, so he went left, up a small hill, and trees everywhere, it was getting later, as the road, came to its highest peak, he stopped the car to say, "Listen up girls I need you to stay here, I need to check this out?"

Jill pleaded with Jack to allow her to go, so he said, "Alright you can come, just stay behind me?"

"Gladly, she said with a smile, Jack got out, and started down the small hill with Jill behind him, he noticed two tracks at the bottom of the road, it was getting a little darker, then heard a car, coming at him, he dove out of the way while, tackling Jill and the two went into a sand bank. Jack looked back at the small sedan, to whisper, "Stealth mode", then stood up to help Jill up to see the car fishtail it up the road, for her to hit him in the arm and said, "What did you do that for, now my hair is all sandy."

"Hush, you wanted to come, now be quiet", as they continued to follow the road that faced the ocean, next to a raised railroad track, the lights of the cabin above shined out as the darkness became thick, to the rumblings of a high speed train was fast approaching, the noise was deafening as his plugged his ears, as it went by, realizing he needed a distraction, he said to Jill "Come here closer."

"Yes Jack, now that you got me all alone out here what do you wants to do to me?" she said as she was stroking his arm.

"Listen not now" said Jack, as she was looking for his manhood, for her to say, "So there will be a later time?"

"What about your boyfriend?"

Who cares about him Jack, why worry about a wild boy when I can have a man, especially one who is a Bounty Hunter?"

Jack just looked at her, to say "Call Carly and have Austin and her walk up the hill to and wander into the woods, to see the Ocean; there is a cabin up there."

Jill did as to what she was told, her silhouette was very noticeable under the full moon, and she was pretty sexy, thought Jack, to hear, "Alright they are on their way" she said.

Jack's phone rang, he answered it to hear, "Jack this is Clarence, we got the sedan and the two guys who said they were having a party and your girl is the main attraction, however, there is another problem, they are bomb makers, and that whole place is wired?"

Jack closed up his phone to say, "Jill call off your girls and get them back into the car?"

Jack waited, as she said, "I can't reach her she must not have her phone with her.

A loud explosion was heard as it vibrated through the ground, as Jack jumped onto Jill, while on the hill, he was somewhat sad, that meant either or both girls were dead, to hear, very loudly, "Hey we got two girls out here, shut off the fields."

Jill said, "Now this is what I like allow me to spread my legs for you, I'm not wearing any panties?" while Jack laid on her.

"Hush up, were going, and I think the girls are safe as another said, "Jimmy go down and escort the lost girls up here, we will have fun with them, as Jack saw Jimmy close by, and jumped him, striking him in the kidney's and with his weapon, delivering the knockout blow as Jack took him down, he zip tied his wrists, and then saw Jill there holding his feet together, Jack zip tied them together, as they were off, Jack felt wires he ran through, with Jill right behind, to the top of a wall that over looked a driveway where several cars were parked, Jill was next to him to say, "What do you think it is?"

"A hide out of sorts, here on a reservation, that no one uses, so they can do as they please, Ssh."

Jack and Jill heard another man say, "Look at these two their hot?"

"Leave us alone or my boyfriend will kill both of you?"

"Tough talk for a prisoner" said the other, to add, "Take them to see Johnny, he probably knows them, their age, also tape their mouths shut, they have a tendency to want to scream, and you know how it echoes through here."

Jack pushed Jill away from him, so that he could make his move, down the wall, to a bench, and across the parking space, Jack, used his weapon, like a club, and struck the guy, who went down, Jack, pulled him away from the door, to see Jill was there to help, she said, "Leave me those, I'll do this, go get the girls."

Jack entered the lavish looking house, gun drawn, and ready, room by room, it was quiet, then there was the stairs down one level, and all the noise was heard, Jack caught a glimpse, of what was going on, over twenty men naked, with a partner, a younger female companion, going at it, off to his right was a full length bar, then he sensed someone behind him, he turned to see it was Jill, who said, "What's going on?"

"You wouldn't want to know."

"Try me, Jack, as she peered around to see and turn back to him to say, "Come on it looks like fun, besides that could be our cover, let me lead you in," she got up to begin to undress, off went her top and skirt, to allow him to see that she was nude and comfortable, to the point, that she took his hand as he holstered, and zipped up, to see the action all around them as the other men, OooH and Aah'd over her nearly perfect body, as she saw some of her friends even, who saw her, a door past the pool table, she tried it, it opened to a bed, as she turned on the lights, she said, "You can take me here lover, over there, or where ever, as Jack closed the door, and turned out the lights, Jack crossed the room. To the other door, to hear, "We need to keep our cover, come do me on the bed", as she held her butt out on the edge of the bed, she was on all fours.

"Hush up" said Jack as he opened the other door to hear, "There are the two running around out there."

Jack sees a young guy turnaround in a black high back chair to see Carly, naked say, "Who did you come with?"

"His name is Jack, said Carly.

"Sorry don't know him, was he on the invite list?"

"Yes according to this list it says Jack Thompson and others?"

"Oh him, so why aren't you girls down in the dungeon, playing with that group?"

"Carly held Austin, who still wore her panties and bra back to say, "We told Jack that we wanted to go skinny dipping in the hot tub?"

"Sorry we don't have a hot tub?"

"That's why we couldn't find one, Duh?" said Carly.

"Yeah duh, if you girls want to skinny dip, then why don't you do it for me?"

"Sure I don't mind, but not in front of your friends?"

"This is an orgy, had you not seen the girls here before?"

"Sorry we don't roll that way, it's either her and I and you or nothing?" said a confident Carly.

"Doesn't look like you're in any position to make any demands" said Johnny, taking a deep breath, to say, "All right fella's, out with you."

"You sure Johnny, that one's looks dangerous."

"Don't worry about me; turn the mine field back on."

"Yes Johnny" said another, as Jack watches them leave, he motions for Carly, to see him as she winks, to say, "Alright Johnny, come over here so Austin and I can service your needs." Johnny did so with his back to Jack, began to undress, instantly Jack put Johnny in a sleeper hold, to whisper, "Where is Keisha?"

"In the dungeon?," to add, as he pointed, "Down there", as Jack put him to sleep, Johnny dropped, then Jack zip tied him, to say, "Now girls, I need you to lure the three others into here, I'll nail them at the door, Austin go get Jill to help you."

They nodded their head in agreement, as Jack was tempted to go down below, but knew, he could deflect the use of gunplay if he could only take down all these men, one by one, the very nude Jill and Carly used their charm to lure the men, into the room, and one by one, Jack used his pistol to knock them out, while Austin, finally herself who was naked, joined in on the fun, and zip tied them up in the adjoining bathroom.

Then when Carly told Jack that there were five left, they seemed agitated, Jack stepped out and held his gun out, as the girls all scattered, as both Jill and Carly zip tied the remainder, of the men, they even put a sock in their mouths and taped their mouth shut."

Something both girls felt and they thought was no fun.

Jack then asked the girls to get dressed, and to wait, because the outsides had booby traps, they all nodded, as Jill, Carly and Austin, did as well, Jack led, to the door, that said dungeon, he opened it, the solid stone wall, was damp, as they went down the stone steps, to see a bevy of woman, in different positions, and some large guy, dressed in all black latex, with a mask on, using a whip on all these girls, some were laughing others were crying, and others still were caged, with a male partner, then there was his girl, Keisha, spread out on a wheel, naked, her wrists and ankles pinned to the wood, blood was everywhere, as the guy, would spin it, then strike her with the whip to say, "Are you ready now to get fucked?"

"No I want my daddy" she pleaded for help.

Jack knew this was painful to watch, especially for some other young girls in cages, he thought he could just kill these sick bastards, or have them rest in their own prison, he moved, and tackled the big man, who was caught off guard at first, but was huge, he kicked Jack, as Jack lost his gun, the guy picked it up, and began to shoot at Jack, and the other girls, who were letting some other girls go, as the ammo ran out, he tossed it aside, Jack dove at him, catching his shoulder on his knee, a pain shot through his body, as he lay motionless, as he heard a crack of the whip, and then a thud, as he saw Jill and the two other girls pull the beast down, onto a half spear and was impaled on it.

They came to Jack's rescue, helping him up, he said, "Let her down, and let's call in the Calvary."

Jack was on the phone to Lisa to tell her that the place was rigged, and that Keisha was found, she told him to rest up and help was on the way."

The three girls helped Jack up the stairs, into the bed, of Jonny's, Jack was sore and tired, he fell fast asleep.

CH 4

Assembly to Belarus

The next morning, the sun was up and agents were all over the place. Jack awoke, to see Lisa was sitting on his bed, to say,

"Well done, another twenty five captured, I know Clarance is in high heaven, he is doing what he does best, so far there is a lot of people connected with his scheme, from the looks of it you have a separated shoulder, that fight downstairs with that beast must have been one for the ages, Erica said your quite a hero, trying to preserve lives rather than take them, a true spy, just kills people without regards to any life, but no, along comes Jack Cash, who saves them, then there is Clarance, who gets the information out of them, he is now part of your team."

"What about the girls?" asks Jack.

"What about them, they were merely a distraction for you?"

"Where are they at?" asks Jack.

"They had to get back to class, forget about them, they served their country and now their leading their own lives."

"I'd like to do something for them?"

"Like what pay their tuition?" asks Lisa.

"Yeah, how did you know?"

"Tami worked it out with the university to get three full ride scholarships, for the full term and forgive their already large debt."

"Good, only problem, Austin wants to go to Wisconsin University, in Madison."

"So it will happen. Don't worry, look your all beat up, you need a spa treatment, a place to rest and relax" said Lisa.

"I agree with that" said Jack sliding off the bed, as Lisa helped Jack through an empty room, and up the stairs, past the kitchen, to the door to the outside, Lisa said "I want to take you to the hospital's to have that shoulder checked out, outside stood a tall woman, cute, to hug Jack on the other side, she kissed his cheek, to say, "Thank you, My husband and I are very grateful for finding our daughter, is there anything I or Jim could do, just let us know?"

"Thanks, but don't need a thing, said a tired Jack, as Lisa helped Jack into the back of a suburban, as she took the front seat, he looked over to see it was Blythe, who said, "Hi Jack, nice to see you", the suburban stopped across where Jack's car was under cloak, Jack eased out, to hear, "I can go with you" said Blythe.

"Nah, don't bother, I'll be right behind, Jack made it to his car, which opened for him, he slid in, sitting in the cup holder was two energy drinks, he popped their tops, and drank them down, feeling better, he took it off cloak mode, to turn around, the energy drinks woke him up, and he could smell the girls presence, which put a smile on his face, to think it would be nice to see them again. Then thinking he needed to take advantage when it was available to him, not wait till later, he knows he always does that, now he was driving, better, he thought about his gun, he felt it under his arm, it didn't do its job, but as he followed the suburban, off to the left he saw the reservation, and the mass of heavy equipment, thinking I bet living on the flood plain isn't very good for you", they exited onto the freeway, and drove a bit past a major brewery, then turned off, in downtown, to a hospital, Jack parked, near the suburban, then saw Ramon, and Lisa come to his aid, with their help, to a wheel chair, Jack sat, and was wheeled in, it was like the spa, hospital staff members, lined up, to begin to say their thanks, as he was whisked into a room, the door shut, the light came on, standing on the other end of the room was a man of some Spanish descent, who spoke perfect English say, "Great Job, Jack Cash."

Jack just looked up at him to smile, to hear, "Do you know who I am?"

Jack shakes his head, no.

"Well I'm the President of the International council for worldwide corruption, and I'm here to see how are you doing and ask, "Where is your survey?"

"Jack shakes his head, to say, "I don't know."

"Really that isn't why I'm here, it is my job, to help those who help us, your efforts are so commendable, that I personally wanted to come visit you, to congratulate you for the job in Brussels' and to let you know that you have two options from the King himself, first he would like you to receive a trust in your name, and marry his youngest daughter, as a gift to you or make you a governor?"

"Is this something I have to decide right now, I'm somewhat in a mission, will I see you in two weeks anyway?"

"Yes this is true, but the King would like an answer?"

"Fine, the trust then" said Jack.

"And his daughter?"

"Sure, do you have a picture?"

"Nah, you'll have to see her yourself in person" said the President.

As Jack looks at him, and he hears, "When you get to the meeting, you'll have plenty of time to rest, take care."

The President left, and everyone piled in, especially one person, Doctor Elizabeth Snyder, from Washington D.C., who said, "Now as your physician, let's get you to the x-ray room, he smiled as he looked at her, as she administered a mild sedative.

Meanwhile outside Jim was at his car, he disabled the car's Jack mode, to his, and drove the car out, the smell of energy drinks, and perfume was intoxicating, as the drive was short, as he made it back to the hanger, to see Brian was kissing his new girl friend as he pulled up, she was excited to see that car, that Jim asked her to leave, Brian and her parted ways for him to say "What is your plan now, are you thinking of quitting the service to spend with her?" asked Jim.

"I'm going to ask Miss Meyers if I could bring her to Quantico."

"What is this Brian show, now?"

"No, I was thinking that if everyone else had someone why can't I?"

"First off, because it's the Jack show, besides shut up and help me with this car, as he popped the trunk, to get a whiff of that smell, for Brian to say, "Do we throw this away?" holding the saturated piece of carpet."

"No, you're going to go wash it and dry it, we need to keep everything intact, were going to Belarus."

"Really" expressed Brian.

"Yeah, in an hour or two".

Jim thought to himself, "How can I get this perfume out of the car, it smell, although nice."

Back at the hospital, two big men, with charts in hand said, "Jack the prognosis looks good, we could pop your shoulder back in, and no further medical treatment is necessary, as you can see there is plenty of room, to move the shoulder in and out of position."

"Yeah, it can help you get out of a strait jacket" said the other Doctor.

"Doctor Mike we agreed not to tell him that, so stand up as Jack did, and face me, I'll hold this part while Mike pushes on the other, "Pop" it went back in, at first it hurt, then subsided, to hear, from Doctor Mike, "From now on, it may be painful, but as the inside of the saddle gets worn, it won't hurt as much."

"Well take care, I'll send in your doctor now."

Moments later, Elizabeth came in, to hug Jack to say, "Everything looks good, are you alright?, you have turned this place upside down. How do you feel?"

"Well now that you asked, got anything to keep me awake?"

"I could prescribe some amphetamines, but there addictive?"

"I'm just way too tired; I take energy drinks as it is?"

"Alright wait here I'll be back." she said.

Jack sat on the bed, to wait, only to see Lisa come in, to say, "Looks like your getting some treatment."

"How is the buffet here?"

"They don't have one, this is a city hospital, and they don't have time for that."

"How do you know all of that" asked Jack.

"I saw the food and it looks disgusting."

"Your hungry and I'm thirsty, at least I have my backpack outside, with some protein bars in it."

"About that, the car is gone."

"Great, now what, how about steak and eggs, I saw a sign coming in" said Jack in a near panic mode.

"I guess we could hit that on our way out" said Lisa.

"What do you mean by that?"

"Haven't you heard I'm going with you to Belarus, actually your whole team by order of the President, two more terrorist cells have been discovered, were going non-stop to Minsk, a thirteen hour flight, also we got another problem?"

"What's that?" asked Jack.

"It's about Brian the armorer" said Lisa.

"Yeah, I know about him wanting out of the field."

"Yes, but what you don't know is that he had inappropriate relations with a member of my team?"

"Was it consensual" asked Jack.

"Yes, that doesn't matter, it jeopardized the mission. That is no excuse."

"So let him have his fun, heck bring her along, I don't care, but what I do care about is Blythe."

"You wanted her, so you got her."

"That seemed like an eternity ago, I've actually moved on, if it were me I'd take the three girls who helped me out at Johnny's place."

"Really you don't say, why do you say that?"

"Well to begin with their fearless."

"Who's fearless?" said Elizabeth coming in to say "Now Jack take two of these two times a day till they run out."

"What are they Doctor?" asked Lisa.

"Their for his headaches?" she smiled at Jack.

"Is he free to go now?" asked Lisa.

"He is, but when you get back I want to give you a full physical?" she continued to smile.

"You got that doc," said Jack passing her, feeling it kicking in, to say to Lisa, "Where to now, to get something to eat?"

"Well you tribe awaits?"

"What did she say? said Jack follows Lisa and her crew, down the stairs, to the sidewalk, to walk across the street to the Bell Gardens auditorium, to see them hold the door open for Jack as he enters, to see a crowd of people, who stood and began to clap, then a bigger man stepped forward to say, "Thank you on behalf of my people, for eradicating the evil in those bikers and that crazy man, who use, to use us for target practice, we had no where to turn, even the police were against us, then there is you, the President of the UN international, came and gave us a talk, and suggested we appoint you as our trustee, to handle the rebuilding and growth of our reservation, in exchange we will give you, some land, a percentage and any of our daughters you find interesting?"

Jack looked at Lisa as she smiled back at him, to continue listening, as he said, "Over the years the bikers depleted our savings and welfare checks, and now we are asking if you could help us?"

"Sure, I'll be your trustee" said Jack loudly.

The people all cheered, to hear, "So mister Jack Cash, which of our daughters would you like?"

"How about I choose later, let's focus in on, rebuilding and helping your current situation, shortly I have asked my trusted builder to come here, but in the meantime, let's talk about what you need" said Jack as the leader went on to tell him, the school is in a shambles, no clinic, and all the house are on the flood plain. Jack says, "This is what I think we should do, first raise the land six feet, and create a network of drain culverts."

"Nah, it smells down there" said a senior elder.

"Alright, let's find high ground, like where Johnny lived, flattening it off, and put the school on one side, housing on top, and along the road, and where you once lived, build a community hospital/clinic, what about a casino?"

"What's that? I'm not familiar with that term?" said the high elder.

"It's where you make money, on chance."

"That is gambling, and we can't do that?"

"Fair enough, said Jack, "How about a farmers market?"

"What is that?"

"It is a place where each of your family has a location, say on Wednesday, and Saturdays, to sell what you make?"

"That I like?"

"Fine I will have Robert, come see each of your families to decide on a house and a community auditorium like this, actually hold on a minute, I'll call him now, as Jack dialed him up, he told Rob, he wanted the soil raised six feet, on a slope, to a catch culvert, then a school on the further most spot, to include a community center and a hospital, like three story, along the hill side across the plains, there is an exit from the hwy, to help, next, place fill and top soil along the edge of the hills, to the river, by the railroad tracks, then on the hill build enough homes for all the clans, to go south, along the road, back west to the original settlement, and you have engineers here in place to demolish those houses I want a farmers market, with, lockable shacks, and a front counter top, so that guest may park, in a parking lot, any other questions you can coordinate with my assistant Tami, who will be here overseeing this process."

"Really that long, well alright then."

Jack slides his phone shut to say, "The builder said it would take two weeks, but until then I'm putting you all up into a hotel?"

Another cheer went off, as Jack began to yawn, to say, "Alright I must go, see ya" said Jack as they all waved good bye.

The doors were open as Jack exited, and into the suburban, as Jack got in he saw Clarance, a bit dirtied up, as Lisa and Ramon got in, Jack said, "Where's Blythe?"

"Didn't you say to me, you don't have much interest in her?" said Lisa.

"Yes" said Jack.

"Well she is staying here to help out our efforts here, while we fly overseas."

"Well I thought the more the merrier."

That was the last thing that was said, as they passed the steakhouse, Jack was beginning to think this was the Lisa show all over again, so Jack kept quiet, for the rest of the trip to the airport they went.

Lisa instructed Ramon where to go, passing all the available fast food places, all the way to the airport, into the awaiting hanger. Everyone exited, last was Jack, he got out, to see Brian, for him first to say, do you have a moment?"

"Yeah, sure, what's up?" said a bothered Brian.

"You seem cocky" said Jack.

"Oh not much, I'm sorry I failed you out in the field?"

"No you didn't, your job is plain and simple, you're my armorer, if you feel there is something I ask of you beyond your abilities then let me know, hey I heard you found somebody you really like?"

"Yeah, I just sent her away."

"You don't have to, it's cool with me, just ask me next time."

"Cool, cool, should I ask her to come?" "Yes, that's fine, there now, that's the Brian I know and care about, and so did you load up those weapons I asked about?"

"Yep, in the new armory/lab, do you want to see them?"

"Nah, but you better go get your girl, and oh by the way, I don't want anyone else touching them?"

"What's going on?"

"I think we have a plant, spreading his/hers roots among us all."

"Oh I get cha," said Brian.

"So were going to allow your girl to come with us in hopes she may uncover who that may be, and another thing, my weapon somewhat failed me?"

"When we get off the ground let me check it out, all I know is to charge it, it never needs cleaning, instead of the white box, I have a direct to the batteries, charger."

"Thanks, said Jack patting Brian on the back, and then going inside to see the car is secured, he walked past that to the galley, only to pause to see a screen up in the flight cabin, then said, "Hi Trixie, I was wondering if I could have a meal, milks and coffee brought in?"

"Yes Jack" she said, a bit upset or so Jack thought, he opened his door, then stepped in to close it, he took off his jacket, to discard it, then his holster, and weapon, he put in the box, to see the white handle was green, then changing to a light red, he closed the box, to undress. Meanwhile outside the hanger door stood Barbie her arms crossed, to finally see the gullible boy, Brian, come out to say, "He went for it, your on board", as he went to hug her, she side stepped him, to go back in as the plane started up, Brian, ran to the ramp, he took the controls, to say, "All clear for take off, as the ramp lifted up. Jack was told of the lift off, over the intercom, he sat on the bed, to see the door open and hot fresh food came in, as Trixie carried it to him to say, "Here you go Mister Cash."

"Whoa wait a minute, what is going on here?"

"You'll find out later" she said as quickly left, she closed the door.

"Strange" thought Jack as he quickly finished the food, and two chocolate milks, and was wondering where the coffee was at, when he set his tray down to see the door opening, he saw Gia first, then Jill and then Carly, all step in, to close the door, as Gia spoke first, "Were here to serve you in any capacity as you see fit?" she smiled.

Jack just looked at them all dressed in military gear, with names on their lapels, to say, "That was quick, so you joined the Army?"

"No silly, the three of us joined your team, I guess you told Lisa how much you liked us, so when she asked us to join we all said yes, except Austin, she was through with all of this, but did want to let you know, if you ever go by Madison, she would give you a free pass, but for the rest of us, who wouldn't want to work for the most famous of all, a super spy."

Jack looked them over up and down, to think about this, to say, "Alright I have a mission for each of you, first for Carly, I want you to go into the flight cabin and sit and observe everything that they are doing, do you have cell phones?"

"Yes Lisa gave them to us."

"Excellent, use the ear piece portion, to communicate with me, go ahead and go, Jill can you help out with serving as a hostess."

"Yes, I've done something similar to that."

"And Gia, well, I need you to sit out in the cargo bay and observe those around you and let me know if there is anything going on outside these walls, the other two nodded, and then lingered, then left, as Jack waited, then went in to take a quick shower.

Meanwhile at the galley Trixie was serving the MRE rations, to the people on board, only to hear, "Hi, my name is Jill and Jack asked me to help you."

Trixie turned to see this stunner of a girl, at least four years younger than her, to say, "Sure, there isn't many trays to go around, so I'm serving those higher ranking than those of workers."

"Alright who should I bring those to first?" asked Jill.

"Jim and Lisa, in that order, I'll take this to Brian and Mark, as Trixie passes Blythe, who sat with Barbie a blonde girl, next to her was a large Hispanic guy, to see Brian in his armory, she say, "Brian, I got some chow for you, where do you want it?"

Eagerly, He comes around the corner, towards her, only to take the chow platter, to say "Thanks" and smiles at her.

As Brian steps out of the cage, he smiles at his prize, Barbie, as she doesn't acknowledge him.

Brian, set his tray down, to lock up his cage, to see her, he went to her, gushing himself to her, and she was having none of that as she ignored him for him to say, "I'm glad your on this flight."

"So am I and I just got a huge raise, so if you please leave me alone, I'm here for Jack Cash", she said, as Ramon, felt the tension, and moved a seat or so away, to hear, "Where are you going spick."

Ramon, wasn't having any of that, and went to hold her, to hear, "Enough, Ramon sit back down," said Lisa in a stern voice, to add, "So your just in it for the money, this whole story of you liking Brian, she then stood and pulled her weapon, to point it at Lisa, Gia who saw all of this, called Jack, but got no response, but it was Jill who took the initiative, to use the tray as a weapon, to knock the gun out of her hand, then it was Ramon and Brian, who subdued her, to the floor, a clean and refreshed Jack opened his door to see them to say, "Wow, what did I miss", then said, "Do you guys need help?"

"Nah, we got it" said Brian, looking back at Jack, as Lisa took a seat, and for Casey, to react to what was going on, as he zip tied her up, much to Lisa's satisfaction. Lisa looked at the girl then towards Jack, she thought she needed a place to escape this drama and relax, knowing now, that she was too close, and better back away, as she had her hand on the flight cabin door, only to find it to be locked, she kept trying it, as Trixie said, "It won't do any good?"

"Why's that?"

"Were lining up for a refueling run, see the light above you indicates, cabin is secure, once it goes out, then you can go in, from the looks of it, you want to go in and we could probably use Clarance out here."

After the refueling run, the flight cabin door opened, Mark slept through the whole thing, as His friend Trixie offered him up a plate, he looked at her, to smile, both knew their was a line that has been drawn, as she placed the plate down next to him, to walk away, he looked over at Casey who was man handling the pretty looking blonde, as he tossed her into the lower bunk, then zip tied her ankles and mouth, but was smelling something a lot more sweeter across from him, as Mark saw a quite striking young lady the military outfit did her no justice, as she too turned down a plate of rations, from Trixie, Mark was tempted to say something, as his phone rang, he saw who it was to say, "What's up buddy?"

"Heard you're going overseas, why wasn't I called?"

"Because your on vacation, so how is it with the wife and kids?" said Mark.

"Oh you know their loving it here in the Bahamas, how's it going with you guys?"

"Ah, you know same old thing, go in and rescue someone, and free a nation."

"What's wrong buddy" asked Mike.

"Oh, we got some heavy's with us, and three hot unknowns, and one out of place?"

"I sure wish I could be there with you now" asked Mike, to add "You know me I get bored with all this rest."

"It's only been a week."

"Precisely, that's all I needed, I'm ready to get back in the game."

"I don't see why you couldn't link up with us, ground support is always helpful, no one really needs to know I guess?" said Mark.

"Thanks, I will show you my appreciation."

"Not me, just being there for Jack, I'll call Erica, and confirm a flight out", said Mark.

"Thanks buddy."

Mark closed up the phone, to scroll down to see the words of Miss Erica Meyers, and pushed send, with the E-mail written sent received, and responded, she said "Mike is currently under investigation for going into a hostile area without prior approval, from the UN and two are on their way to the Bahamas to pick him up, and then onto Switzerland for questioning."

Mark closed up his phone to remember when he saw Mike, messed up, now that was funny, he thought, he also began to think about a more wilder time, when guns for hire was popular, as he knew his father was a mercenary, but those days are past, long gone actually, now that the UN has come together to create this super force of personnel, designed to help the super spy, but it does one thing it eliminates any outside interferences. Mark looked up to see that cute girl in front of him saying something, for him to say, "I'm sorry what did you say?"

"I said my name is Carly" with her hand out to shake.

"Names Mark", he said as the two shook, he immediately felt her warm soft hand, to hear her say, "I'm thirsty, and do you know where I can get some bottled water?"

That made Mark smile, then chuckle, to say, "Stay here, I'll get you one."

Mark sees her take a seat, he walked out of the flight cabin, to the galley to see Lisa and Trixie, instant awkwardness, as Trixie, allowed her into the head, which she then closes the folding door, for Mark to get close to Trixie, to say, "Could I get a couple of water's?"

She looked at him, and then walked off, with a pot of fresh brewed coffee, in one hand and a cup of lemons in the other.

He watched her leave to say, "Now where does she keep those water's?"

A tap on the steel door, Jack looked up as the door swung open, Jack saw Trixie, for a moment then Jill, in the background who smiled at him, as the door closed shut, Trixie stood in front of Jack, to say, "I made a fresh pot of coffee, and cut some lemons, would you like a cup?"

"Sure, thanks" said Jack, his chest exposed as he held a encryption book in his hand, along with several other books, she poured him a cup, to drop the lemon in it, to say, "May I join you?", a pause, for her, to say "For cup of coffee?"

"Absolutely, come on over here" he said with excitement in his voice.

She brought over two cups and handed one to him, to sit next to him on the bed; she drank, and saw all the books, to say, "I didn't know you read so much?"

"Only before a big job, it gives me some insight on the city, culture and customs."

"That's fascinating, she said honestly and with enthusiasm.

Jack said, "Help yourself, read anything you like, your part of my team."

Trixie, set her cup of coffee down, then reached across him, to lose balance and land on him, she was apologizing, as Jack said "Don't worry about it, that's alright for you to grope me, I don't mind."

"Really" she said, with a book on Belarus in her hand, and Jacks hand on her arm, he began to stroke it, as she left it there for him to continue, then she spoke, "I'm sorry."

"For what?" asked Jack?

"For becoming attracted to you?" she said in her sweet unassuming way.

"That's alright with me; I'm getting attracted to you too."

"What do you mean?" she asked.

"Well on the ride over here I thought how nice is it to know Trixie will be there waiting for me."

"Shut up, your such a bad boy", she tossed the book aside and went in to kiss Jack, as two adults, they went at it lipped locked, she was shredding her clothes, as Jack dropped his pants, he was at the ready, as she took all of him, and did it like rabbits, finally Jack dominated her body, as she collapsed, while he was still going, but realized quickly, it wasn't a game, so he pulled out and collapsed on top of her, as he fell fast asleep with his arms around her.

It was in the daytime as Jim announced one hour away from landing, Jack awoke from a nice dream, only to feel nothing but firmness and softness, his hand was all over her body, as she lay next to him, with her back to him, leaving his hands to wander, she opened her eyes to turn, to say, "Of all the girls outside that door, why did you choose me?"

"Because, I like you and this was the first time I have had a chance, so why not enjoy it."

"Like, I never ever heard that before" she said it more as a statement, but it felt nice to be appreciated, and although she was awake for the last four hours, she too liked the intimacy for which he held her and stroked her, even Mark, wasn't like that, it was in and out and done, but for the last twelve hours of holding felt nice too, she thought as she got up to say, "Thank you for choosing me, but I better go back to work."

"Really, then come back to bed" said Jack.

"Your not one to beg, besides, were landing soon, we could do this later, as he watched her dress, she faced him, to allow for him to see it all get covered up and said, "You better hurry up, were going to be on the ground soon."

"Alright Mom, "said Jack rolling out of the bed, and getting dressed, as she exited.

Jack stood in front of the mirror, finishing dressing, as he placed his holster on, then his gun, white pearl base, then his grey windbreaker over, thinking, "It was getting heavier and heavier to wear, but as he felt all the right places, he felt secure knowing he had his backups in place". Jack, turned and made up the bed, or so he tried, he slipped on his comfortable shoes, then sat down, to pull up his pant leg, to insert the two knifes, in the protective sheaths, then stood, to hear, over the intercom, "Prepare for landing", Jack sat back down, to begin to think about Sara, then Maria, and then Alba, to smile at Alexandra, four beautiful and phenomenal woman, and of his most recent acquisitions, the two twins, Cara and Christina, Isabella and her older sister Maria Ingles, she was actually the oldest of them all by twenty years, she was cute, but weak at the elbows, then there was Daphne a real gem, she needed to find a place which once supported her life style, and this is as close as it comes, and there was Tia Riley, a 5foot titan in the bed, the one out of place was Lindsay, but once she said, that whoever took her virginity, would be her man, so can't argue with that, then there was the model, Samantha White, another rich girl, who needed a real man to shape her up, the ones he really remembers as the ones to fuck were India, who is now pregnant, and Melanie, all have cleaned up their acts, drug and smoke free, living a secret life as Misses Jack Cash. He went on to think, "Maybe Trixie, nah, Mitzi, Blythe was a choice, however she has become this selfish bitch, what to do with her, a totally hot girl who has gone bad, maybe she's the mole." The plane lands, then taxi's into a hanger, as the plane shuts down, the ramp lowers, everyone is running around, Casey and Clark and their men, Jim, and Brian, undo the car, and Jim drives it out. Jack opens the door, to see his friend Lisa smiling back at him, to say, "Are you ready and refreshed?"

"Sure how bout you?" asked Jack.

"I wish, with all the drama going on out here."

"All you had to do was ask and I'd let you come spend the night."

"Oh not in you bed" said Lisa.

"No that's not what I'm saying; I have a pull out bed in my sofa."

"Really" asked Lisa.

"Sure, Have Trixie make it up, and while were off, rest a bit, under one condition?"

"What's that?", as she continued to talk as Jack said, "If you could fill out that pamphlet, and fax it in to the President of the UN."

Jack tosses it to her; she catches it to say, "From the cover it wants to know who will be your one guest?"

"I don't know who wants to go with me?"

The only one who raised her hand was Blythe, so Jack said, "So it shall be, put Blythe down."

"Really, thanks" she said as she literally jumped onto Jack as the other three coed's looked on, for Jack to say, "Alright Blythe, wait by my car."

To hear from behind him, "Jack there are two UN inspectors who wish to have a word with you."

Jack turned to see two smartly dressed officers, for Jack, to say, "Jim can you escort them into my room, I need to see Brian."

"Right this way" said Jim.

"Trixie" said Jack.

'I'm way ahead of you; I'll have fresh coffee brought in."

"Now for you three, who wants' to be part of the action, who likes danger, and who likes to be on the outside?"

Jill stepped forward to say, "I like it all, what do you have in mind, you and me going a round?"

"Can you go with Casey and Clark, and his men, ever fired a weapon?"

"Yes, and strangely you knew that didn't you" she said with a smile, to add, "You knew my father was a Marine, and that I've traveled the world."

"This is true, that is why you're here, and your new assignment is with them, the strike team."

"Thank you" she said as she jumped at him and gave him a kiss on the cheek, to leave.

"What about me" said Gia?

"You're joining her, what are you waiting for?"

She leaned in, to say, "You know, you could have either of us, or all of us at once" she kissed him on the cheek.

He responded by saying, "I know, this is a time to get to know how you are, so stick close with them and work as a team.

He looks down at Carly to say, "So you're the outsider, but your more than that aren't you, you're a communications major, so I'd like for you to coordinate all voice traffic to me, via our command center, work with Trixie, and she will help you, as for Clarance, I want you in the field is that cool with you ?"

"Yep, you're the boss, what about her?" pointing back to Barbie, zip tied, whom was in the bunk. Said Clarance.

"Let her go" said Jack.

Clarance looked at Lisa as did Ramon, back to Jack as Trixie past them to hear from Lisa, "Jack she pulled a gun on me."

"Yes, but did she fire it?"

"No, but" stammered Lisa.

"Listen it was probably an honest mistake, looks she is in your club, if you don't want her, I'll take her, undo her mouth, let her decide", as Clarance, yanks off the duct tape, she said, "I want to work for Jack Cash."

"Then it's settled, she is on my team, cut her loose, to see Lisa to say, "I gather you're staying behind?"

"Yes."

"Well do you want to hear what the UN inspectors have to say?"

"Sure" said Jack.

Jack led, Lisa in to his cabin then they both go in, then Jack shuts the door.

The two girls stood at the top of the ramp seeing the men work to resupply the plane, and one man named Captain Clark, supervising with a clip board, as they went up to him to say, "Jack asked us to join you guys what can we do?"

"Stand over there, till they are done, please" said Clark.

Inside the room, Jack saw the two UN investigators drinking coffee, as Trixie kept them company, then exited, as Jack and Lisa came in, they waved at Lisa knowing her, but seeing

Jack was a whole new thing, as Jack said, "Sorry to keep you waiting, what do you have for me?"

"First off, My name is Roberta, and this is my partner Gene, Jack waved at him as the two knew of each other, for her to continue, were your assigned attaché for you, although we have not been in contact with you, we are the liaison between the country you are in and its people, the President of Belarus has given you unlimited access anywhere you see fit, and you may arrest as many as you see fit, his only stipulation, is that you are the only one that may carry or fire a weapon."

Jack just looked at her to decide, what to say, as Lisa even looked at him, to try to get a read on him, Jack shook his head, to say, "I guess our visit is over?"

Jack turned to exit as the two UN inspectors, were caught off guard, as Jack opened the door and left, to yell, "Alright lets load up" he stood on the ramp to see Clark, for Jack to say, "Get everything on board, were heading out."

"Mister Cash" said a voice behind him, he turned to see a panicked looking woman who said, "Alright have it your way, I didn't think you would go?"

"I'm not, but if I can't have some ground support, it's best they fly off."

"No, listen to me, please" as she was in near hysterics

Jim was at the ramp controls as he lifted it up, as it closed shut, Jim said, "I'll get everyone in the flight cabin."

Jack looked at both of them, and Lisa even backed away, for her to begin, "Please don't get me wrong, it is not my position to tell you a thing, how you conduct your operations, is yours and we as the UN team are yours, not the other way, as she had tears in her eyes, as she began to cry.

Jack looked at Lisa, as the Gene stepped forward to say, "Can we talk man to man" said Gene.

"Sure, come into my room, have your partner come as well."

Jack led Gene in, then it was Lisa, helping Roberta, as the door closed shut, Jack poured some coffee, and added a wedge of lemon, as she still was crying, for Jack to say, "What do I have to do to make her stop?"

"Listen, can you have a seat?"

"I'll stand" said Jack his back to them.

"Fine, our role is to oversea an air and land force designed to support the whole world, with its aid to their people and antiquities, riches and wealth's, but ultimately we work for you, there is none higher than yourself, as you enter any country on this earth, you have the UN finalizing all the deals, from this point forward, you no longer work for your Supreme Court, your classified as an International Super Spy, and work with a council of members, that oversea your actions abroad, through your record, you have been labeled the preserver of life, you would rather shoot someone in the leg, then just put one in the head, so think of us as the legislative branch, but as for the confrontation's, well that is up to your country to support you with what you need, and with spy club following your every move, we as UN inspectors even have to watch our own backs, so, what my colleague was asking of you, was that the President Lemane, of Belarus." "He requests that only you, fire a weapon, they are merely wishes, if you entrust someone, to protect you as in any case, that is your prerogative, or to allow them to defend you, do you know what I mean?"

"Yes, I guess, it was a communications thing" said Jack.

"Yes, that's it; please forgive us, if we implied anything other than that."

"So what you're saying is, I'm allowed, to fire on anyone I so choose, in the event I'm shot, or down, my support team can protect me."

"Well yes, and no" said Gene, as Jack throws his hands up, Jack pulls out his phone, and goes to the French translator, to say, "Alright Roberta, if you please, tell me in your native language, what you are saying?" asks Jack.

She spoke clearly as it translated to a written and voice repeat, for Jack to understand, for him to say, "Alright, it was a miss-understanding, as the two thanked Jack, as Jack opened the door for them, he dialed up Jim to say, "Open it up and assemble the troops."

Casey, Had his personnel ready as the two UN inspectors passed by to hear, "What had he decided to leave?"

"Then we would have been killed" said Roberta.

"Who would have done that?"

"UN assassins", she said quietly.

Casey overheard her comment, to give her a stare down, as the ramp dropped, as Jack jumped on it, and rode it down, to say, as he saw, the hanger door open, and the UN suburban drive off, to see the hanger door go back down, to say "Alright, Casey, I want these two girls to join your teams, and Clarance will join you in?", he nodded in agreement. "Everyone wear an earpiece, I want the following teams, Paul, Tim and Jill Hoyt." "Casey, Scott and Gia." "Tony, and Jared, and then Art and Brooks, you go lose yourselves." "Then Morris, Bauer and Spancer, Rick and Clarance, then Mark and Roxy." "Blythe will be with me in my car, the President of Belarus has asked that no one will fire their guns, at anyone, or cut anyone up with a knife, if they are in your way, zip tie them up, wrists and ankles and mouth, yes I know about that ruling, so each of you carry a roll of silicon tape, and an all- purpose tool, what I need from all of you four groups, is to scour the city on leads, that will be coordinated by Carly and Trixie, the only person authorized to shoot their weapon is Me, any questions?"

Jack looks at the teams that have separated themselves to their groups, as Jim appeared, to say, "Here is your communication devices, and each of you has the new sat phone, turn it on, coordinate the channel listed in this card, before you leave the building, I would also like to say, "This mission is like no other, dangerous cells have threaten our President and we need your help."

Casey and Mark began to laugh.

"What's so funny" said Clarance.

"It's a joke, he did that to fire up the new girls, that's it, its no big deal, we know that anytime Jack is somewhere it is very important" Mark said looking at the stern and tough Clarance.

Jill walks over to a huge pack, to say, "You want me to carry that, what it is?"

"It's a secret device, exclusively for Jack, and I'm the one who has been tasked to carry it, Morris and Bauer, are assembling your packs and in it is a taser gun and holster, can you fire?"

"Yep, my dad was a Marine."

"Excellent welcome to the team" said Casey, as Jim pulled off the tarp of the car; Jill said "Wow, does that go where ever he goes?"

"Yep, that's his secret car, as she sees Blythe, standing by it to say, "What's her deal?"

Casey looks at Jill to say, "I don't know, her well, I can't really say?"

"Why not is that a secret too?"

"Look Jill, this is not a social call or whatever you think this is, we all work for Jack, we do what he wants and that's it."

"Alright sorry."

"About what?" asked Jack, as he veers over to them, as the trunk opens, Casey puts his hand on her arm to hold her back, to say, "Careful, tread lightly", as she fought him off, Jack looked over his pack, to see a case, he stuffs it in, to feel someone behind him, to see it was Jill, who says, "What are you doing?"

"Nothing" said Jack, to add, "You better stick close to Casey, this is your first test, make me proud, he is waiting for you, so you better get going", she leaves, un-willing, then goes as Brian appears, as the hanger door opens, to show four black vans, as the teams began to leave Brian says, "Everything is ready."

"Then load it up in my trunk, as he lifted up the trunk, to pull out his backpack and see the duffle bag of cash, was still there, he opens the door, only to see Blythe a bit annoyed, to say, "Go ahead and have a seat, but don't touch a thing."

Jack went up the ramp, to see Brian, hustling the weapons out, as he saw Jack to say, "Your gun is still charging, but pull it off if you like, I got it in the middle of the night."

Jack set his bag on the counter, and then pulled off the gun, it hurt from the electricity, but felt warm to him, after he placed a clip in and loaded and locked the chamber, he re-inserted it back in its holster. Jack zipped his jacket, the lining held, magazines loaded, and marked, twelve, he inserted in and then Brian helped him, with the rest, to say, "What do you want me to do with the duffle bag?"

"Just store it for me" said Jack.

"Oh that reminds me" said Brian, to add, "Here is a package for you, from Erica", as he hands it to Jack.

Jack opens it up to see two credit cards and two packs of thousands, to say, "What am I suppose to do with that?", as Brian looks on, to say, "You mean the cash?"

"Yeah, a thousand dollar bill?, Euros would have been better", as Jack stuff's them into their place, to say, "Can you place a blanket over those weapons, in the trunk?"

"Absolutely" said Brian, as Jack exit's the armory he sees Barbie who says, "Thanks Jack for this opportunity."

"Don't thank me, thank Lisa she is you real boss."

CH 5

Special call for help

Jack drove out of the hanger, to say, to Blythe, "So you want to be a spy?, well the UN may open up a place for you, to be in such a way, but in the meantime let me show you how we do it", as Jack took his hands off the wheel, to place the phone into the dash, as Sara drove herself, while Jack pulled up the portable computer screen, to see the three highlighted area's, he spoke, as all the other teams were on line, "All right I want Paul, in car 1 to the north, Casey in car 2 to the south, Tony in car 3 to the east, and hold on, I got another call."

Jack, unplug, his phone, and he answered the call to say, "Sleep", and out went Blythe, to say, "Slow, to a stop," Is this Jack Cash? "I'M Vladimier Ecklon, and I'm the President of Russia, I ask if you could come to my country and find my wife who was kidnapped and recover her?"

"I'd say when and where?" asked Jack, as he received the instructions. Jack pulled up Casey's number to call him to say, "Will you follow Mark's command and continue the mission of finding these terrorist?"

"Yes."

"Thank you, out", Jack ends the call, then he dials up Mark to say, "Mark this is Jack, I need to leave this country, can you continue the operations?"

A long pause, then he said, "Yes, I'll try?"

"Great, I should be back in a few hours or so", to add, "But call me to keep me informed, out", to add, "Turn around back to the plane, looks like were going to St Petersburg, Jack realized either he was in over his head or his team lost their fire for all of this, Jack thinks, "I just wish Mark would come out of his shell, and for Mike to be that daring firefighter, he once knew, good people are hard to find, wait Carlos, he is a Cuban spy", Jack searched his name, but before he could make that call, was a call from Mitzi, he answered it, to hear, "Hi, honey how are you?"

"Oh a bit ruffled" said Jack.

"I heard; guess who I'm on the plane with?"

There was silence as she said, "Erica, and Mike, refreshed and ready to go, in addition, Kelli the CIA agent has agreed to be your partner, and Simone, we heard that you were unhappy with Blythe, so we should be there in twelve hours."

"That is good news, but I'm off to Russia, the Premier's wife has been taken, and has asked me to come rescue her, but if you could get up to speed, by joining the mission in progress, and take over ground operations in Belarus, I'd be very happy with that."

"You can count on me" said Mitzi.

Jack slid the phone shut, as he said, "Phone up, dial Jim, to hear "This is Jim."

"Pull the plane out, and get ready for takeoff, were on a new mission, get Trixie on the phone."

Moments later he heard, "Here Jack, what do you need?"

"A flight plan into St Petersburg."

"Florida, Jack?"

"No Russia, it will be a hot landing!" said Jack.

"A stop and drop?" inquired Trixie.

"Yeah, are you guys ready to leave, I'm around the corner, as Jack saw the plane on the tarmac, with the ramp down, as Jack commanded traction tires, and up he went into the spot, and the ramp went up, as the plane was moving, it turned, and took up speed, and just like that the plane was off the ground.

Jack rode out the lift off, as the car moved a bit but the traction tires held it in place, as his phone rang, he saw where it was coming from, so he said, "This is Jack go."

"Jack, this is the President of Russia, Vladimier Ecklon, I'm sending you a picture and information, about her, also I just received demands of one hundred million Euro's, and if the demands are not met they will rape her repeatedly, until I either pay or resign, she was last seen at the palace in St Petersburg, I myself is moving around with my guards in tow, I will tell you this there are three main forces or groups here in Russia, 1st one being our own guards, and the red army as one, the second is the renegade forces, led by the former party leader, then there is the invaders, that provide the chaos, watch out, both those parties have a super spy like yourself, and both have pledge not to help, so that is why I asked for your help, as I first asked the UN for help, and they suggested you, are you still coming?"

"Yes on my way, less than two hours away."

"Good the air space is cleared, for your arrival, we are now tracking your plane, and you will not receive any greetings, except my best wishes good luck."

Jack closed up his phone to see both Jim and Brian pulling straps, as Jack exited, to see a hoist lift up the car, turn it around, then set it back down, as he went up to the galley to see Trixie and Carly, as a plate of hot food, was set down on the portable table, he said, "Thanks, and could you both do me a favor, pull Blythe out of the car, and put her on the bed, thanks."

Jack ate and drank the chocolate milks, as he looked at the clear refrigerator to see the energy drinks, as he slowly ate the pot roast, and vegetables, apple sauce, he sees Trixie who said, "It is done, she is really out."

"Hey could I have some of those energy drinks?"

"Sure we have lots, ever since we found the one can, they had been stocking up on them."

"Excellent, can you have Jim put a case or two in the car?"

"Sure I'll get right on that" said Trixie, as she takes Carly with her, to see Jim and Brian, securing the car down, to say, "Jack wants to know if you have a case or two of those energy drinks, he can take with him?"

"Yeah there in the Lab, the door should be open" said Brian.

Trixie leads Carly, in to the armory, and to the place, as Trixie accidently knocked over the duffle bag, and cash went everywhere, she panicked, to say, "Help me pick all these up, literally thousand dollar bills, all over the floor, as Carly, helped herself, and stuffed them, in her bra, and in her pockets, as Trixie on her hands and feet, to hear, "What's going on here?" said Brian."

"Sorry It must of just spilled", as Brian, helped Trixie, while Carly, saw a lone one thousand dollar bill, she picked it up, and slipped it in her pocket, as she stood with a smile on her face, as Brian and Trixie finished the rest, this time Brian, zipped up the bag, opened up a locker, and set the bag in there to say, "Look around is there any other pieces of cash?"

On the floor was a bin, as Brian, pulled up two cases, to say "I got this, get going on, girls please."

Brian, carried them to the car, as Jim, held the door open, to allow, Brian to place them behind the seat, to say, "He will need a heavy jacket and gloves, go in and first see where Jack is at, then bring them to me, as Jim sat down, at the steering wheel, to change from warm weather to cold settings, he did a quick diagnostic check, as Trixie came back with the Jacket, gloves, hat and scarf, and a pair of cold weather boots, while Carly, took a seat across from Jack as he looked at her, but still ate, for her to say, "That smells so good, you know your lucky."

"Why's that?" asked Jack.

"Because, you have all these people helping you out."

Jack just looked at her, as the flight cabin door was open, radio chatter was going crazy, to hear, Bill say, over the intercom, "Jim I need you up here we need to send an answer, now."

Jack got up, and went forward, to pick up the mic, to say, "Stand down, this is International Bounty Hunter, Jack Cash, and were coming in", in perfect Russian. He hands it back to the pilot to say, "I don't think we met."

"Well sir, I'm Air Force Colonel Bill Bilson, and was asked to be your pilot."

"Well thank you very much, for agreeing to be my pilot."

Trixie turned the corner to see Carly sitting where Jack was suppose to be at to say, "What are you doing?", in one sweep, she pull up the tray, and inserted it into the recycle bin, to turn, to say in her meanest look ever, "Go over there and sit down."

Jack stands behind Trixie to touch her hips, and she jumped but settled down, to see him, for Jack to say, "Hey what happen to my tray?"

"Oh I'm sorry, I thought you were through."

"Nah, but do you have any more of those sweet tasting rolls?"

"Why yes I do, hold on, let me get you another tray", as Jack took his seat, Jim past them, as Brian also came in, the flight cabin to sit, leaving the door wide open, Jim sat to look at his instrument panel to say, "Brian we got an alarm going off, check the screens."

"What the hell" said Brian?

"What do you got boy" said Jim sliding back out of his seat, to see what Brian was looking at, on the monitor, during all of this commotion, Carly, went into the lab, Brian, was ready to go, when Jim said, "Hold on, what is she up to, what do we have in there, that she could want?"

Brian was tensing as he saw her close to the weapons cage, for Jim to say, "Hold on what is she doing?"

"Is that the cabinet, what is in there, look it is opening, as Brian looks up at Jim, to say, "Money???"

"What money?"

"From Cuba" said Brian.

Wow, why would she do that?" said Jim, to add "I thought that bag was in his trunk? As they watched, Jim went to the door, to say, "Hey Jack do you mind if I close this for a second."

"No, but I would like you to cut that girl free, I'd like to have lunch with her."

Jack said in between bites of the sweet roll.

Jim did as he was told and pulled Barbie out of his bunk to cut her free, she pushed him away, to take a seat right by Jack to say, "Thanks, I was wondering when I could go out with you?"

Jim closed the door, while she was talking to Jack.

Jim looked at Brian, to say, "What do you want to do?"

"If it were me, I'd tell the boss, that is thieving I'd throw her off the plane, that's just me" said the new pilot, Bill Bilson.

Jim looked over at Bill, knowing he was right, regardless of who's money it was, "Jim take a look" said Brian, as they both looked on, there was a gun, the .45 combat colt commander, for Brian to say "So that's where my gun went to."

"Hey guys were coming on approach, the landing lights are on, and we got an reception," said Bill, as Jim hopped into the co-pilots seat, to click on the intercom, Jack were ten minutes to touch down, we will set you down, then fly off."

The door opened, for Jack to say, "Are you ever going to let me finish my dinner?"

Jack saw they were coming in hot, to say, "Thanks guys, I gotta to go."

"Brian, unsecure, the car, and lower the ramp" said Jim.

Brian, was right behind Jack, as Brian, with Carly's help undid the straps, and turned up the raise wheel position, Jack got in, overrode the system, to say, "Its all me Sara, hold on, as he saw Brian, lower the ramp, to the flat position, as the car, was on and in the ready position to launch, Jack inched closer to the edge, the ground came up quickly, and just like that, Jack shot off, the car, roared off, and onto the tarmac, to say, "Drive us to this address, defense measures up, as the plane lifted off, as the car, went into stealth mode, and through a section of perimeter fencing, and onto the street, while in the distant horns were blasting, but soon drowned out as the car quickly was gone, as the traction control was on extreme, ice and snow pack, and just like that the roads faded off as the car continued towards the palace, in the background a sole helicopter was being tracked, as the sound of heavy gunfire ricochet off the car, Jack pulled up the head's up display, looking at his options, he choose the letter M, and selected rear, and said, "Fire, and just like that the ground to air missile, was launched at the target, seconds later it exploded, Jack saw on his display it was the USS Nimitz group patrolling the waters in the Baltic sea, as Jack hit speaker to hear, "This is the Admiral Cates, according to your position, a rocket was fired, do you need support?"

"Not now, but maybe in the future can you assemble a ground force team?"

"Yes I can" said Admiral Cates.

"I'll let you know when and where, out" said Jack as the car slowed, to see the gate was blown up, Jack slowed to a stop, to see the dead bodies, and he exited the car, as he looked around. Then as he saw, it was probably that helicopter, he thought. Jack got back in, and went up to the lovely semi half circle, to see two men, and got out, and went up the stairs, to see a striking red head, emerge to say, "You must be Jack cash, were expecting you, come in."

Jack entered the warm retreat, he whispered, "Cloak mode", and the car disappeared.

Then followed her to a room, where there was blood on the bed, for Jack to say, "Was she cut or raped?"

"I believe it's the attacker's blood, from probably the nose, as she probably fought her attackers off."

"How many do you think there were?" asked Jack looking around, and assessing the situation.

"From all the bullet holes, I'd say fifteen, probably in three teams" she said from her expertise and knowledge.

"So it was a well prepared attack?" asked Jack.

"Yes, I think so."

"I'm sorry I didn't catch your name?" asked Jack.

"Its Lexine Gobel, I'm a Russian professor of criminal activities, and over here I have a data base of known criminals, and of course the good ones, like yourself."

"It says three?" asked Jack.

"Yes, it is our two Russian spy's, and now you, so if you wait a second, I'll tell you who and where, and then we should be done here" said Doctor Gobel., as Jack saw a printed picture of the Premiers wife, the lovely Victoria Ecklon, to hear, from her, "She is pretty isn't she?"

Jack held the picture up to her to say, "Nah, you're about the same."

"Stop it, your making me blush."

Jack was looking around the place to say, "This place is sure huge."

"I'd give you the tour, but I know your in a hurry, and I'd imagine if you get her back, you'll spend some time up here, skiing, wait here it is, Oh, my god" she said frantically.

"What is it, Oh your right he is ugly, what's up with his nose?" said Jack.

"That Mister Cash, is our well known spy turned traitor, he is a former KGB operator, named Varfolomey, and he is a professional assassin."

"Really, a professional assassin, doesn't leave behind his blood, are you sure it's not a plant?"

"No I don't think so, the spray, is consistent with being struck, by a fist, or a flat hand, I'd say she broke his nose, oh here is his current known address, it's in Moscow, as she allows Jack to put it in his phone, for her to say, "That would make sense" she said in a round about way.

"Why's that?" asked Jack.

"It's suppose to be the international destination for all the world's shipments, to anywhere in the world, Moscow international airport is the world's largest's, there is even a US military attachment there, I think it's an air wing."

"Thanks I should go," said Jack.

"Yes you should," she said.

"Do you need a lift?" asked Jack.

"Nah, I need to stay here to finish the cleanup that is what all that smell is, they killed over fifty guards and fifty staff, and it's a shame."

"Alright thanks for the information" said Jack on his way out.

"Wait do you need his picture?" she asks trying to catch up with him.

"Nah, I'd seen it once, it will still give me nightmares."

Jack went outside, to see on the horizon, was a group of helicopters coming his way, as Jack slid into his car, it fired up, and drove off, as he increased his speed towards them, the next stop was the blown up helicopter, he went off the road onto the roving hills to the helicopters location, still in cloak mode.

As the helicopters came closer, they flew over his position, as Jack hit the hand brake, and did a spin, he tracked their position, to survey that they carried ammunition, so Jack, said "Display, missiles, it showed five left, there was six helicopters, showing bad intentions, so he spoke and said Target one, fire, target two, fire, target three, fire, target four, fire, and target five,fire, as he watched all five made contact with each helicopter and was blown out of the sky, just as they opened fired, on the palace, all five blew out as the other one turned away from the Palace towards him, he hit the J button, and off went the pigeon, he guided towards the rear rotor, and then let it go, it struck and blew out the rear rotor, and the helio was coming down fast, it hit and ejected close to Jack, as he got out, and ran through the snow, with gun in hand, two lie dead, and two were wounded, he kicked the first one in the throat, and tackled the second one, with a fatal strike to the head. Jack went back to see that the guy was bleeding, he rolled him over, and zip tied his wrists. Jack was on the move, he checked the dead, that littered the outside, their uniform had no markings, as he took a picture, inside the helicopter, he found a gem, a long bore, long range Russian sniper rifle, with a ten mag clip of .50 cal rounds, looking around, he found an ammo can of rounds, he slung that over, his shoulder, to check those of the dead, and searched their bodies, for wallet's and collect I D's, he holstered his gun, and zipped up, although he was now about done, he dialed up Jim, to say "Yeah I need a pick-up, like in DC?, that was fun?" asked Jack.

"We got you here, yeah, we can try, the Nimitz just refueled us, we should be there in ten mikes, deploy the balloon".

"Sorry I used all my missiles, and lost a bird" said Jack running back to his car.

"No worries, I'll have Brian ready, to reinstall them, we have more" said Jim.

Jack slid his phone shut and put it away, to grab the prisoner, and the pair was on the move, back to the car, he said trunk". It opened to see the blanket over the weapons, Jack took off the rifle and laid it down with the ammo box, to think, "I forgot all about these, darn it", then spun the prisoner around, to the side door, the door open at the passenger seat, and Jack put him in the seat, to close the door, to say, "Sleep."

Jack trudged through the snow to the other crash site's, and began to sift through the bodies, pulling ID's, he had twenty, as he slid them in his pocket, all in about ten minutes.

"Wow that is some debris field" said Jim when Jack saw his ride fly over, loop back, Jack made it back to his car, got in to see, the prisoner was out, started the car, and off he went, up to a crest, then said, "Deploy balloon."

Jim was at the controls, as they made the final approach for pickup, the arms guided the wire into the catcher, and just like that the car took off, but not going higher as the plane drug the car, over one hill, and through a snow bank, the plane dipped, inside, Jim was screaming, as the catcher wasn't responding, as he said, "Abort, abort."

Jack held on as he was at the mercy of the plane, as he was in a valley, when all of a sudden the car came to an abrupt stop. Jack got out to assess the damages, he called for the balloon to retract, it started, as Jack saw the plane fly over, as the balloon was close, he untwisted it as it deflated, he stuck it back in the center of the roof, and then looked over his situation, so he got back in, and took control of the car, and, using traction tires, he drove out of the snow bank, going towards the road, the road was getting higher than he was, and over head the plane just past him again, he was on a down hill slope, as he picked up speed, he remembered seeing, hydraulic lift system, he thought back to the manual he read, where it lifted the car up, so just at the right time he said Y and in that instant the car lifted up, just then the car deployed seat belts, and said, "Crash is imminent." as he sailed onto the road, he turned the wheel, and slid off the road onto the other side, the car ended up on one side, he was at a 90 degree angle, looking over the display he was still in traction mode, but the display, kept registering "Malfunction", so he tried to move but it was no use, he was stuck. Jack pulled his phone and dialed up Jim, he said "Jim, and seconds later Jim was on to say, "Yeah I got you, were making a landing, will back up, to ad, "Looks like you're off the road?"

"Yeah, I put it in the ditch, looks like no power lines" said Jack.

In that next instance, as Jack waited, plane slowed its air speed, touched down, it to be squiggly, as it slowed to a stop, a mile past him, Brian pulled out the ATV, to set the ramp half way, and out the back were Brian, and Jim, on an ATV. Brian slid the ATV, to a stop. Jim was at Jack's door trying, to help Jack. Jack was confined to the car, with his hands up and free, Jim immediately, saw the problem, the car was on a high side, jammed on a rock, when Brian yelled, from under the car, "I see the problem, it's a stuck hydraulic lift arm, broken." Jim went down into the frozen stream bed, to see the damage, for Jim to say, "What did he do?"

"Looks like he jumped the road" said Brian.

"Interesting, he used the hydraulic lifts, to propel the car up, brilliant, I know what we need to do, go back and get the plasma torch, we will cut this off" said Jim, yelling at Brian.

Back on the USS Nimitz, and an operator said, "Admiral Cates the Russian Air force had just launched two MIG interceptors, and should be over our VIP in five mikes, sir?, what shall we do?"

"Do not, do a thing, we need confirmation from Mister Cash, still nothing?"

"No sir, either he is away from his phone and not responding?" said the operator.

"Have AWAX fly the border, I want pictures of the situation, who do we have up there now?"

"Dens and Whitmore" said the first officer.

"Alright put the super hornets in the air."

Jack, forced his way out, through the passenger side window, that was finally down, he was out with Brian, as a loud roar, buzzed their position, Jack looked up to say, "Now we have trouble?"

"Brian load the car, with the assembly of missiles" said Jim, as the huge plane was close to them now, making talking nearly impossible, then on the MIG's second run, 20 MM guns went off, as Jim dove under the car, as did Jack, as the bullets ricocheted off the car in all directions, Jack scrambled around the car, to pull his phone, he sync it up with the car, to see the display, as his phone kept ringing, he answered it to say, "This is Jack" as a loud cheer was heard in the background, to hear, "This is Admiral Cates, we see that your having trouble what support can we offer you?"

"Find out who they are and have them stand down."

"What about we shoot them down to give you support?"

"No not yet, thanks, but it may trigger a war, get back to me on their intentions, I'll leave this line open" said Jack.

Jack noticed a button on the top right, he pushed it, and it showed the enemy track pattern, thinking, "I knew that", then he said small display, and the letter K, within seconds, the right

Stewart N. Johnson

side flap opened and a bird was shot out, it soared upward, Jack slowed its progress, by spreading the huge wing of the bald eagle lookalike, Jack flew the single bird, in the jets flight path, enough so, they changed their course, to hear, "There bugging out, their heading home, the reception has been called off" said Admiral Cates.

Another cheer went off, to hear Jack, this is Admiral Cates, is their anything else we can provide you?"

"Yes, how are you coming on the ground support team?"

"Assembled, you want us to drop them off at your location?"

"Nah, there is an air wing, at Moscow International Airport, can you have them secure a hanger and a helicopter?"

"Yes I can, were already ahead of you."

"Oh Admiral one more thing, do you have any surveillance footage of the helicopters earlier?" asked Jack.

"We will assemble that for you as well, we could map that area if you like?"

"No, but if you could also, wait one I have another call, Jack placed the Admiral on hold to see that it was Mitzi, he answered it, to say, as he watched Brian, load a missile at a time, to say, "Interesting", then answer Mitzi, "Yes, how may I help you?"

"Were on the ground, we just heard, I want to send our boys to your location."

"No, keep them there" said Jack.

"But you have no one, there to support you."

"I have Trixie" said Jack.

"True, alright, let me know if there is anything?"

"Nah, right now were stuck and trying to get out of a mess."

"Is it something I should be aware of?" asked Mitzi.

"Nah, were good, as Jack saw the huge plane back up towards the car, he recalled the bird and it gently came back to him, he caught it, and handed it back to Brian, he put it back in. Jack went back to his main screen, as he saw a huge gantry system extend, as the straps were set in place, by Jim, after he cut off the hydraulic arm, next the car was lifted up, as Brian

90

guided the car up, to the top, then it went inside, where it sat back down, in the wheel wells, Brian, held the trunk position. Jack walked up the ramp while on his phone, as Brian raised the ramp, everyone, was on board, as Jim yelled to Bill, "Get this plane off the ground." The plane straighten, and begin to gain speed, as everyone held their place, as Bill lifted off, and slowly upwards on a flight slope, the car was turned around, facing out the back, the straps removed. Jim took the driver's seat to do a diagnostic check, as he looked over at Jack's prisoner, who was out. Jack said, "I have a prisoner, can you help me out Brian."

Brian hauls out the guy, and drags him towards the head, and sets him down, he was still out, then over the intercom, Bill said "Where to?"

Jack was at the intercom to say, "Moscow International, U S armed forces hanger."

Jack looked back at the car with the front left was flat, then saw Brian, had air tools, as the car was lifted, the wheel taken off, as the plane leveled off, Jack watched their precision, of reloading, and repairing, as he held on. Jim and Brian were hard at work finishing the car, the tire back on, spun tight, Brian broke out a torque wrench. Jim, was doing and performing a diagnostic test, as Jack, went to his room, turned the handle, he opened to see Ramon, to say, "What's going on, here?" for Jack to see Lisa was on the sofa bed.

"Lisa is sleeping soundly," says Ramon, pointing to her.

"Alright why don't you come out and guard a prisoner for me?"

He looks back at her and then to Jack to say, "Alright, I Imagine she will be fine."

As Ramon stepped out, Jack held his arm to say, "So you were here the entire time, the plane landed, so why didn't you come out and see what was going on and help out?"

"Help out, I'll I do is drive and guard Miss Curtis."

"Alright I gotcha, the prisoner is in the rear head."

Ramon turned the corner to see Jim and Brian loading weapons, to say, "That car has missiles?"

"Yeah do you want to help us out?" asked Brian.

"Nah, I never signed on to do that either."

Brian looks at Jim, as they went back to work, for Jim to say, "I got a lower than average reading on the sleep gas, can you get another canister" Brian shakes his head, and goes into his cage. Brian, passes, the hung up, Carly, he found the canister, and took it out and came back to see for the first time the super sharp engine, as Jim reattaches the new canister, to say, "To bad for the hydraulics, their dead, and causing the whole system to be off", for Brian it was the first to see such a beautiful machine, with the four turbo chargers, the engine and inside was sparkling clean, as Jim looked back to say, "When we get to Moscow, a technician, is flying in, to tune it for the cold weather, it seems to be running rough and have him bringing a new arm" said Jim.

Brian looked at all the gauges and the huge computer box, every space was used, as wires were all attached as Jim finished the test, and having reset the birds in the hood, Brian helped him out with that, for Jim, to say, "I'll finish the test if you can tie the car down?"

Brian did that, as the danger was over, for all, to hear, Bill say, "Were in international flight space, all the way to Moscow, we will be there in thirty minutes."

Meanwhile back in Minsk, the jumbo jet had landed carrying Mike and Mitzi, along with two new strike teams, unarmed except with tasers, and long range support, it was Jack's new partner CIA Kelli and Simone who took the lead for Jack.

All the teams were at their intended targets, as Mark and Clarance was recalled, the strike team took the lead, Gia joined in with Scott and Casey, who had one of the UN inspectors, Gene on the scene, Paul and Jill had a terrorist, who they took by surprise, was out on a smoke break, who told them, where to go. They were ready to go in, local and sectional police were on the scene to supervise, then they gave the signal to go, as the element of surprise, took them around midnight, not a not a single shot was fired, 48 men were taken, without incident, as they were mostly asleep, they were all arrested. Mitzi called, to get an update, then asked Casey to stay there till they get back as she said, "Were on our way onto Moscow, with Mark and Clarance."

CH 6

Operation super cell blow up

Jack's plane landed first, as it taxied to the US side, right by a huge U S packaging facility, the hanger door went up, and the plane went in, and to the left it went, to park, facing out as the hanger door went down, an Air force ground crew went to work, looking over the plane as the ramp was lowered, Jim drove the car out. Inside his room, Jack and Lisa just finished a long conversation over Ramon, and the network, for Jack to say, "When Mitzi gets here, you and Ramon can go, and take the jumbo back to Minsk."

"Well again, I'm sorry that Ramon didn't help you out, but your wrong he is too a team player."

"Wait till you crash and see if he is the one pulling you out" said Jack.

"What do you mean by that?"

"I think he will be the one running away."

There was a knock on the door, Jack opened it, to hear, "The other plane has landed."

Moments later, the plane landed, taxied, then parked in a hanger next to them, the door opened and a team of people exited, troops out and a young boy, went to the Mercedes. Up the ramp went the VIP's, to Jack's cabin, in walked Erica, followed by Mitzi, and Mike, who stood by the door, it was Mitzi who jumped into Jack's lap to give him a kiss, to hear, her say, "Miss Curtis you can go now, that I'm here."

"Hold on, I want both of you, out of here, this one is a dangerous place, your both, over worked, look what it did for Mike, and while I have the two of you, which one informed Jim to give me sleeping pills?" asked Jack.

Erica raised her hand, for Jack to say, "Why?"

"I was just thinking you need to rest."

"That's what you get for thinking, both of you I want gone, and take that no good wanna be girl Blythe with you."

"Sorry we can't, you know both of us" said Erica, as Lisa stands.

"Why not" asked Jack.

"Well when you had me fill out the pamphlet for you, I put her down as you plus one, so it will take at least a week to change that?"

"Oh I thought you said it was a week?"

"No, silly, it will be three weeks" said Lisa.

Jack set Mitzi aside to say, "Whoa, no way am I staying with her for a week, let alone three, and sorry I won't stay but a week."

"Then you won't want to hear what's next" said Lisa.

"Hit me, while I'm still in a good mood" said Jack, pacing.

"Well to replace her, I have Trixie going in."

"That's not so bad" said Jack.

"Then in the event she goes down, I chose Jill as the first alternate" said Lisa.

"The girl who we just recruited, that's like throwing her to the wolves" said Jack.

"Sure, but no one knows her and besides she volunteered, what do you have to worry, you seem to find all the right girls, now find us some men" said Lisa.

But isn't that how it should work?" asked Jack.

A knock on the door, Mike opens it, to see Clarance, to say, "This Varfolomey, is a KGB operator and trained professional sniper, has a prisoner he has been with, although she is covered up, they are in a little flat a block from the Kremilin, off the M10 into the main city, here is the address, he hands it to Mike, who in turns hands it to Jack.

Jack looked at the address, to say, "What's this?"

"Clarance took it from his prisoner" said Mike.

Jack put it in his pocket, to say, "Times a wasting."

"What do you want to do with Blythe?"

"Have her rest up, when I'm done we will go together I guess" said Jack confused.

"Sure, you don't want her to go with you, now?"

"Nah, I can't afford if there is collateral damage, besides I don't feel she is on the same page as I am, look we can go round and round all day, I gotta to go."

Erica, stepped forward, to hold onto his arm, leaned in and whispered into Jack's ear "Jack I don't like this, this country is dangerous, and you're putting all of us in danger."

Jack looked at her, to say, "I hear what your saying, and will take it under advisement, but as I was asked out of respect to rescue the wife of the President of Russia, one Vladimir Ecklon."

"Whoa wait a minute, you said your on a rescue mission, what happen to the terrorist cells?" asked Erica.

"That was in Belarus, that's why I left a team behind."

"Well alright, I will give you two weeks, but no more, you need to get to that council" said Lisa, who sided up to them.

"You got a deal, but I'll be done in less then this week."

"O Kay, as she let go.

Jack went past every one, to see Mike opened the door for him, Jack stepped out, and he went around the corner to see that the cage was closed, and behind the door was Carly hung by her wrists, her mouth was taped, wearing only a see through bra and panties, for Jack to yell, "Brian."

Both Jim and Brian looked up, as they were at the front of the plane, to see that the catcher, solenoid was in the single position, not the dual, as Jim said, "Go find out what he wants, I'll fix this." Then Brian went up to the ramp to see Jack at the cage to say, "Did you need something Jack?" he said inquisitively, but knew he needed to further explain, as he walked towards him.

"So are you gonna to tell me how she ended up here?"

"First I want to say, once we dropped you off, that one came at us in the cockpit, we subdued her, and took her into the cage." For Jack to look around, for Brian to say, "The other one Barbie, we gave sleeping pills to, and then zip tied her up, she is in the cabin, back on the bunk."

Jack looked at him to say, "Let her down, give her some clothes, and tell me why she is hung like that?"

"She is dangerous, and we searched her for more weapons? And besides we caught her stealing money" said Brian.

"I want her cut loose, I want to talk with her, as for Carly, let her have the money and send her back to the US, where we found her, besides what did she do that was so bad?"

"She stole the money?"

"You sure it wasn't an early payment?" asked Jack.

Brian looked at him to say, "What, oh by the way, I found the .45 cal."

"Yeah it was in the duffle bag, I know that, so how is she like this?" asked Jack, making all this to be some coincidence.

"After we lifted back off the ground, she came at us in the cockpit, as she threw her tray at us, it hit pilot Bill in the head, so we took her down, zip tied her up, stripped her down."

"Well cut her loose", said Jack, as Brian does and leaves the cage as Jack hands her clothes to her, she begins to dress, as Jack motions for Brian to further leave.

Brian acknowledged him, by getting off the plane.

Jack pulled the tape off her mouth to hear her sob as she dressed, Jack said, "What would you like to do? Go back or stay with me?"

She looked him up and down, to say, "I'd like to stay with you."

"Then it's settled, your in my room" said Jack proudly.

Jack left the cage, with Carly in hand, and dropped her off at his cabin, while he went into the flight cabin, to see Barbie; he pulled the tape from her mouth, as Bill, quickly exited the cabin, and closed the door.

Jack said, "You're a field agent."

She shuddered then said "Do you want me to go with you?"

"Sure why not, your an agent aren't you?"

"Yes, I am, and yes I loved to go with you, just to get away from these guys "said the feisty Barbie.

"Good I know you'll be an asset to me" said Jack.

"Finally someone who believes in me, as Jack cuts off her bindings, and tossed her clothes to her, she dressed, in front of him, as he turned his back to her, she saw a knife on the counter, and she slipped it into her pocket, to say, "I'm ready to go".

Jack saw Jim, as Jack opened the flight cabin's door, who said, "The car is ready for you, but lowered his eyes to see Jack wasn't happy with them, as Jim held the door open, and Barbie slid past and gave Jim the finger, as he closed the door.

Jack went out to his car, only to see the young technician, who said, "Everything, is running fine, as Jack got in, with Barbie in passenger seat, as Erica flew around the corner, to see Jack drive out.

Brian stood by Erica to say, "He doesn't look happy."

"He shouldn't be, take a look at this" she hands it to Brian who said, "Shit I knew that girl was dirty, we need better intelligence, how can something like this happen, as Jim, Blythe and Lisa came up to say, "He is gone, but you could still call him?"

"Yep afraid so" said Jim, as he hands the Intel sheet back to Lisa, who says, "Listen from now on we need a better line of defense; I'll give him a call."

"Besides, what are you complaining about she is your agent" said Mitzi behind Lisa.

Lisa and Erica just looked at her as Lisa said "Now what?"

"Now, you two take the jumbo jet back to Minsk, wait for us, as we need to stay here and support Jack, with only those we trust, as she was looking at Lisa.

Both Lisa and Erica nodded their heads, as Mitzi called her team towards her to say, "Alright Jim, what do you need off the jumbo jet for supplies?"

"I could use some help with crates."

"Alright, Mark, Clarance, Rick, and Mike, help him out, Brian can you help out?"

Jack drove with ease, as Barbie, was extremely nice to him, by placing her hand on his arm, and stroking it, as Jack could see something in her pocket was bulging out, but as he punched in the coordinates, the car followed the route, the city was alive, but as the sun was setting in February the cold was setting in ice was on parts of the road, Jack had his phone in the dash, as two possible ways was available to him, as he slowed off the M10, out onto the streets, cars were everywhere, as was the police, as his shiny new silver car was visible, he flipped the plates to show embassy, to ensure no one would stop them, a group of canals ran through the south part of the city, as his destination was coming up fast, the parkways, were lighting up as he crossed the Moskva, as he saw on his radar he was close, so he said, "I was wondering if, you could go out and provide a distraction, while I go inside." The car came to a complete stop, as Jack was reaching for something in the dash.

"Sure what do you have in mind?" asked Barbie.

"Go out to the edge, of that building, put in this ear piece, as I have one, so that you can tell me if you see a crooked nosed ugly guy approach", she tried the door, as it opened for her, she immediately felt the cold to say, "I don't know it seems cold out there."

Jack points to the back seat to say, "See if there is a jacket back there and put it on?"

She found it, and got out, as Jack watched her get to the corner, as he slipped out to feel the cold, he said, "Secure", as he tried the door to the flats, and went in, with address, and phone in hand, he put the phone away, as he made it to the stairs and up, to the second floor, he pulled his weapon, he was ready, as he tried the door, knob, it opened, it was dark, as a shot rang out, as Jack dove, behind the kitchen cabinets several guns fired wildly, as Jack was on his hands and knees, to the edge, thinking a concussion grenade would be nice now, it was as moments went by, but through a window, a missile struck the wall, and erupted, and exploded, as Jack and everyone else, landed on the first floor.

Jack stood first and with weapon out, he shot, and hit the first one in the leg, as the guy was wounded, and then Jack nailed the other one in the head, he was dead, as he dialed up Mike to say, "I got a prisoner can you come to my location, and bring Clarance, as Jack pushed his prisoner through the merchants door, only to hear the sound of sirens in the night, Jack yelled for Barbie to come, who was fraternizing with a Guy, as she came back to him, as Jack zip tied the guys hand, he knew he was too late, so he told her, "Come on, were going to have police here any minute, she scrambled towards him, for Jack to say, "In the back, he gets the front seat."

She dove, into the back, as Jack wheeled the guy around into the passenger seat, went around, got in, backed up, and drove the other direction, away from the trouble, he drove in a circle, only to see from his military map, that he was crossing into hostile area, he knew this when cars were behind him, and then the chase was on. He pulled up his head's up display, he placed the car in the cloak mode, and he was invisibly, then used a 1/4 of letter F, and oil slick was in place, as he went back to S and traction tires, then let the car drive itself in Stealth, a car pile-up was behind them, and according to his radar, he was clear, the drive was short, as a motor inn, appeared close to the M2, that he pulled off, and parked. It was getting later, as Jack said, "Wait here with the prisoner, I'm getting us a room."

Jack got out to say, "Secure", then went inside, to speak Russian, like he was a pro, to ask for a rear room, on the first floor, Jack looked in his pocket for his expense credit card, which he paid, and was given a key card, he went out into the cold, got in, to see that they were still how he left them, he got in and pulled out, drove to the end, back up, and park behind the building, then got out, went around, and pulled the prisoner out, as Barbie said "I can get the key for you", Jack hands her the key card, she inserts it in, and opens the door, so Jack can, pull him in, and the door closed.

Barbie announces, "I'm hungry?"

Jack set the prisoner on one of the beds, to pull out a zip tie, for his ankles, then with the other zip tie, he was ready to use it on his mouth, when the guy pleaded in Russian not to do it, that he would be quiet, as Barbie was looking at Jack, and he hands her some Euro's, he had Brian change out and out the door she went.

Some time had past, she knocked on the door, Jack let her in, to see the spread, she got, to say, "There was a diner across the way."

They ate together, as she was kind, to him, but sinister in some sort of way, when she announced, I want to take a shower, do you want to join me?" she said coyly. Jack watched her, to say,

"So, go ahead."

She went into the bathroom and closed the door.

Jack pulled up his phone, to see that Erica and Lisa were back in Belarus, as it was the first thing on his phone. Jack saw that he had fifty five missed calls, he scrolled through them to see one was from Sara in Mobile, next to hers was Carly the homemaker, it was a text message, he pulled it up to read "Jack, its CC, I've been through 1200 and still no sign of those plans, will continue the search."

Jack sent her a text back, saying, "Continue to search, then we can talk about your future, when I'm back in town as for now sit tight, and I will get in touch with you."

The shower stopped running, moments later, the door opened to see her standing there in only a towel, one on her head the other around her breasts, to say, "Are we staying the night, I'd like to wash my clothes?"

"Nah, get dressed, were leaving soon enough."

Only to hear the outside door, was a knock, which she quickly went back in and closed the door, for which Jack got up, and went to the door, to see it was Mike and Clarance, Jack opened the door, and they came in, instantly the guy knew something was up, and began to scream, as Clarance was on him, showing the guy his Irish side, while Mike hands Jack a message, to say, "It's from Lisa."

Jack reads, "That over in Nekrasovka, is a branch of the terrorist group, that has been stirred up, they have tanks and artillery, you need to get out of there ASAP, over a half of million men force, the streets will be full, wait till morning, I'll have a Russian contact waiting for you. Lisa."

"That was nice of her to think of me, but maybe I ought to go and stir things really up."

"What do you have in mind?" asked Mike.

"Hey Clarance can you get some information out of that guy and ask him where is Varfolomey is at?"

"Meanwhile I need you to drive to Nekrasovka base and get me a tank, I think I want to have fun, here" said Jack handing him an ear piece, then to Clarance, Jack said, "I want you to wear one too."

Clarance had his large hand at the guy's throat, to insert with his other hand the ear piece.

Mike was gone, as Jack closed the door, Barbie opened the bathroom door, only to see Clarance, who looked up at her with a growl, for her to step out, to see Jack go in and close the door, she witnessed the dirtier side of interrogation, as Clarance got the information needed, but in the process the guy strained his heart and died. Much to the horror of Barbie who had never witnessed such a horrific event that she began to cry when Clarance told her "Keep quiet, or you will be next".

Jack emerged to see Clarance was carrying off the guy, out the door, as Jack checked the fridge, to see a well stocked bar, only to see Barbie run to the bathroom, to vomit, as she was doing her business, Clarance came back in, to say "I tossed the body in the trash bin, here is what he told me" he said Varfolomey is on the run, as he found out that You, Jack Cash was on his trail, he has the wife of the President and she is unharmed, he is going to look for refuge at Nekrasovka, military installation, ran by terrorist their leader is Aleksander the second."

Jack agrees with him, to say, "Alright, you can come with me?"

"No I can't" said a serious Clarance.

"What do you mean?" asked Jack?

"Well I was told, at all costs not to ride in your car, let alone participate in any actions especially here in Russia, for they will kill me on sight, and as you can see I'm un-armed, also I want to apologize for yelling at your woman, but she wouldn't keep quiet."

"That's alright, all she is, is a trainee, as she wants to learn to be a spy."

Clarance didn't say a thing, so Jack said Barbie let's go, I guess you'll be alright here" Jack said to Clarance.

"Yeah, Mark is on his way to pick me up, have fun on the base."

"Yeah, thanks for the information" said Jack.

"Come on Barbie, let's go."

She emerged looking better, as Jack grabbed her arm, and the two went out, as the door was closed shut, Jack escorted her to the car, then he got in, and took off, moments later Mark pulls up, and Clarance comes out and gets in, as Mark backs up, to see in his ear, Mark stops, to say, "Jack gave you a ear piece?"

"Yeah, do you want it?"

"Hell yes, what's going on, hand it to me" said Mark as he closes it up, in his hand to say, "Did he ask you to participate?"

"Yes, but I refused."

"What are you crazy, if he asks you to join, that's what you do?" said a stunned Mark.

"But, Jim told me not to get in his car at all costs."

"Yes, that is true, you will never sit in that car alone, but if the boss asks you to join him, then that's what you do, what are you some pussy?"

Mark received a punch, that Clarance delivered, that glanced off his face to hear, "Drive I know where he is going, looks like I need to make that up to him, let me have that ear piece back."

"No, you need to stick with me; I'll show you what we need to do."

Meanwhile Jack was driving towards the Terrorist base, as he was searching for plans of some type, or recognition, of exactly what the base was, as it had none, nothing in his data base. Military troops were all present, carrying weapons, as he drove right into the hornet's nest, as in the distance he could see huge lights on, as the car was tracking the best way in, instantly Jack noticed something on a higher road, then in his ear, he heard, "Jack this is Mark, Clarance and I are at your service?"

"Great, thanks, I need you both to the north, for a pickup Barbie doesn't look so good, and I also need a man on higher ground, to cover us on the ground, I have a Russian sniper rifle."

"Clarance said he would do that" said Mark.

"Great," out" said Jack as he slowed to see a tall woman, on the side of the road, with a flat tire, trying to change her tire, he past her, then parked in front of her, and said to Barbie, "Stay here."

Jack got out leaving, the car running, he went back to say, "Miss Do you need help?"

"Finally it's about time you got here" she has her weapon pointed at him, to add, "So the famous Jack Cash we met again."

"Sorry I don't remember you" said Jack stopping in his tracks but moved slowly towards her, as he sensed there was no danger.

She said, "So you're here in my city, blowing thing up and killing people, that's not the Jack I knew, they said you're the preserver of life, do you still not recognize me, then come closer, you're a hard man to track, you always did the unexpected."

Jack eased forward to see the pretty face, to see her smile, then say, "Come on Jack, you sat right next to me in class, it's the Ice Princess, Rebecca Adams, still don't remember me, that's right your too busy with that girl named Allison, how was she Jack, you know in bed?"

Just then the side door opened, and Barbie fell out, as she was hurling again, as both Jack and Rebecca looked at her, for Rebecca to say, "No way, stand aside Jack Cash, do you know who you have, oh my god, that is Serena Babington, from Jacksonville, Florida, isn't it, come closer you bitch, as she approach the trembling Barbie who was on all fours, looking up, to hear Rebecca say, "You don't know who she is do you, Jack, no because your way to interested in their outside beauty to realize the devil themselves, that bitch and I have had our run ins, she costed me two huge bounties in Jacksonville, and you know that she works for the notorious gang of biker thieves called the Rednecks, don't move bitch or I will drill you where you stand, so Jack why is she here?"

Jack shrugs his shoulder, as he was trying to catch up with Rebecca, getting closer to Barbie, for Jack, to say, "She is a trainee and wants to be a spy."

"Ha, Ha, Ha, Rebecca laughed, to say, "This double, two timer is in everyone pocket, you see Jack she is a whore, did you do this one too?"

"No" said Jack, as they watched as Barbie fumbled her hand in the jacket, as Rebecca had her gun out to say, "You see Jack while you were preoccupied, with this one, you didn't get the memo, she was bad, and your boss Lisa Curtis, contacted me, to help assist you, as Rebecca saw, as Barbie, was trying to pull out something, as she had a strange look on her face, and began to scream, only to be shot in the head, and fell down, she was dead."

"What did you do that for?" asked Jack.

"I was told to, she is a counter agent, and Lisa asked me to put her down, she said that you were in trouble and needed some help" as she holstered her weapon, she went to her, and pulled her out of his jacket to say, "This must be yours you will need it out here."

"Yeah", said Jack putting his hands down, to see her lift up the body and pick up the life less body and toss her into her car to say, "Come on, I'm here to help you out.

CH 7

Rescue Victoria, Russian style

The Navy Seal teams, sat around the empty hanger, wondering what was up, the Black hawk helicopter, pilots sat at the ready, when a sergeant asked the Captain, "Hey Cappy, what's up, we have been sitting here for two hours now, do you think he might be somewhere else?"

"We tried him on the dial up and no response."

"Had you thought he might be in danger, and can't respond, can we open the bay doors?"

"No, if you're that concerned, go outside, but without your gear, and only you Sergeant Turner."

"Aye, Aye Captain", he dropped his gear, went out a side door to see a huge military jumbo jet, with its tail wing of the numbers that he was looking at, Tom went running after it, only to hear, "It won't do you any good, did you miss the flight?"

"Nah, were Seals, and had asked to come down for ground support, for Mister Cash."

Tom looks at the other plane in the hanger to say, "That tail wing is the same as the one that just left."

"Yep" said Jim wiping off his hands with the rag.

"Do you know where I could get in touch with Mister Cash?"

"Sure I'll do one better, I'll take you to see the one in charge" said Jim waving him along, as Tom follows in, to see the huge hanger door close behind him, he could feel the gust of cool wind, as he ascends up the ramp, Tom saw first a gorgeous woman, it was hard to look away from her, when a short blonde, equally stunning, then a superior hot brunette, for which he store at her, still has his mouth open to say, "Where am I ?"

"Your on the Jack Cash's prop plane, my name is Mitzi and I run the ground support operations, so you're a Seal, how many more are there of you?"

"Fifteen and two pilots."

"So two teams then?" asked Mitzi.

"No three, of five, Miss" said Tom, being a bit sassy. As he looked over at Jim who had a stern look on his face.

"What is your name and rank Seal?"

"Ma'am, its Sergeant Tom Turner."

"Alright, seeing you're the only one who decided to find us."

"We were sent by Admiral Cates, aboard the Nimitz battle group, I guess were his escort."

"I know Sergeant, will you shut up and let me finish" said the frustrating Mitzi.

"Yes Ma'am."

Mitzi pulls out a topographical map, to show Sergeant Turner to say, "Now, your three teams, need to bring up some support to Jack, on the north side of here, Nekrasovka, there is the Chornaya river, where one team will provide an eastern flank, to the north is tank row, I need a team there, then the last team on the western flank, I want you Mister Turner to coordinate all the teams, here is seventeen ear pieces, very powerful, just speak when spoken to, the way it works is, Jack will tell you what he is doing, then other agents in the field will call out support strategies, and it will be your job, to back them up, do you understand this Mister Turner?"

"Yes Ma'am" he looked somber.

"Jim do you want to take them in?"

Before Jim could answer Brian, stepped up to say, "Mitzi I'd like to do it, I feel like I have been slacking off."

"Suit yourself, take what you need, and call me when you land."

"Yes" said Brian, leading Tom out.

Jim looked at Mitzi who said, "You know I would have never sent you in, the boy is getting to soft, besides this Tom Turner, I like."

Brian, went to the door, as the other Seals stood, to see Tom following, once in they surrounded him, to hear, Cappy say,

"So, are you Jack Cash?"

"No, sir" said Brian.

"Our specific orders were to meet up with Jack Cash."

"Alright" said Brian, as he turned around, and went to the door, to hear, "Wait" said Tom, to add, "Hear him out, I'm just saying we go back to the Nimitz and Admiral Cates asks what we did?"

"We waited to link up with Jack Cash."

Brian turned to use a new tact, to these overly stubborn Seals to say, "It's a code name for these covert operations are you still interested?"

"Go on" said Cappy.

"Well as Brian turned to say, "As we speak a group of our people are on the ground, trying to prevent a war, and it will be your job to provide back up support for them, as Sergeant Turner has been briefed, it is totally up to you if you decide to help."

Brian was at the door to hear, "Wait, our job is to support this mission, when we go?"

"Right now."

Jack with Rebecca next to him, drove down to a road, then backed in, as Jack pulled his phone out, to say, "I got some gear in the back, we may need all of it."

"What do you want me to do?"

"I'd say find something that can provide us some backup, here is an earpiece so that you can talk with me."

"What is all that noise?"

"It's one of my men getting a tank for me, just talk normal, let's go" said Jack as the two exited into the cold of the night.

Jack says, "Trunk", it opens, for Jack to pull out the long sniper rifle, to say, to her, "Can you shoot this?"

"No, you got anything smaller?"

"I got a rocket launcher, to hear, "Jack, its Mark, we will be there in a mike."

"Alright sure, park somewhere not close to me?"

Rebecca chooses an assault rifle and hand gun, to hear, Jack say, "Were going to scale that wall, so take what you can with leaving your hands free."

"Yes sir" she said in a smart aleck sort of way.

Moments later a car slides to a stop, on the gravel, as two men get out and run towards Jack to say, "Were here to serve you what do you need?" said Mark, with Clarance right behind.

"Do you have an ear piece?" he hands one to Clarance to say, "Which one of you, said you're a sniper?"

"I am" said Clarance, as Jack hands him the rifle and the ammo box, he shows Clarance on his phone a topographical map of the area to say, "See this hill, can you get up there, and set up?"

"Mark, you come with me, and grab that missile launcher, as Jack and Rebecca goes to the wall, Jack has his back pack on, he gets to the wall, reaches his wrist up, spins his watch face, and aims for the highest point, and it shoots out, the ring, it sticks, moments later, he is whisked up, once on top of the wall, he touches the two sides and it releases, it retracts back in, next he pulls out some climbing rope, and tosses an end to her, the other end he throws to Mike on the other side, on the ground waiting.

Mark finishes loading to say, "I didn't know you were a sniper?"

"I'm not" said Clarance.

"Then why did you say you were?"

"Cause I'll do whatever I can, that's why," said Clarance, running toward the hill, as Mark broke away from him.

Jack used a ring clip to slide down, the still rope, as Mike tied it down to a tank. Jack jumped at the last moment, and slid, then rolled into a kneeling position to hear from Brian, for Jack to say, "Excellent, have them as designated, send the best shooters to the west hill and relieve Clarance.

Jack saw a huge two winged tank buster, with a 20 mm Gatlin gun, as Rebecca, was next to him, for Jack, to say, "Mike help Mark over, then pulled Rebecca aside to say, "How would you like to get into that thing, and tear up the ground troops?"

"It looks like a suicide mission."

"Fine I'll send Mark over there."

"Hold on, I didn't say no, how about a kiss first?"

Jack nodded, as she gave him a passionate kiss on the lips, as Jack laid back, against the tank and she was climbing on top of him, to hear Mike say, "Jack we ain't got time for this."

She let him up as she wiped off her mouth, to say, "Now that was worth it, as she was on her back scrambling to get up, she said, "Alight I'm going, with you guys" she was behind the remaining tanks, as Mike said, "Are we going?" motioning for them to get into his tank.

"What about the other tanks?" said Jack?

"Oh I took care of them, here are all the keys?"

"What if they have a master key?"

"I took care of that too, I cut the inlet wire, on all 49 others, now get in, I'll drive, I told Mark he is the loader, and we need to drive over to the ammo dump to load up."

"Then what are we waiting for?" said Jack, climbing up the side into his position as the commander, it was night, and the night vision goggles were out, Mike drove the tank like he owned it, it moved flawlessly.

Jack was talking to someone, as the noise was deafening, to say, "Keep the helicopter away, till the surprise happens, I need a team at the ammo dump, one that can help blow it up, on the other side to support the hill, and lastly from the tanks position, out. As Jack looked at his phone, the location of the ammo dump, using occasional commands to Mike as, "Left

111

and Right, Straight, and Halt, as Jack jumped, out, and down, to see a guard shack, He shot the guard in the head, and then the other one, went and used the button to raise the gate, just then as the tank passed by, he lowered it, going to the large chain link fence, he pulled in one side then the other, to read it was suppose to be closed anyway, a chain, was available, and he locked it shut, Jack ran across the grounds to the underground bunkers where usually there would be guards but it was empty, something was up, as he ran to see Mark and Mike were loading tank rounds, individually, but that was till Jack got on the middle of the line, and it went quicker, both Mike and Jack were constantly looking around, only to hear a honk at the main gate, the noise was loud, then it all stopped, next was the 20mm rounds in belts, for the commander's gun, Mike and Mark, set it in place, loaded up the first one, down to the chute, where ten more belts connections await, as Jack found something he wanted, a case of fragment grenades, and a case of incideraries, Mike took them, from him to say, "Jack were full."

"Then put them on the outside."

"You got it" said Mike.

Jack hauled his prize on top of the tank, to a storage position, as Mike took the last two cases, and gave them to Mark, in the rear to arrange, rounds sealed him in as Mike set the rear armor down, to secure it, as Jack slid into the commanders seat, his hand on the safety switch to see Mike climb into the driver's seat, as out from the grass was a group of soldiers, to see one say, "We got the ammo dump will wire it and blow it, give us ten mikes."

"Drive on" yelled Jack begins the diversions Rebecca "who held a position, above them to give them cover.

The tank lurched forward, to turn right to see the gate was open, as the tank was moving now, "Load the gun, with bouncing Betties."

Jack placed on the gunners sight helmet, to guide the gun, and hit the switch, and off the rocket went off, as Mark, was pulling and reloading, the first was a direct hit, and the huge building blew up, as Jack continued the rounds, as fast as Mark could reload, Jack had it firing, as they made it up to the top of the hill, phase one was complete the ground forces were severed, but onto the next hill was the sniper, Clarance, was pinning the Air Force pilots and personnel, from getting their planes up, especially, Rebecca, who moved on the ground above and was using scatter fire, on the Planes, Jets and ground personal, and they were lighting her up, as well. Jack was on the other hill, when off to his right the whole building collapsed, a wave of dust engulfed them, as Jack closed his eyes, and everything was at a standstill till Jack yelled, "Get her moving Mike". Jack set his sights on the last jet, and fired, the plane blew up. Jack was going down a hill, then back up, to see a wave of Armored Personnel Carriers with rocket launchers, lobbing rounds at them, Mark was back at it, loading and reloading, as Jack returned direct hits, but the far superior tank, was on the move, and while, Mark rested, by throwing out spent rounds to make room, Jack was on the gun, as spent rounds were building up, thousand down, Jack ran out, as the gun spun dry. Mark said, "Hold on, I'll clip in a new mag box, and Jack was using the missile rounds from the side launcher, he engaged with the enemy, then Jack noticed a huge hanger bay, so he tilted the gun up, and fired off his main missile round, to hear your clear" by Mark.

Jack was back on the 20 mm cannon, adjusting its burst rate, then off to his right the hill of where Clarance and Rebecca were at, blew up, and now no one had said a thing, but behind Jack, the Ammo dump blew, sending shock waves through the terrorist compound, so much so, the ground opened up, like an earthquake, as Mike drove towards the sniper hill. Just as if there was not so much as to a delay, but that round Jack last fired, exploded, then a much louder, and concussion effect occurred, as the ground rumbled and the tank shook, Jack and Mike went down to seal off there hatches, to ride out the fallout. It lasted a good five minutes......

Moments had passed, as Rebecca called out that she was injured, could she get help?" SEAL team, north, responded first, getting to her and providing her some assistance.

Jack found the gas mask at his station, he put it on, as did Mike, to hear, "Drive us out of here", as Mike drove, through the little windows Jack could see her, standing, with others around her, for him to say, "Go pick her up", as the plane's were blown upside down, at least 200 hundred feet in all directions, all the jets on the other side were in shambles, as the tank gained momentum, over the hill, to see that the sky was lit up, and clear from the air indicator, Jack popped the top, and went up, out, to see the camp below, was in ruins, bodies were everywhere, Jack popped the hatch, and lifted it off, he stood up to see the carnage he created, a huge gaping crevice, showed the floors below, as he had the tank stop, to allow Rebecca on, it continued, as he said, "Let's go, said Jack, "To the admin offices, let's see who is alive, the tank, stayed on the left side of the huge gaping hole, as Mike came to rest, in front of the base admin office, Jack unhooked and jumped out, and pulled his gun, as he went into the partial collapsed building, to see a trail of injured or dead bodies, to the commanders office, on the corner, stood a gentleman, his head was bleeding, he was dirty, he just looked at Jack. Jack entered, with his gun drawn, he spoke Russian to him, he said, "Who are you and what right do you have for all this, how many men you have, this is an act of war, Mother Russia will not stand for this."

In his best Russian, Jack said, "Give us Victoria Ecklon, and I will let you live?"

"This is what this is all about, her kidnapping, we did it to scare the President into financing our operations, she is unharmed, and who are you?"

"Names, Jack Cash."

"Oh, you created all this, there is a half a million men and women underground that nearly ninety percent are dead or severely wounded, and you did this to us and what force?"

"Me and my small team, now hands behind your back, as Jack zip ties him, and yanks him out, to hear, "I am a descendant from Alexander the Great."

"I thought he was Roman, aren't you Russian?"

"Yes, but I said I was a descendant."

"I wouldn't say that out to loud."

Jack hauls him out, as SEAL teams open the huge front gates, as Russian red army storm, in, as Aleksander says, "If you want Varfolomey, he is on the Kostroma peninsula on the hill top, where you can see many miles, but you better watch out Fyodor, will be hunting you, and if you take the road to the north it will take you to the M3 and up to that part of the country good luck."

Jack gave Aleksander up to the commander of the red army, and got back on the tank and rehooked up to say, "All other troops fall back and regroup, thanks, as the tank took off, to the east, and the firing ranges, into the country, the tank plowed through barbed wire fences, to hit a street, then Mike, took a left, as Jack led him via a commands, a report came back to him, four SEAL's dead two wounded, Black hawk is behind them, with eight plus Clarance, and the reports came back, that the bomb that went off was two 1800 pound hydrogen bombs, under the ground, twenty floors of secrets, uncovered."

Jack slowed Mike, to say, over there is a huge open space, Mike took a residential street, to a dead end, that the tank flew off, onto the grass, pasture, from where they were at, you can see for miles, but according to his map, the hills were to his left, as was the rivers and lakes, Jack realized the Tank was losing its purpose, and said, "Let's go off to the right, and back to the road, as it was in the middle of the night, he kept his phone on his intended targets, as Mike found a gravel road, and took a right, nearly a zero turn, to a solid newly paved road, to see a sign that said, "Welcome to Ivanovo, the land of caves and cliffs," Jack said, "Drive across the street", Jack looked at his watch that said it was 0400 in the morning, he wished he had an energy drink, as he spun his back pack around, to find, a meal bar, he tore it open, and began a single bite, as Mike had the Tank at idle, Jack said "Check out over there", Mike hopped out, to run toward the edge to see the drop off, and the water, rushing over, but he also saw what appeared to be a guy with a woman and a man, on the other side, as he ran back towards the tank when a single shot rang out, as Mike rolled, the round missed him, to say, "We got him, that bastard", Mike hopped back in, and backed up, then spun it around, took a right, and then judged where he thought they would be at, and stopped, at a pedestrian bridge, to hear, "Jack I think our guy is in there".

Jack was unhooked, and took off his helmet to give to Mike to wear, as he offered the rest of his meal bar, Mike took it, to watch Jack running across the pedestrian bridge, he jumped the entrance to the caves, he held his phone out to see that the cave system was updating possible routes, as he ran, he gained speed, as his phone led him to the three people going very slowly, Jack was close, as he went further down, then back up, he slowed to hear voices, Jack pulled his weapon, he was ready, as he eased the gun against the handler, who spoke "help", as Jack hit him with his gun, in one sweep he took Victoria from the laid out guy, took a picture of her, for confirmation, who she was, it came back true and draped her over his shoulder, and retraced his steps, and ran back wards, as his phone provided the light, he carefully climbed over the short fence, onto the pedestrian bridge, to see Mike, to say, "All right, get out of here, and take that tank back, I've called in the Black hawk, moments later Jack was standing in the field as the helicopter touched down, and they helped the woman in, to a seat, and Jack as well, it lifted off, as Jack, took a helmet to say, "Next stop, south of the Archangel Cathedral, the helio soared down, as Jack pulled up the President of Russia, to text him, he has her safe and sound, in route to the Kremilin palace, in Moscow."

He texted back, "Thank you"-- "and for the take down of the terrorist network, what a job."

Jack held on as there approach was close from, the President of Russia, it said, "And the men involved?"

Jack hesitated, to write, "Still at large."

"Can you bring them in?" asked the President of Russia?

"Yes" said Jack, thinking he should have just put a bullet in each one.

As the helicopter, set down in the square, for a brief moment, long enough for Jack to help Victoria out and into his arms, a team of royal guards, signaled the helicopter away, Jack carried her inside, to a awaiting hospital bed, as he laid her down, she was whisk away, as Jack himself was on the move, back, outside, as the guards were scattered, Jack saw a car in the distant who had a familiar smile on his face, Jack jumped the fence, and was across the street, as he slid in, next to Clarance, to say, "Drive me back up that hill!"

Jack was on the phone, to Mark, who answered, to say, "Stay up there, and actually go back to that location, and set the tank up, I want to blast those hills, we got a mouse hunt."

Clarance drove the car, as Jack looked at his phone screen, He told him where to go, Mike took several turns, then onto a gravel road, where it was blocked off, Jack spoke, "Come to me, to say, pull over, Clarance, park over here.

He stopped the car, for which Jack said, "Do you still have that sniper weapon?"

"Nah, I left it on the hill, as Jack's car was across from them he said, "You go to the other side."

"What are you talking about, there is nothing here."

Jack ran over to the invisible car, opened his door, to say, "Resume", as the car mystically appeared, as Clarance, got out of his rental, over to the Mercedes, the seat automatically adjusted for him, as Jack sat next to him, for Jack, to say, "Don't touch a thing."

"I got that lecture earlier" said Clarance who had his hands together.

Jack set his phone into the dash, to say, "Take me to the tank, and the car took off, as the road seemed to be disappearing, and the next thing Clarance knew, the car sprinted over a creek, as the traction tires, were in place, and instantly onto the former tanks tracks, up the road, to a clearing, never once stopped, as Clarance sat in amazement, as this super car, was doing all the driving, as Jack was at his lap top, he pulled out, as he was talking to Mike, they were ready to go track him, so Jack said, "Yeah, go ahead, he saw he was still ten minutes away, to say so, and Mike and Mark, were armed, Mike said he parked the tank, under a carport, and took the two keys out."

From his vantage point Clarance could not see a thing, let alone, what Jack was doing, he just kept looking outside the window, as night was turning into morning, they were close to the street, Jack went back to tracking Mike and Mark, the car, turned left onto the street, as cars and trucks lined the two lane highway, as the car drove the pace of the slow traffic, a news alert hit his phone, it said, "Super Spy Jack Cash, rescues Premier's wife Victoria in less than twenty hours ago, after she was taken. And brought down the last of the great KGB organization and destroys their last remaining compound."

Another incoming message was from Lisa, that said, "Jack get out of Russia immediately, it was a trap, it was suppose to be a test that you were the pawn, for you to rescue the premier's wife, however from our sources say it was a ploy, but what you did was the last thing the President of Russia, could of ever expected, you exposed his secret network and illegal nuclear weapons grade operation, every minute new discoveries have surfaced, your life is in danger......"

Jack slid the phone shut, to think about this, to say, "Clarance I know you new to my team, how would you like to help me out?"

"Sure, I owe you, what would you like me to do?"

"What would you say if I left you behind and say you lied low for a week or so, here in this town?"

"I'd say whatever you wanted, I'll do it."

"That's nice to hear" said Jack.

"Sure, I won't let you down, that one time, it won't be again?"

"Good, I'm going to drive out of town, pull off to the side of the road, and you get out, Jack reached in and pulled out at a bundle of 1000's to hand to him, to say, "Here is ten thousand dollars, do what as you feel, blend in be a tourist, take up cave exploration, find me clues on this Varfolomey, and call me on my phone, better yet call Tami at this number, as Clarance punches it in the phone Jack gave him, for Jack to continue, "Let me have that ear piece back?"

Jack takes it and puts it in a box on his console.

Then says, "Mike and Mark, recall were pulling back."

Moments went by when Mark said, "Yeah this is Mark, we understand, good thing there are booby traps all over this place, come on back, I'll be in front of the pedestrian bridge."

The traffic was lightening up, for Jack to say, "You know this may take a few weeks or so..."

"I'll be here, for however as long as it takes" said Clarance.

"Good that's nice to hear" said Jack.

"Do you think I should keep any receipts I get?"

"Oh, I hadn't thought about that, you know it could make for a good cover, like business expenses" said Jack.

"No what I meant for all this cash?"

"Nah, have you been paid yet for your services?"

"I don't know, when I joined, they told me, that I'd be paid every other week, by direct deposit, and gave me a credit card to access the funds."

"Then consider this a gift from me."

"Alright thanks" said Clarance smiling at him.

"Do you have a weapon?"

"Don't need one, I have my hands."

"Yes you do", as Jack pulled off to the side of the road, the men got out, as the trunk opened, Jack looked through the remaining weapons to hand Clarance a 9 mm berretta, and a few clips, Jack tidied up then closed the trunk to see he was gone."

Jack got back in and turned around, and drove south, with little or no traffic, then turned out, and parked, he scrolled his phone for the world feed and the fallout was gaining momentum, some called this the largest cover-up the world has ever known, one carefully placed tank round couldn't have left that kind of damage, but as a another news agency just reported, a secret nuclear weapons grade plant was destroyed along with nineteen sixteen hundred pound hydrogen bombs went off, the effects were felt to the Volga river, as half of its level is gone and felt the effects as far south as Ukraine, definitely something was up, the United Nations, announced that Russia may lose its charter and be expelled from future activities, as if the reports are true, they were used to be part of this game, a press conference is scheduled for 1600 hours, Eastern standard time, to allow the President Vladimir Ecklon a chance to tell his side of the story, either way it doesn't look so good. Thought Jack.

Jack closed up his phone to see Mike and Mark running, Jack lowered his window, to say, one in the back and one beside me", as the window went up, the door opened, as the seat was forward, and Mark dove in, Mike took the front to say, "That's why I'm the slower......"

Jack drove on, as the road, was going away from the compound, his two men kept quiet, while they watched as Jack didn't drive the car, but instead was on a lap top, looking over surveillance, he pin pointed what he was looking for, to say, "I have a new mission, seeing the last one wasn't even my idea".

Jack positioned the car, to turn, as Mike said, "Are you going back to the compound?"

"Yes, we left something there I want."

They turned to go along the north side, past the crater that was once the Ammo dump, to the West, by the rope he left behind, he changed the car into cloak mode, as he zig, zagged, parked trucks, to see where he need to go, the heart of the huge explosion, Jack was ready to go, when Mike said, "Hold on, I'll get that." As all three saw the rifle.

"Really, you want to do this?" expressed Jack, seeing his monitor indicated some radiation was present.

"I owe you" said a reluctant, Mike.

"Wait" said Jack, as he went to his display and hit K, and in that instant, a bird shot out, as he told the car to go in reverse, and it zigzagged backwards, the car turned, as Jack parked it, to sync up the camera on the eagle, as it spread its wings, using the external receiver, it picked up speed, to soar, as Jack caught sight of the rifle, Jack tested out the claws, the eagle went in, landed, grasp the rifle, as several UN inspectors, wearing gas masks, saw the bird, and pointed as it was trying to grasp the sling, Jack transferred half power for lift, as it snatched it, the bird was struggling to lift it up, so Jack gave it all, it's power, inverted its wings, and everything shot up, the bird made the beeline to the car. Jack didn't know if he should go out and get that, when Mike said, "I'll go out and retrieve it."

Mike exited and went to the rear as Jack controlled the soar, as it dipped, then leveled off about ten feet above Mike, Jack released the claws, and the rifle landed into Mike's arms, and then Jack let the bird lift back up, it circled, as it slowed and saw what it was looking for, and lowered down, to the ground, to reach out to snag, the ammo case handle, using all of its thrust, it was having a bit of trouble, as the UN inspectors watched the bird struggle, but was able to lift off, and over the wall, it was on a slow descent downward, as Mike realizing the bird was going down, he raced towards it, as the weight of the ammo can, took the bird down, to the ground, Mike picked it up, and Jack said Trunk, it opened, as Mike still cradled the long rifle, as Jack got out to assist Mike, put the ammo can inside, with the bird, as Jack found a black bag, he set it in it., Mike handed Jack the rifle, as Jack, set the rifle butt end in, at an angle, then said Close." Jack saw Mike get in, as he slid in, Jack said, "Let's go to the hanger."

Several hours later, it was noon, at Moscow International Airport. The car drove, and followed the traffic in, right behind a huge packaging truck. The car was under the cloak of invisibility.

The Red Army was all over the place, as the car was still undected. Nearly, hitting a car, his car swerved to miss them, near crashes occur, from the car behind him, hitting his bumper, Jack hit letter G, that deployed the magnet, then the car closed in and stuck to Jack's car, as he followed right behind, with the car in tow, as the gate was raised, the truck went in, and the car went in behind, it, as it left the other car behind, as the gate came crashing down, he went to the left, and sped it up, as Jack was on the phone with Jim, to raise the hanger door, it went up, as Jim waved to those watching, as Jack past by, then Jim hit the button, the hanger door went down. Jack parked the car, got out to see Brian, to say, "Can you scan us for radiation poisoning?"

Jim comes over to him to say, "We got a small problem?"

"What you heard about the bird?"

"No, what happen to the bird" asked Jim.

"Oh it wasn't nothing really, have a look, said Jack as the truck opened, as Mike helped Mark out, Jim just looked at the pair, as they went past. Only to Brian, waving a monitor, over them, to say, "There all clear" as he went to Jack and swiped him, to say, "The level is non-existent, but if your exposed the watch should take as much as it can."

"Good to know" said Jack.

"Do you know were stuck here, till the President of Russia opens up the air space above, I imagine the fallout from the bombing will result in several days of waiting?"

"Wait a moment", said Jack as he went up the ramp, to see Trixie, then he knocked on the door, of the flight cabin, it opened to see Mitzi, who said, "Nice to see you made it, you know they have your picture posted everywhere, and now were all in trouble, no flights in or going out."

"And how is that my fault, my mission was to rescue the wife of the President of Russia, and I did that, now it's time to go back to Belarus." Said Jack thinking.

"Alright, but they won't allow us to fly out, especially if they think you are on the plane" said Mitzi.

"That's it, the President of Russia, asked me to find and capture the attacker Varfolomey, well what he doesn't know, is that I'm here and my last location I reported from was Ivanovo, this is what I want you to do, "Call in to say your flying off to resupply Jack Cash up in Ivanovo, and need a clearance to fly off, to a carrier to resupply, then I will create a diversion, making it know I'm still there."

"How are you going to do that when you're here?"

"Trust me" said Jack smiling.

"I will try" said a concerned Mitzi.

Jack slid his phone on to call Clarance who answered, "Yeah."

"I need a diversion, can you go down the road, I see where your at, go down two blocks and on the left, is a tank, get inside, you may have to hot wire it, to get the electrics working, turn the barrel towards the hills, and fire one round off, then get out of there, and go north to town of Kostroma, there should be some answers to finding Varfolomey., do you understand this?"

"Yes, will do" said Clarance.

As Jack looked at the Russian satellite feed, on his phone, to watch Clarance at work, the heat signature resonated in and around the tank, the fire of the round was captured, as it struck and blew out some chunks of the hillside, and could see by satellite him running, it also showed police swarmed in, in and around the tank. He closed up his phone to see Mitzi was all smiles to say "Were cleared to take off."

"Did they say why?" asked Jack.

"No, they didn't need to, I will tell Jim, we will be underway soon, "So mister, pilot, Bill, get us out of here."

"Yes, Ma'am.

"Hey where is Clarance?"

"Oh he is on a little assignment for me" said Jack smiling.

"Are you going to tell me where?"

"Nope only need to know", as Jack gets up out of her seat, to hear, "Oh Jack just wanted you to know your friend is in the hospital, and she is doing fine, the President of Russia is going to visit her today."

Jack went into his room, to see that the bed was made up with one exception; a very nude Carly was in the middle of the bed, smiling, for Jack to think, "Yes its time to relax."

Jack entered, closed the door, he went and sat down, as she came to him, then laid back and two went to sleep.

Jim and Brian unloaded the trunk, and Brian took the rifle in, admiring the one of a kind, and set it down by the replica bird, as Jim drove the car in, Jim called up to Bill to get the plane moving, the ramp was half up, then all the way as they left the confines of the hanger, as the go ahead was given, Bill throttled up the plane, and off it went, out to taxi, and turned, set the run, and off, for a quick flight to Minsk, as the plane climbed, and turned like it was going south, when all of a sudden, it went west over the mountains, and into Belarus. Jim and Brian were hard at it with the car, they turned it around, on the plane was a visitor, who was under the hood, the special technician who designed the engine, transmission, and drive train, he adjusted the idle and throttle controls, to discover that the car is learning, the driver, as Jim discovered from the on board computer the two, sat and watched the video of the eagle performing the task, as Jesse said, "So Jim what is that birds lifting capacity?"

"I believe we never measured that before, Mister Carter".

"You have to give it to this spy, he is unlike Ben, seems like every week I'm out in California rebuilding his cars he crashes or blows up."

"How many are you on now?"

"Going on his fifth year, I'd say one hundred" said the young engineer.

"One hundred cars" asked Jim.

"Yeah, but he doesn't have what Jack has either, Ben's cars are beat up to match his environment, you see to me this is the super spy's car, it's an indent statement."

"And no one can drive it" said Jim.

"Yeah and no one can drive it, because it drives itself, this is a prototype that came from NASA as its supercar of the future."

"And now it's synonymous with the world's best agent."

"I'd second that, what is your opinion on the bombing" asked Jesse looking at the figures.

"It's really none of either of our business, is it really, our jobs is to keep the super spy well equipped."

"And speaking of that where are all these hotties I keep hearing about, it must be like a magnetic that he draws them in" said the eager young man.

"Well not so much lately, it's really staying in house, and I will leave it at that" said Jim.

"I hear you."

Mitzi watched the world feed like all the rest of the world as the President of Russia, Vladimir Ecklon, was to speak, since the bombing, that left over five hundred thousand dead, as a reporter spoke, to add, in the aftermath of the UN inspectors went into this compound, of all places, the former home of the underground or secret police, some say the former KGB operations group has all been destroyed along with the detonation of two 1600 pound hydrogen bombs, and nineteen smaller ones to include a weapons grade plutonium, and credit for all of this destruction, was Super Spy, Jack Cash, who was asked to come to Russia, when the top two soviet spy's turned the President of Russia down, and asked the UN to allow Mister Cash in, but what the President of Russia, could have never expected, Mister Cash exposed the secret bomb building enterprise, some twenty floors under the ground, to having the wife rescued unharmed, in less than twenty hours after her abduction, here now is the President of Russia, Vladimier Ecklon, he came to the podium, to say, "Ladies and Gentleman, members of the press, military and of course the United Nations and the World Council of International Corruption, I want to start off with a story, about how this government was held hostage, by the KGB and its affiliates, and in their demands they wanted one hundred million dollars, well since the bombing occurred all those responsible has been captured, and from this moment forward, the secret police is dissolved, my wife and I would to personally like to thank Jack Cash of the United States for her rescue, and who was instrumental in the take down and destruction of the KGB, he worked closely with one of our top agents who was injured in the fight, but will recover with no limitation, as for the bomb making underground, I was not aware of it, nor had any idea such a thing was happening, we feel, like our door is open to the US and UN Inspectors, to sift through the wreckage, and allow them to come up with there own conclusions, any questions?"

"Where is this Super Spy, you call Jack Cash, who is he?"

"Well, since he freed, my wife Victoria, from her captors, I asked him to track down the very man who held her."

"So he is still here in Russia?"

"Yes, as far as we know."

"Good job, Jack" said Mitzi, she said to herself, seeing her phone was ringing, she saw it was Lisa, to say, "Yes."

"We got a bigger problem" said a frantic Lisa.

"What's that, what you are saying?" asked Mitzi.

"It's Jack, the whole secret police is onto him, and we need to extract him from Ivanovo, which was his last transmission?"

"Who is this?" said Mitzi.

"Mitzi I'm not joking around, if they catch him, were through" said Lisa.

Mitzi was stalling to see how long to let her worry, as the pause wasn't helping either.

"So what the President of Russia, said wasn't true?"

"Well No, and Yes, but Jack is in danger" said Mitzi, seeing Jim and Bill who were being amused.

"Not from where I'm at, but maybe soon" said Mitzi as she got up and went to his room, she went in and was looking at the pair of them, to finally come clean, to say, "Calm down he is fine."

"Are you seeing the feed I'm seeing it looks like their collapsing on him" still saying the frantic Lisa.

Mitzi sees Jack, lying with Carly, she stands by Jack's side to say, "Jack wake up, its Lisa, she wants to say Hi, as she tosses the phone on his chest, as she goes to the door, closes it and locks it down, and begins to get undress, first her blouse, then her bra.

As Jack watches, he puts the phone up to his ear, to say, sheepishly "Hi, this Lisa its Jack, how may I help you, he said in a seductive voice as Mitzi comes closer to allow Jack to touch her amazingly firm breasts, as she pulls her stretch pants and panties down, she unbuckles his pants, unzips them, and removes his shoes, to pull off his pants, while Lisa went on and on, as Jack watched as Mitzi climbed up on the bed, walked over to him, spread a bit then sat down on his manhood, she did all the work, while Lisa and him talked, his breathing was heighten, by her action to him, till Jack said, "Look I'll see you in Minsk, Bye", closed up the phone and pitched it aside, so he could concentrate on her hips and how beautifully she was working them. She had all the control, as she spoke to say, "You know I really missed you, while I lay in that bed, and not once did you come and visit me" while she looked at Carly who was asleep, she turned over, away from them.

"How could I I'm still on a mission, I can't even go home, even as three days has since passed, I'll be in Minsk, till the end of the week, where at least the King likes me."

"And, so do I" as she leans over to kiss him on the lips, for Jack to say, "I like you too."

"Yes but do you love me, like I love you."

"Sure, I have feeling for you" said Jack.

"Yes, but are they the same feeling you have for all your wives?"

"Well yes, I really only have feeling for one, that would be Sara, the rest of them were gifts, what was I suppose to refuse them, if I'm allowed wives, I'll take them" said Jack with his hands on her hips.

"Yes, but what about cheating on them or her?"

"What are you saying, and what are you implying I'm cheating on someone, before I married, I told each and everyone of them, I may want other partners, and they were fine with that, so what are you saying, you want to be a wife now?"

"You know I'd like to be, but then I would lose my position, and you would be out your ground support and all those little details I give to you and your computer, and plus you can have this anytime you like, but wait you're a bad boy, and bad boys don't go looking for it, it comes to them, and that's why I'm here to share in some of that power you received from doing all that damage, for a guy who's reputation as the preserver of life, on this one you tarnished that and your reputation" said Mitzi.

"I never said that I don't kill others, I just try to salvage those that I can help, not some radicalist who will still try to kill me, even after I wound them, besides after this summit I may have one more mission I may have you look into."

"What's that another secret?"

"Yeah, sort of, I left Clarance behind, under cover, to spy on Varfolomey."

"Wait, Lisa just told me that someone was captured in Ivanovo."

"Wrong Intel, my man, told me he set a delay timer on the gun, and is now in the town of Kostroma, posing as a wine dealer, for an Irish organization, his family owns" said Jack.

"Really."

"I don't know that's your job, to keep in touch with him, while I go into the summit" said Jack.

"So you're still going?" said a surprised Mitzi.

"Yep, I wish it were you and I, but I need you to look after them, and inside I heard, no phones, no nothing, for the next three weeks, what a bummer" said Jack. "I don't know if I can last three weeks without doing this to you."

"Shut up, and now it's your turn and take me from behind this time" said a demanding Mitzi.

Jim and Jesse finished the diagnostics, to shut the car doors, everything was replaced, for Jesse to say, "What if I just came to work exclusively for you, do you think Jack would approve it?"

"Maybe, but what would you do?"

"Continue building super cars, and fixing them, looks like you guys are having all the fun?" said Jesse.

"This is fun, we haven't had a bit of down time at all" said Jim.

"I know but your supporting the world's greatest spy, who cares, someday he will retire, as will all of us, look at my hair, I was good looking with brown hair, now I have silver streaks, and I'm only 24 yrs old."

"That's the youth now a-days, you need to find a woman, to take off some of that edge" said Jim.

"True, true, but you have Debby, and if it weren't for Jack what would you be doing?"

"I would be retired, your right about that, but you know, even after we get the approval, with Debby and I, he could still sleep with her, did I just say that, listen your right kid, there are hot and sexy girls tied to Jack, and for Jack alone, Debby is special, as is other girls that work for us, just awhile back we had two wildcats aboard, and we had to take them down, one actually liked Brian, but turns out she was just using him to get on board."

"I'm still interested" said Jesse.

"Let me ask Mitzi, meanwhile can you wash off the car, using the wet cloth" said Jim.

"Yes sir" said Jesse. As Brian came up to him to see him using the cloth to say, "I overheard you want to get on board, is this true?"

"Yeah, who wouldn't?"

"Well me, I'd love to get off and go back to being just an armorer."

"Then I'll take your place" said the eager Jesse.

"Easy, I don't know why you want to do that, and it's not my place", Brian leaves him to do work.

Jim sees Trixie to say, "Can he be bothered?"

"Why, you can go see him."

"What bothering you" asked Jim?

"Mitzi is in there with him."

"Well if it's what those two went through, said Jim at the door with Trixie, as they saw, Jack, Mitzi and Carly. They were sound asleep, for Jim to say, "They spent the last twenty hours on a woman hunt, as Jim tries to push Trixie out, and closes the door, to feel it closed, to say, "I guess we will wait till he comes out."

CH 8

King of Belarus and Spies

The next morning, he had awaken, as his overnight sleep was eventful, upon, waking, Mitzi was dressed, and said, "If the reports are true, then you Jack, have left Russia, for now you're here in Belarus", as she shows him the recent wire news that he was on all the front page news of all eastern European countries detailing exactly what he did, and his newest mission from the UN was clean up Minsk, at all costs, which meant door to door fighting, and complete wipeout of all known terrorist cells, tied to the secret police, and Russia, as the President of Russia had asked for a complete surrender, so the helpers to Jack Cash, were gathering and processing all those that were the followers and were given immunity from prosecution, and was able to return to their country's to see their loved ones, and that meant over one hundred and twenty five plus. The 48 people earlier, for a total of 173, so they let Jack sleep, and he did, for another two days, same for Mike and Mark, who awoke as did Jack, from Mitzi, who told him, that everything was going according to plan, and that he could rest. Finally he awoke for good, he got up, emerged refreshed, from his room, to step out, to a hanger that was open, a pretty open airfield, his car, was under a cover, as he stepped out on to the tarmac, not a soul was around, except long passenger buses, he looked at his watch to see that the date must be wrong, as Jim made his way over from the other hanger door, to say "Hey Jim, what day is it?"

"The twenty second of February."

"What, how could that be, what happen to the last four days?"

"I guess you were really tired."

"You did it to me again, it was those damn sleeping pills" said Jack.

"Yep, by orders from the boss" said Jim.

As Jim was on his phone, for Jack to say, "Who are you calling?"

"It's me Jack", Jack turns to see Lisa, who looked pretty good, for him, to say, "Wow don't you look good."

"What did Jim give you, he needs to wake you up" said Lisa.

"Nothing I'm fine" said Jack.

"Yes, you are, so we thought it would be best if you went earlier than later, so tomorrow, you and your team will be flying to Geneva, to get your rehabilitation started, on your manifest, you have Blythe, going first, then it will be Trixie, although I thought now that Mitzi's here, she would of taken her place, then there is this girl call Jill, what a fiery dynamo, a former Marine's daughter, she can shoot and defend herself well, for an aspiring agent, she even enrolled with the FBI, they sent us her file, very impressive, so from now on, she and Gia, will join the strike team, I sent the SEAL's back to the Nimitz, that battle group will still be your main backup, as they will sit in the Mediterranean sea, and Admiral Cates, is awaiting any order you so have, like once your done their a short trip to the Ural mountains for a game of cat and mouse."

"I have six days, till I officially have to be there."

"No you don't, after we process everyone, it will take at least two days, we need you there to authenticate, it's really you, besides the King and Queen of Belarus, wants' you to visit them, to thank you for visiting, we chose Blythe to accompany you?"

"How about Kelli?"

"She left, as did Simone back to Puerto Rico, both didn't like the cold weather.

"Great the help is dropping like flies" said Jack.

"Well you have Jill, who I think has promise and Gia, maybe or not so much and Jesse?"

"Boy or girl?" asked Jack.

"Boy, he is the one who designed your car, so he is a real genius" said Lisa.

"And how does that benefit me now?"

"I don't know, but I need to ask of you one more thing, will you waive the charges against Claire Montfork?"

"Who is that bitch, the one from Puerto Rico?"

"Yeah, but I talked with her and she is reformed, and why would you care so much?"

"Then let her go?' said Jack.

"We can't, the order only can come from you" said Lisa.

"So what do I need to sign?"

She shows him an official document, which he signs off on, and she says, "I'll get Mitzi to authenticate it and send it to them, so when you go to Switzerland, the team will take her home."

"So what do you have going on next door" said Jack getting a look at the modern jet.

"Ah not much, were just processing the detainees to transport."

"Do you need help?" asked Jack.

"Nah, don't worry about it, you better go get changed I believe Trixie has your outfit laid out for you, and Blythe will be ready when you are, have fun".

Jack steps up on the ramp to see a young looking kid, he just walks past, to see Trixie, she says, "So what will this thing be about, having to dress up and all?"

"Come inside and I will tell you".

Jack saw the tuxedo on a hanger, inside the room, as Trixie closed the door, to say, "So what do you think of our new hire?"

"Who is she?" asked Jack.

"It's not a girl, silly; it's a guy, finally someone new to look at?"

"Getting tired of me already?"

"Never, so aren't you excited about going to Switzerland, I heard that you're going to the Alps."

"Really cause last I knew you were going too" said Jack.

"Well that is alright, it just kind of frightens me, you know with all those spies, there in all."

"Don't forget, I'll be there too" said Jack.

"I know, but what will I be doing all day while you're in class?"

"I don't know? activities I guess."

She helped him finished dressing, then helped him with his holster, and then his dinner jacket. Trixie adjusted his tie, to say "You look quite handsome, try not to have too much fun."

"I won't" said Jack sarcastically, as he turned the handle, to step out, into the empty cargo bay, then down the steps to the concrete surface, a stunningly, well dressed Blythe appeared, in some ways she looked like Devlin, but a slight prettier, she took his arm, as Jack led her to the passenger side of the car, the door opened, as Jack let her in, then closed the door, went around to see that young kid looking at him, then got in.

"It's not nice to stare", said Brian, who was cleaning off his hands, to hear, "So what do you guys do all day?"

"It's simple really, we do our assigned jobs, like for instance me, I'm his armorer, gunsmith, weapons and ordinance handler, not to mention ground and aircraft maintenance and refueling, sometimes a runner" said Brian.

"What about the girls" said Jesse?

"Well I can tell you it's no love fest if that's what you're looking for."

"What about that blonde?"

"Which one", said Brian looking around, to see who he was talking about, to add, "Let's just say, every girl on this plane has someone already, and four of them, you want to stay clear of."

"Who's that?"

"Well first is Lisa Curtis, assistant CIA director, then there is Erica Meyers, she works for our nation's supreme court, usually on this plane is two girls you want to steer away from, that's Mitzi the brunette and Trixie the Blonde."

"So what about that really small hot blonde, with that sexy mouth."

"Oh, yeah, I forgot her too, she is Jack's personal assistant her name is Tami or there is Carly.

Jack watched the road as the car droved to its new destination, Blythe was quiet, her dress was hiked up a bit, but neither she nor Jack cared, she knew that he had lost faith in her, and she it, it was a sheer accident she was going to this conference, let alone a state dinner, as she turned her head, to say, "So what went wrong with us?"

"What do you mean?"

"Well it just seems to me, that you're not that into me anymore?"

"Well I don't know, maybe it was the fact I gave you the opportunity to become a spy, and you deserted me on your first chance."

"What do you mean by that?"

"How about the boat, to Santa Isabel, what happen there?"

"I was sea sick and laid down in the front cabin, next thing I knew we were back at port."

"It's convenient how you go missing, when there are more desirable candidates for the job?"

"What job is that?" asked Blythe.

"To be a stand alone spy, to go on your own missions and become successful."

"Really, you mean that?"

"Sure why do you think your name was on the manifest to the council in four days?"

A smile went across her face as she thought, to say, "Just think I did it without ever sleeping with you."

Jack's car turned a corner, to see, a gate guard, as the window lowered the guard, took a picture of them, to say, "Welcome Mister and Misses Jack Cash, go on up and park, in the garage on the right, an entrance is below", Jack tried to drive the car, but it was having none of that as it went the designated speed, into a parking spot, they both got out together, as Jack held her hand, as they came to the door, where inside sat a lady, who had two tags ready, as she hands them to him, which he gives to her, and places the card on his pocket, to read Jack Cash, for her it was Blythe Cash. They continued on, past a security guard station, and a metal detector, Jack walked right through, as Blythe followed, to a set of stairs up, then on the main floor, was round tables, on either side was a stage, one was for the band, setting up and the other was for the King and Queen, and their distinguished guests, to include, a place setting for Jack next to the Queen, and Blythe was on the other side with the King, then his cabinet.

Jack left Blythe by the seating area, as guests came in, Jack went to the restroom, upon his exit, he noticed a short haired black-haired Italian looking woman, who smiled at him, wearing a pearl necklace, into the side restroom, Jack, continued on, to see a hostess carrying glasses of white wine, she said, "Sir would you like one?"

Jack takes one, puts the glass next to his watch, no, nothing so he took a sip, it tasted refreshing, as he made it back to where Blythe was at she too was talking to some other ladies as the place filled, then the band played and in walked the King and Queen, under announcement, the Queen looked magnificent, as she was half his age, then it was the King, as a lane was cleared for them, up the stairs, then an usher, motioned for Jack to follow the Queen, up, he walked slowly trying to avoid her train, then a matron, helped her in position, as Jack assumed the chair next to her, he could have been on the other side of the room, he was so close he could touch that delicate flower.

The announcement to sit, and Jack waited till the Queen sat, then he squeezed in, to sit as attendants pushed them in as necessary. Jack saw others raise their hand to stop the pushing, he did as well. His patron stopped, in front of him were plates, silverware and glasses, in front of them, was a server pouring the wine first, then water, then a juice of sorts, to hear from the lady on his right "That's cranberry juice, it's very good for you."

Jack turns to see that pretty black-haired girl, her named tag read,

"Ingrid", and her title, "Foreign Secretary of Affairs", but said nothing, as the music played, he could hear Blythe's voice and that cackle of a laugh, to think, "She was sure living it up", as one by one courses came and gone, some barely a bite, while others way too much, he mimicked, the Queen, even though, the dinner was a mere show of hospitality, and a way of getting out of their huge home and grounds, on this days event, a person spoke, it was a foreign language, Jack used his phone to translate, with ear piece in his ear, told him what he what he was saying, a gift from the people of Minsk, for the capture and suppose freedom, they are going to build him a shrine and 640 acres of farming land, for a new palace, built for the arrival of a new son. They all stood up and cheered, the girl on his right kept talking and suggesting thing to him, she was annoying him now, then all of a sudden things got quiet, as a time of silence was given, for when they flashed on the screen the devastation, in Moscow, then all of a sudden it was a cheer, as it gained momentum, to a song, something like, over and over again, we are free, at last from the KGB. A toast was given, they all stood, as did the Queen and King, Jack followed suit, then as dinner was nearing, Ingrid leaned over to say, "Now they are going to award you, this is a special time in our country, since the occurrence, there has been a forty percent drop in crime, just in our country alone, peace is on the horizon, for us and other countries still under Russian law, and you're the one who saved us, look over there" she said as the image was that of the tank, with Jack's arm stretched out, moments before the blast, was on the wall.

"That picture will be made into a life size replica and displayed in front of the government's building here in Minsk."

"Wow that's nice" said Jack.

"It's more than nice, it's probably as great as when Charlemagne himself was here, your being idolized, and that palace you saw being built is for you" said Ingrid.

"Really come on, they don't have to do that."

"Do that, its already done, your reputation alone got you that, if when you decide to retire you can come live here and become King, is what they are saying now, and it will be taken to the administration, to become adopted, tomorrow, I will take you out there and show you your land" she said as she was the only one talking, to see all of them was looking at him, she said quickly "Get up and give a speech, hurry."

Jack rose, as everyone below him kneeled, as did the Queen and King, the chairs were pulled away, he heard her say, "Kneel, before them."

Jack did that, as the King stepped forward, to say something, in a dialect of Russian, as Jack tried to figure it all out, but was recording it, a gold sword was pulled from its scarab, to set on each shoulder, then his head, to signify he was a Sir now, or a Knight, as Ingrid kept telling him, he had powers within the government, regardless if Jack wanted it or not, it was his, as the Queen presented Jack with a jeweled box, Ingrid said, "Reach up and hold your hands out for her to place in them."

Jack could feel the weight of the heavy box, only to hear, "Now raise my son, for you are now of my family."

"The King has just adopted you" she said, as Jack looked at the magnificent gift.

"You can put it down, that red cashmere cloth will be placed under it, as for the sword, you must wear it, I'll help you with that, Jack raised as the King handed him the scarab and gold sword, Jack set the jewel box on the cloth, then undid his belt, to slid on the scarab, to his right, as the chairs came back in place, Jack sat down to hear, "Isn't it exciting, your third in line to the throne." as Ingrid, placed her hand upon his, to rub, for her to say one last thing "I know you have many questions tomorrow I will answer all of them, enjoy tonight."

The meal was finishing, everything was great, then it was the pastry desserts, a platter to choose from, which started with the Queen, then it was Jack's turn, as he used his tongs, he chose a cinnamon twist like pastry, to hear, "Good choice, there is marzipan filling inside", moments later a liquor was poured, then a bell rang and they all ate them, drank the liquor, and coffee was served, black as a servant held a tray of condiments, like milk, sugar, but no Lemon, he whispered to Ingrid, "Can you ask him for Lemon wedges?"

"Yes," then she spoke her native language, he left as another came up, as did others to see Jack take a lemon wedge, and put it in, and that was all it took, the Queen and King took it that way, even Ingrid liked it that way, Jack sensed the coffee was way strong, but the lemon balanced it out, it was a perfect fit, to hear, "Do you like our coffee?"

"Yes, may I have another?" said Jack.

"Of course, that pot in front of you is filled with chicory, we roast it, and chop it up and it marinates in a vat for 30 days, then its dried, ground up and then seeped over springs water, that's why it's so good" said the King.

Moments later, outside chairs were cleared out, leaving, the King, Queen, Blythe, Jack and Ingrid, as the front table was taken away in favor of a shorter one, about knee high, where coffee, cookies, and pastries were placed, the tables were cleared, for the dance floor, as the band, began the love songs, then it was the King's dance, he chose Blythe, they danced a waltz, as Ingrid said, "Next dance you must ask the Queen for a dance, then perform a waltz, keep your frame straight and your hold tight but at a distance." She moved in closer to whisper, "All eyes will be on you, then at the end of the dance she will either curtsy you or kiss you on the cheek, to grade your performance, then it's the King's dances, where he chooses lucky ladies from the guests below, to dance, the more he chooses, shows how well he, likes the dinner, well the less, the least he liked it, then it will be your turn, dance at least ten times, to show your appreciation, many more, if you really liked it or all of them, then there will be a line up."

Jack watched the King with Blythe who struggled to keep up, sometimes drug her feet, Jack thought of Mitzi, who taught him, how elegant she was, the ten minute song ended, with Blythe ready to collapse, as the King bowed, for Ingrid, to say, "He was displeased with her."

"It figures" said Jack, As he rises, to take the Queen's hand, he escorted her down, and onto the dance floor, as Jack synced his phone up to his ear piece to the waltz, as the coach spoke, he followed flawlessly, for the extended dance no one wanted to end, especially the smiling Queen, but as it came to the end, Jack swayed her away, waiting a response, it was on the way back when she kissed him on both cheeks.

A round of applause, by everyone, a smile on the King's face said it all, as Jack turned, to signal for all."

The King agreed, as women lined up, as there was a separation, to show the women were hidden from the King's view, to be present now, stunningly beautiful, and of all shapes and sizes, but there was one distinct feature, their sturdy faces, long triangular with deep piercing eyes. So from both ends they were on parade, the King chose the first, each lady would state their name, and the region they were from, in hopes of some recognition after the short one minute dance, then the King would hand them to Jack.

Jack, who danced with whom he choose, as he saw the King reject some over others, while the King choose another, this first girl, said her name was Marie, she was eloquent, she had a fine smell to her, next was, Anna, another stunning brunette. Next up was Leonie, a blonde, tall; the hold was difficult, as his head was at her bust line. Next was Maria, black haired, green eyes, smiles a lot, Lena, was similar to Austin, a cute smile and really pouty lips, she kissed him on the cheek when finished. Next was Emily, if there could have been a perfect match dancing wise it was her, they swung their arms, and was in sync on the floor, she was his overall, choice, in the back of his mind he knew what was coming, so he went along with it. Next was the shortest, by far, her name was Lea, or Leah, it was uncomfortably, for him, as the song ended, either by the band who saw how uncomfortable it was for Jack, as his eyes lit up with Laura, a brown hair beauty, he was back on track, for the next one was the jackpot, an extremely cute, girl named Julia, long flowing brunette, who wore a constant smile, one to always remember as her touch to his was delicate, but her palms were sweaty. At the end of the dance, it was as if Jack wanted an encore, which was allowed, much to the clapping of the crowd and the King himself, as he stood and waited, Jack and Julia to finish, as Jack realized it was time to let that one go. Next up was Nina, a black haired, somewhat polish girl, cute to look at and other things, she was the most sexual with him, as several times, she fell into him, purposely, till the end. Jack realized she was flirting with him. Next was a passer, an ugly girl, named Olga, he toughed it out with her especially when she told him, she was a cousin of the King. Next was Tatiana not at all of the name of his former partner, she was Russian all the way, tough, straight back, small bust line, definitely a fighter, next was Alexandra, brunette some what pretty, she left, and it was Ekaterina, she was Russian tough, she led Jack around the room, he was glad it was over, next was Anastasia, a gem, delicate, pretty, and really flirty, and smiled a lot, Jack was sad to see her go, next was Raisa, black hair, nothing special, that was till the line was thinning, and the real stars were seen, and the next one for Jack, was Natasha, super cute, a real gem, dancing was fun and professional, he just couldn't stop looking at her, she was just like Austin, but more mature, something was between them, and after she left, it was Daria, a tall short hair, to shoulder length kinda blonde, brown dyed thing, extremely beautiful, next was another looker, her name was Bianca, a stunningly gorgeous lady, with dark piercing eyes, as she went, and the last one was Brigitte, a another stunner, brunette, hard to keep his eyes off her, as the final dance ended, she kissed him on the cheek, and went away. Then the King and Queen took the very last dance, and Blythe was no where to be found, as Ingrid was in Jack's arms, as she showed him she was jealous of all the ladies, this joyous night ended as all clapped the Queen and Jack, the King and Ingrid.

The party broke up, and everyone was exiting, as Ingrid went up to Jack to say, "Jack, the King and Queen would like you to be their guests for the next three days before you must go to Switzerland, will you accept?"

"What of my date?"

"We don't know where she is at, besides I'll be your date?"

"Sounds good to me, let me make a call."

Jack dialed up Lisa, who answered to see it was 0200 in the morning to say, "We know, we picked her up, wandering the grounds, go have fun, your ride will be waiting on Friday, have fun."

Jack closed up the phone, to pick up the jeweled box, and the cloth, to see Ingrid, who takes his arm, to say, "The motorcade is waiting, as Jack made it to the parking garage, he opens the door for Ingrid, looking around he notices Spy Club was in place, goes to the trunk, it opens, he undoes a flap, and a combination, and then places the cloth and jeweled box inside, then next to the combination, he adjusts the sides and closes it up, he takes off his sword, then closes the trunk, gets in, to say, "Valet mode", then drives the car out, to fall into line, behind the King's car, as motorcycles were all around, the drive was relatively long, as Ingrid slept, peacefully, she was actually pretty hot, the plunging neck line showed off her assets, then they started to climb, up to a mountain top, where it leveled out, a huge barn, doors were open, and the Kings car drove in, as Jack nudged her, she awoke to say, "Follow him in, and you will park on the right."

Jack did so, to park, he waited to see the King and Queen exit.

A Porter, stood waiting, for Jack, as he motioned for them to exit, he said, "My name is John, I'll be at your service, while you're here." Jack just looked up at the huge man, to nod, "Yes, the name is "Jack Cash". Porter John led Jack and Ingrid inside as Jack said, "Secure".

In through the foyer, was a grand staircase upwards, as Porter John, continued up, then to the right, then stopped to say, "If the lady allows, here is your room, and the gentleman, is on the other side."

Porter John opened the door for Jack, who heard, "I'll see you tomorrow morning", said Ingrid. As Porter John, walks in to say, "This wing, is all yours, it is quiet so if you like you can play the piano, here is a closet, full of clothes, as we received from your people, through this door is your bedroom, fireplace, it gets drafty up here, I can start a fire if you like?"

"Nah, I'll be fine" said Jack at the door.

"Through there is the bathroom, and out onto the patio, connects to the other side, so rest and if you desire anything, just pick up the phone, good night sir".

Porter John left, as Jack was looking at this magnificent room, with its high ceilings, and rich décor, paintings on the wall, looked new, and the tapestry, Jack went into the bathroom, to see everything was polished, a toothbrush, and razor, he felt the bristles, they were new, Jack used his watch, to check for any poisons, then went over to the magnificently large tub, and decided to run a bath, he plugged the hole, and adjusted the hot water, and then saw the bubbles, so he poured them in, turned around to see a woman standing there, smiling to say, "Sir I'm here to assist you in your bath?"

Jack looked around to say, "How did you get in?"

"Through a door, it's a secret passage, between the walls; I could show you if you like?"

"Nah, that's not necessary," said Jack, admiring how beautiful she actually was, to say, "I can do it myself?"

"Here in our country, it is very rude for a gentleman to refuse a woman."

"What is your name?" asks Jack looking her over.

She smiled, to say, in her best English, "My names, Nadia, I'm the Queen's chamber maid, I service all the Queen's needs, she said with her hands out.

Behind her stood, Ingrid, not happy, as she missed out on an opportunity, and left without being seen by Jack who was preoccupied with Nadia, who was watching him.

Jack tried hard, to resign himself, to say, "Alright I will allow this."

Jack takes off his Jacket, then his holster then his shirt, and pants, slips off his shoes and socks, then his underwear, to set the holster on the shelf by the tub. He turns to see Nadia, herself had disrobed, pulling off her sheer dress, to reveal her nude tight body, Jack himself was rising, He leans over to shut off the water, as her hands are on his back, which made him jump, to see that she had moved in to press her body on his. She was fierce looking, with a near perfect body, and red lips, her dark hair showed her real strong side, she was a Russian woman no doubt, Jack thought, as he set down in the middle of this huge tub. Nadia spoke very good English, she said, "Turn around and I'll wash your back", so Jack turned as she slid behind him, he relaxed back into her arms, as she took care of him. The bath was over, as he was tired as she said, "I placed Valerian in the water for you to sleep." She helped him up, dried him off, and took him to his bed.

CH 9

A day out on the back 400

Next morning came with the sound of a single rooster croaking, the cool breeze on his head, the covers felt luxurious, his body smelled sweet, he was alone, Jack thought of his own protection, he looked for his gun, he sprang up, and went into the bathroom, there on the shelf was still his holster and gun. He stood there naked, he went to the mirror, washed his face, shaved and brushed his teeth, then went back into the bedroom, to see that the bed was made, and his clothes laid out, as Jack looked around, wondering if they came through that secret passage or what, he dressed in clothes, that fit perfect, and went into the bathroom, retrieved his holster, slung it on, then saw a light gray windbreaker on the bed, he placed it on, to feel, inside was his badge, and phone, then saw that his tux was gone.

Jack exited the room, to see array of servants, with trays, to hear, "Mister would you like your meal on the patio?" said Porter John, who held his hand out to show the way.

"That's where I'm having it Jack" said a voice, of that of Ingrid's.

"Sure why not" said Jack, a bit over whelmed by all the staff.

The huge doors were open, as a slight breeze could be felt, Jack waited for Ingrid, who led the way, outside, to a chair, as

Jack remembered that this wasn't here last night, to follow suit to sit across from her.

"So did you sleep well?" asked Ingrid.

"Actually I did, it was quite refreshing" said Jack looking at her.

"If it were me, were would of ended up spending the night together" she said in a statement, rather than a question.

Two elegant plates was served, with lids on them, several glasses were placed, as water was poured, grapefruit, then apple juice, lastly was a cup of coffee, with a bowl of lemons.

Jack saw a server to the right of him and there was one in the back of him, as Ingrid, said "I know, you get use to it, but there here to serve any need you have?"

"Such as" asked Jack, reaching for the lid.

"Allow me sir" said the servant.

The lid came off, to see and smell, a wave of different delights, Jack tried, what looked like an omelet, on the left side, as he waved his watch over it still read green, and it tasted like Lobster.

"That is Lobster from gulf of Riga, flown in daily, the eggs Benedict, is all from around the kingdom, and the fruit is flown in from all over the world" said Ingrid, in a statement.

Jack ate while she continued to talk, to say, "How was your service last night?"

Jack looked at her, trying to figure out what she was talking about, to say, "I don't follow, what you're asking?"

"The chamber maid, how was she?"

"I don't know what you are saying?"

"Come on I saw the young lady, there in your room?"

Jack just looked at her, to say, "How did you do that?"

"There are secret passages all throughout the palace, so I know what I saw?"

"All I know was, Yeah, Nadia was there, but after the bath, she tucked me in, and I went to sleep."

"And that's all you did?"

"What are you implying?"

"Oh, nothing, except that Nadia was there to satisfy all of your needs."

"I think she did a good job."

"Really?" said Ingrid.

when some horses began to assemble below them, but slowly, with riders from different areas, or at least Jack thought by looking at them, for Ingrid to say, "Before we go see your property, the King is arranged a hunting party, for the morning, are you interested?"

"What do you mean?"

"Well the riders below, are Men, for which you danced with their daughter's last night, so the ones that were chosen, were now invited, the fathers and sons, from all over the country and some from Lithuania, Latvia and Estonia". It has been reported that all our partner countries, have seen drops in crime, and killings." She paused to see some of the men below, look up at her, for her to continue, to say, "So for that, it's a celebration, the King is putting on this show, if you want to participate, simple raise your hand, it will go far for you to participate, and allow those fathers and sons an opportunity to impress you, so eventually, you'll select their daughter to marry."

"Does that mean, I need to go now?"

"No silly, you go when you're ready, everyone will wait for you, just like these servant's are here to wait on you hand and foot, so shall they."

"I don't think I've ever been on a horse" said Jack honestly, looking up on his phone, on how to ride a horse, to say, "Now that looks complicated".

"No worries, they will probably give you the workers stallion, it's a little black one, I ride it all the time" said a confident Ingrid.

With that, Jack raises his arm, much to the delight of those below.

"You can lower your hand now" said Ingrid shaking her head.

"Sir would you like to read the papers?" said Porter John, showing three types of newspapers.

"Sure thanks" said Jack as Porter John, sets them down on a clean plate, as another plate was set for him. Jack reached in to a basket, Porter John looked at him, so he used the tongs, to select a scone, as the server behind him slid the bread plate close to him, he then sliced it open, and applied some fresh whipped butter, and then used another fork to take small bites, "It tasted good" he thought, the butter was sweet, tangy and pure white.

"How do you like the goat's milk, you know their the prize of the King, and are fed a specific diet and massaged twice a day."

"I'd like that, and much more" said Jack.

"Ssh, be careful on what you ask, for you will get it."

As Porter John who left came back to say, "We have summoned a professional, would you care to wait here or have a brief course before you ride, down there, sir?"

"Before the ride" said Jack watching what he says, as Jack uncover the newspaper to see the front page, of the Belarus times, "Super Spy, Jack Cash, destroys the KGB in one fatal swoop" Jack quickly saw that there was ten pages dedicated to the destruction, fallout and aftermath. Next was the London Inquirer, where a little blurb on the front page, and a small announcement, the last paper was the New York Examiner, that showed it was the same morning, today, and not a single word, as he went to page 22, under international news, it said "A massive, 9.0 earthquake hit Moscow, and there was some casualties, but most were safe, still waiting for the aftershocks".

Jack thought "Was that me, or was that real?" he finished the scone, drank, the coffee, sip's a few of the juices, then stood, up, as Porter John said, "Right this way, we have some riding clothes for you, then I'll escort you down to the King."

Jack tried on the riding chaps, and then discarded them, only to settle with a vest, and a whip.

Jack followed Porter John down, to the foyer, then into a parlor, where the King and Queen sat, across from them was the woman from last night, as the Queen said "Mister

Cash, I'd like you to meet, my sister Queen Ana, from Latvia, that's where we grew up together, actually our family controls Lithuania, and Estonia, so we would like you to know you're always welcome."

"Mister Cash, thank you for accepting my offer, in a moment we shall ride through our many forest's, today is Geese" said the King, as Jack stood, not really knowing what to do, until he heard, "Would you like to sit?" said the Queen.

Jack slid in to a chair at the other head of the table, across from the King, who said, "Try the scones, aren't they marvelous?"

"Yes, they are indeed, especially with the white cream."

Jack was served, a small platter of assorted scones, using his tongs, he chose one, but as he tried to grab it, it broke in half, Jack held one piece, and well the other and the whole platter was gone and a new platter replaced in mere seconds.

Jack took his and set it on his plate, then smeared some white goat cream on the top, as coffee and lemon were served to him.

"So you like this coffee with lemon, have you been drinking that long "said Queen Ana. Who was smiling at him?

"Not really, it balances the caffeine, in American coffee, with a little citrus."

"Were not too familiar with this American coffee, but if you could send us some we could try it" said the King.

"Sure, when I get back, I'll have some delivered to you, but it's a lot stronger than the chicory" said Jack, as the King finished, and stood, as did the other Queens, and Jack followed suit.

"Come my boy, we need to talk", Jack fell in beside him, to hear, "You know my sister in law really likes you, and if you were to marry her, you would have all of Latvia, to do as you please, she has a family palace ten times the size of this, and she rules over a million and half people, what do you think?"

"Anything is possible, I'd need to spend some time with her to see if it's a good fit" said Jack smiling.

"In our country, when a Queen likes a powerful man, they usually get that man, but I can understand your reservations, here you'll be King, without trouble, there you'll never be King, because, it is in the bloodline, and although she has power, you'll only be her husband, and the children you bore, will be entitled, as you won't be, but once we past, then, you'll receive this kingdom, and any woman you choose may be Queen, so what did you think of the ladies last night?"

"There was a few I'd choose."

"Fine, who were they and where were they from, we will hold a dance for them, and then you shall choose."

"How will all that work?" asked Jack, as the King placed his arm around him to say, "My wife is childless, we try every day with no results, and now she has grown wearily, and in a state of despair, so when we adopted you came with its own set of rules, first being someone of great importance, second one who the people idolize, and erect a statue of them, we simply don't go around appointing a son, especially you that has a fierce reputation, of the one who has a lion's heart, no you were chosen, and from what my sister in law says about you, your well equipped."

Porter John opened the door, to the side where a hundred men, and horses assembled, all in different colors, in the middle was a huge white stallion, no saddle on him, on it a rope around its neck, for the King to say, "Here you go, my Son, your first present, get on and tame it" said the King laughing, but in a respectful manner.

Jack looked at it, to see it stood at least nine foot tall, he thought for a moment before he reacted, and went to his phone, as he typed in "How to break a wild horse?"

The answer, "Get on and show him whose boss."

Jack slowly walked out to it, as it threw its hooves up in the air, and made a wild sound, then Jack grabbed its mane, and swung on up on it, holding on for dear life, as the back legs, threw themselves out, as all the men laughed, but Jack held on, it was a bit, but soon the horse died down, much to everyone's dismay, even the King was taken by surprise, as Jack steered him around, back to the circle, to hear, "So my son, you have conquered the stallion?, what shall you call him?"

"the Parthian Stranger" as he slid off, him, to receive a harness, which he figured it out using his phone, by diagram, then a brilliant saddle, came out, as Jack took it from the Stable Master, and placed it on him, then cinched it up, as the laughing turned serious, as Jack did one more thing simply amazing, as his reputation was growing, as he slid on the horse, and texted Tami, about the coffee, and where to send it.

The horses cleared a path as the King, took his place next to Jack, on Parthian Stranger, as they walked their horses, others were behind them, through a creek, up and on the other side, to a wide field, where, fifty on each side broke up, for the King to say "Now my son, choose one of your riders, to use their rifle, they are all loaded, and how ever many you shoot, I'll give you another gift."

"Shall I choose the men with whom I choose the ladies, I fancied?"

"If you like, you have ones in mind, I will express to you, those from last night, were my selections, for my mistress's, for you my son, you can choose from my entire kingdom, and fifty of those ladies are representative, here now."

Jack felt foolish, as he back away, to allow the King to decide, as he broke up the men, for Jack to fall in to his side, to say,

"What shall I give you, my King, if you out do me?"

"You'll marry my sister in law."

"Fair enough" said Jack, as he was about to ride to his group, when the King said, "What shall I give you if you out do me in this match."

Jack just looked at him, trying to think, to say, "Nothing, your hospitality has far exceeded my expectations."

"Nah, what I was thinking, If I want you to marry, my sister in law, why don't I give you those that you were smitten by last night, you know, to make this one competitive, you remember,

Princess's, Natasha, Daria, Bianca, Brigitte, Lena, Emily, Julia and Nina, they too have expressed interest in becoming your wives, so do we have a deal?"

Jack thought, "It was a win either way, as he looked over to the rider next to him, who said, "Do you know what that mean's?"

"What? Hand me your rifle" said Jack.

"It means you must for sake all other women, for her."

Jack places it in his hands, to think of only Sara now, and of Maria, Alexandra and Alba, and all the others, to say, "What do we do, now?"

"Nothing, your job is to shoot, it's our job to rustle the birds in the air."

"I thought we were shooting geese?" asked Jack.

"You are, but don't worry, our sons, do this all the time, besides, these are the King's geese."

A panic crossed over Jack's face, as he checked the rifling, as his team went fast, making noise, as Jack was on one side, and about hundred yards away was the king, who was already firing, as Geese were flying everywhere, but Jack knew this was a gentleman's game, which meant he could only fire at what his men could muster up, as Jack waited, he moved forward, and so did the King, cause if it were up to him, he would charge down the hill, but realized it was straight out of the history pages, and instead of men chasing the geese, it was the fox and the hounds, when he snapped out of his dream, to see a bird coming right at him, he fired, and it hit its mark, thinking, it was close enough to use his pistol.

The morning wore on as Jack fired at only what he saw, his count was fifteen birds, he had no idea what the King shot, as the men kept the bids with them, there probably is a prize for how many each one gets, Jack admired the countless sea of natural grasses, even wildlife could be seen, as the King got closer to say, "My son, how is your ammunition, ready to go in and count our totals?"

"One more shot" said Jack as a geese went up and the King shot it."

"Great", thought Jack, "That could be one more than me or many more."

A trumpeter, sounded a retreat, as Jack turned the calm horse, to see more rolling fields as the King closed in beside him to say, "What do you think?"

"About all this" said Jack standing up, seeing the panoramic beauty, in all directions, to say, "Yeah, this could easily get use to, your so very gracious."

The King smiled, thinking he made the right choice for his son, to say, "Yes, and over to the south will be your parcel, six hundred and forty acres, plus some day this million acres as well."

"Why don't you farm this?"

"I guess we could, we spent the last twenty years fighting for our independence, and now that were totally free, maybe we will, any ideas?"

"I have to see who won that wager first."

"You did" said the King.

"How do you know that?" asked Jack.

"I counted your shots, you're a calculating man, one shot one kill, fifteen shots, fifteen kills, and I shot it thirty times and maybe ten at the most."

Jack took a deep breath in and then let it out, to hear, "They told you didn't they?" asked the King.

"What are you saying" asked Jack.

"About the one man for the Queen, it may pertain to them, but because you're an American Super Spy, and you already have fifteen wives, I mean fourteen."

"So you know?" asked Jack.

"Yes, and in the old days it was the truly great men, who had multiple wives, but there are some women who are greater than most men, and we are limited to only one man, you on the other hand, can have as many as you like, and the ones you should seek are the princess's, like at the dance, there the ones who will thrust you into their kingdom's and control, that was my next gift was introduce fifty of the princess, besides the eight that have shown real interest in you, from your team you can choose fifty for you to marry, you can have one or all, its your choice, you may after I pass, move in and assume control over Belarus, of course you'll work with the parliament."

"Of course I will, then you got a deal, you wanna race back."

The King was already gone, but as Jack got Parthian Stranger up, and moving, his strides were magnificent, and quickly he caught up to the King, but held back, remembering a book he read about competition, sometimes you need to lose to get further ahead, so he slowed, but kept on his heels, as the King was in full run, as the Parthian Stranger was in a trot, as they came up and over a hill, and down to an open gate, and into the pen, fresh grass, as the name Parthian Stranger was already on the door, as Jack dismounted, and led the horse into the lap of luxury, fresh carpet and a water trough, for the horse to drink, oats, and hay, as Jack took off the saddle, and set it on the saddle dock, then off went the bridle, on the wall were brushes, and the horse ate while Jack began to brush his animal down, as the King waited, for Jack then, barked out some orders, as a team of men came in, but spooked the horse, as Jack calmed him down, to order them out.

Jack took his time only to hear Ingrid say, "You disrespected your team, it's their job to care for your horse."

"It's something a man's got to do?"

"So when do you think you'll be done?"

"What's the rush, I have two more days?"

"Yes, but I want to show you your present the country has given you, and if you want to make any changes, now is the time?"

"I actually know a builder who can help out."

"Come on Mister Cash, don't you think we have our own builders, architects and craftsman's."

"Sure, I was only suggesting" said Jack.

"Understood, you know you're like no one anyone of us has ever seen, what do you like to have fun?"

"I don't know, I really like to ride the horse, but I'm a little sore down there."

"It happens to all of us" said Ingrid.

"So what's your story, are you married, have a boyfriend, perhaps a lover" said Jack.

"None to all three, I'm a good girl, who is waiting for the right man to come along, so that I can spend the rest of my life with him."

"So you're a one girl guy too."

"What do you mean?" she asked.

"Meaning, only one man can marry you."

"Depends on the guy, if you meant you, well, I guess I could but I don't like to share, and you already have fourteen, how many more are you looking for?"

"Not really looking for anymore, maybe Queen Ana, she seems nice."

"She is and very rich, only one problem?"

"I know" said Jack.

"Her money is tied to the family wealth, and you would not only get a portion at a time, but you would be safe for the rest of your life."

"That's not what I meant, I meant that she was a one woman, for one man" said Jack.

"That is true, but you're the exception, with your name by hers, she would get instant creditability, and that's just from your reputation, not to mention, what you could impose on others, like recruiting an army of men, that sort of thing" said Ingrid.

"What about you, what if I choose you to be my wife?"

"I'd have to decline, one you don't even know me, and second you have to get my fathers approval first?"

"So let's go visit him" said Jack jokingly.

"He lives in Pinsk, in the Marshes Valley, on the southern most part of Belarus.

Jack smiled at her to see she saw him laugh, to hear, "No you didn't just lead me on" come here" she said as she chased him in the horse stall, till she caught up with him, he held her in his arms, to look in her eyes as he bent over to kiss her she turned her head to say, "I can't, not here, not now, were in the King's barn, it would be disrespectful to do that, but maybe once we get out and on that piece of property you just received, well then who knows", she broke apart from him to hear, "Noon Meal is ready".

Jack exited the horse stall, handing his brush, to the team waiting, to have Ingrid in tow, towards the house, when he stopped, to notice a weird looking man standing by the door smoking a cigarette, to say, "You Jack Cash, Varfolomey wants a duel in the mountains of Luga."

"Sorry, he will have to wait, I'm busy" said Jack as he got into his face, to add, "I don't know who you are and I don't care, maybe, you're a KGB defector, and maybe, my new target is the remaining KGB operatives, I suggest you back down or I will kill you."

"Wow Mister, I want no trouble, I'm only the messenger."

As the Kings royal guard surrounded him and put him on the ground, cuffed him, thinking, and "No zip ties, actually nothing, just hanging around in one spot too long could get me killed." Thought Jack.

Jack walked his way back into the Palace, only to hear, "My son, come and let's have lunch."

Jack went through the door, to sense a bit of déjà vue, as he looked to see Ingrid smiling, he wanted to say something to her, as if he knew her in a past life or something, to walk into the dining room area to hear, "Take off that uniform" the King said.

Jack looked himself over, to see that it was his clothes, but for the vest, so he undid that, to let it drop, to hear, "Allow me Sir" said Porter John.

Jack allowed the Porter, to do as they are told.

Jack sat at the head of the table opposite the King, as if he had done this countless times before, as he waited to be pushed in by the Butler, feeling that he was at a good distance, he saw the silver lined up, glasses, and serving plates, then one by one, the guests came in, to take up the remaining chairs along with Ingrid, who sat next to Jack, the portions were many, but only a bite or two, at best, plenty of drink, and coffee, especially, the case Tami had taken from the plane and sent over, that was far better than the root coffee. As lunch ended, the leaders of the top men that won, suggested a social for Mister Jack, for him to choose the ladies from, all were in agreement, except Jack who was in his own world, and thinking about how all this is too familiar.

The men took their leave, as Ingrid announced she was, "Taking Jack down to his piece of property."

The King waved his hand in agreement, so Ingrid said, "Come on Jack let me show you your grounds."

Jack followed, her into a semi long black car, to sit beside her, this was the first time they were all alone, as the car sped off.

Jack looked out among the fields, of the huge estate; his mind went back to that pretty Queen Ana, who returned to her native country of Latvia, something he knew he needed to visit. The sweeping road, zig zagged down the hill, but instead of leaving the estate, the car went to the left, down a road, lined with bare trees, for Ingrid to say, "Wonderful Sumac and chestnut trees, mixed in with Lilacs, all in hibernation till spring, this is the King's road, to the south plantation, which is now yours, starting about here" she said as she pointed, to add, "All along the hill side."

The car went down a slope, into the fertile valley, past an orchard, which she said, "This is the famed apple orchard, where for hundreds of years people have come up to that factory to process those famed apples, now there yours, which means, every year from now on, you'll receive compensation, plus fresh apples, apple cider, applesauce, apple butter, and apple cider vinegar, we use all of the apple, we use it all."

"And what of the seeds?" asked Jack.

"The seeds, I don't know, really why?"

"Seems to me, if their prized and all, why not take the whole area, and put more apple trees on them?"

"Because the King really hasn't ever done anything like that, the trees are just there, and the villagers who support the King, work the orchards."

Jack nodded his head, then kept quiet, as the road, turned one more time, to the semi flat valley floor, where grasses grew, for the car to stop, Jack and Ingrid exited, to see the magnificent valley, with hills all around, yet the factory could be seen, and the valley, was exposed, but trees, were on the south side, to hear "along the trees is a stream, which flows from the upper region, and is the water that flows into a huge aquifer underneath the village, that supports the kingdom."

"Can we walk out there?"

"You don't want to do that, it's all marshy, you know wet, all the time."

"May I suggest something?" asked Jack.

"Absolutely, this is your place now, whatever you like?"

"I noticed last night on our way in that there was huge digging equipment along the road, where is all that dirt going?"

"I don't know, I guess I could ask?, Why do you ask?"

"Well I was thinking, if they needed a place how about over there?" said Jack pointing to the drop off of the village to his new property.

"I don't know, it's illegal to dump anything on Royal property, but I can see your concern, I'll first check with the King, then the villagers, matter of fact, how about I set up a meeting with their council."

"Sure that sounds great" said Jack as Ingrid steered him away from that view to the site, which had stakes laid out, a survey team was visible, as Ingrid said, "That's not the site of your palace, that is only the barn, gifts from all over the country will be brought in, and assembled here, maintained, and accounted for in a report especially for you, that I will maintain. "No, your Palace is well under way up on that plateau, for the King to see, that is how the Royals do it, the King is the highest, then the prince, and princess's, this palace is the King's dream, let's go take a look at it, get in."

Jack got back in, as the car swept up the hill, slightly, for all to see this magnificent looking palace, in all of its glory, they leveled out on a cleared out place on the hill side, as the car parked he got out, to see below was the apple orchards, that lined the hills, between the King and Him, the newly carved out of the hillside, indicated this palace was huge, at least an acre in size, a trailer, was parked on the right side, to see many men pile out from, doing something, to see the main guy approach Ingrid, to say in his native tongue, "Feel free, to survey the grounds, He will show you everything."

Jack and Ingrid, got the tour, to the south side, where the stream was diverted, so that a magnificent waterfall, could be placed in, as Ingrid said something to the guy, which he agreed with, for her to say "Michel, agrees with you, that the land is eroding under ground, and he will build up the soil, and build dams along the way for irrigation, and if you want to build up the area, by the village he agrees too."

Jack says, "Let's see the palace."

Ingrid nodded in agreement, as Michel, was the leader, as they went in, the ceiling was magnificent, the walls were high, and it was warm, not a real dry, it was room after room, of different, complete with a luxurious bath, shower, as Michel said, "You have unlimited amount of water, there is a cistern underground that holds one hundred thousand of gallons of spring water, a special spring was diverted exclusively for you." He said.

Then Jack reached a spectacular room, complete with pool, about three feet deep, unfinished, it had blue mosaic tiles, hand placed in the rectangle shaped, then saw on the end was another smaller on the end, for Ingrid to say, "That is an exclusive a mineral pool, heated to 92 degrees, a place to relax, the King has one, maybe you could ask them to show you it, everything he has, you'll have, in this horseshoe shaped three story palace, comes with servants, and complete staff of thirteen."

"How many rooms will there be?"

Ingrid asked Michel that, and he said, "Fifty-six."

"Really?" said Jack marveled at the size and enormity of the structure, and of the two wings, and the courtyard, and the massive waterfall, that could be seen, to see a massive Olympic size swimming pool, and gardens, as they went out, Jack followed Ingrid, for Jack, to see it was nearing completion. They walked around the pool, back to the west side, as French style doors, allowed them into the massive kitchen, and all the windows, to see out, to a dining room, where a long table like the King's was at, and the kitchen, as the state of the art in appliances, bread ovens, multiple ovens, a massive twelve burner stove, for Michel to say, "Come, this is for the servants, and through the door, was the formal dining room, it was massive, it resembled a ballroom, curio cabinets, lined one wall as that room was near complete, as the wall paper finished the room off., to a set of doors, that opened, and shelves were being built in the wall, for Michel, to say, "This is your library, and the King, has asked for donations, of such and a ten thousand books are being assembled and will be maintained by a Librarian from the University of Belarus." The next set of doors, came out to what looked like a entertaining room, but what Jack liked best about the room, was the stillness of the air and how warm it was, although empty, and without shades, you could look out the huge windows, to see the castle on the hill, as from the top story of the castle looked out back to the palace, was Queen Mary, who turned back to her husband the King, to say, "I wonder if he likes being here?"

"How so what do you mean?" said the King, sitting to see his wife.

"He has such a huge appetite, for young women?"

"Like yourself, perhaps?"

"No, he doesn't even see me."

"Then make yourself known to him, I will allow it."
"And what if he rejects me?"

"Then I'll cut off his head" said the King.

Queen Mary simply didn't know what to do, even though she did make a call out to her sister, of the news, and she was ecstatic, and said, she was going to be sending him gifts, and she said, if he did in fact have such a huge appetite, for women, then she would do what she could do to satisfied it, as she herself, had made a call out to all young maidens in her country."

"No John, this is something of a delicate matter, I will try, and see what our son thinks of such a relationship, as for your new mistress, I'd see who he wanted before you go and break their hearts, first, then choose."

The King stood to resign himself, as he came to her at the window, and whispered, "Shall we try one more time?"

"Sure, where will you have me?, on the bed, as she felt his hands on her hips, as he pressed her, against the glass, as she bent forward, as he pulled down her panties, he was ready for her, as she unlatched the window, it opened, as she held onto the frame, as the King went in easily, she was a screamer, as the kingdom, heard her cries, down in the palace, Jack too had his own idea with Ingrid, as he opened a window to look out, to see up to the castle, and instantly knew what was going on as all he could see was the top of the torso of the young Queen, and her passions of cries, as Jack thought, Ingrid, as she was a bit game, as she spoke to Michel, and he left, as she came to the window, to see the Queen, to smile, to say, "Ah, it's a royal screw, is that what you say in America?"

"Nah, we call that an all out fucking, interested?" said Jack.

"Not like that, if I were caught doing that and the Queen saw me, I'd have my head cut off, no, if I were to do that, it would have to be on a bed, so I could support your weight, but not like that." As the screaming ended abruptly, but the show was well worth it, as they saw the window close, and peace restored.

"I'm tired can we go back?" asked Jack realizing he wasn't getting anywhere with this one, and thinking of those eight young ladies, to see her say, "Yes of course", and he was right behind her.

Jack went out to the car that was waiting, he got in, thinking how nice it will be, but he realized the early horse ride was putting him to sleep, the ride back was silent, as Ingrid said, "I'll see you soon." as the car stopped at the King's Palace and let him off.

CH 10

Flash backs

J ack walked into the King's palace, with Porter John, who was at the door, ushering him in, everyone knew who Jack was, and his title, the men from earlier, were with the King, for an audience, so the main chambers were blocked, as each man exited, excited. Jack went up the grand staircase, to his floor, to walk it back, to his door, where a butler stood, to open his door, Jack went in, and the door shut.

Jack took a seat on the luxurious couch, laid his head back against the pillow and was out, he knew he was safe, and secure, as guards were all over the place. Jack closed his eyes, with his arms crossed and went to sleep.

During the sleep, his mind was a buzz, as all this triggered some repressed thoughts and memories, and Ingrid who was that, she seemed so sincere like something a sister would say to another, she was special, he thought to hear, "My son, why are you sitting in your room, while your guests are waiting?"

Jack said to his Dad, "But I'm so tired from playing outside."

"Come, your guests wait."

Jack got up, went out the door, he noticed the marble tiles, to the stairwell, to hear "Unther, Unther, are you coming down, the Banister's boys are here, and they wanted to play a match on the pitch."

Jack felt the real wood of the custom made railings, as he stepped on each of the hand placed marble steps to hear, "We have a match with the Lorne family, seven on seven, it will be us four, you, Roger, and little Jeremy Sanders."

"All right hold on", said Jack making his way, into the foyer, to see this beautiful woman who was called, "Sophia", by his Dad. Who he recognized, to think that must be Mom, the confident and defiant Jack walked outside, to see a young girl run towards him, she wrapped her arms around to say, "Unther, Unther, Jeremy won't leave me alone.

Jack saw the young brother of the four sisters, and especially the oldest Helen, to who he smiled at, as she was with her friend Mary and her sister Margaret, all stood on the sidelines as the bigger group of boys were practicing with themselves, as he finally broke away from her grasp, to say, "Hey leave my sister alone", as he meets up with the Bannister brothers, two sets of twins a year apart, but all look the same, their family was known as furniture makers, the old style with their hands, and rich, their family has been doing that for over 20 generations, this was no school yard fight, it was a planned event held each year, to signify the start of rugby season, one Jack had been playing in since he was four, the field was regulation, as his father owns a professional team.

Crowds of people have assembled, usually it's the villagers, who sit in the public stands and pay to see this royal event, and Jack was the star, he played fly half, as the Bannister boys were in the scrum, Little Jeremy is the hooker, and dummy half, and Roger was the fullback, he was solid for a 5 year old, and could run like the wind, Jack headed out onto the pitch, the sun was shining, as the Bannister boys, flanked him on both sides, Jeremy was on the left, and Roger the far right, Jack kicked off, the ball went straight into the air, twenty meters, and caught, and the tackling began, Jack shifted to the strong side, as Roger fell behind him, Jack gauged their passing, till the moment came, and shot the gap, to steal the pass, and ran his way to slam the ball down for a try, he and the entire team embraced him, on the sidelines the girls all cheered., as the game progressed it was evident they weren't backing down and by half, Jack looked up at the scoreboard to see the sign say "Cologne 24 and Bonn 0, as he and the others went into the grounds rest center, where fresh beverages, and snacks were set out, each had their own stall, the state of the art equipment, after refreshments Jack's dad came in to give the speech, "Boys we got them were we want them, let's finish them off, now come together, and 1-2-3 say Cologne", Jack went out to see that the weather had turned and it was beginning to rain, the villagers all had poncho's and umbrellas, while his family and other royals sat under a tent, as Jack looked over to see His Dad, his Mom, his sister Christine, next to her was the two girls that liked him the most, Helen and Mary, next to them was Mary's sister Margaret and Roger's sister Elizabeth, then the three other Sander's girls, Victoria, Nicole and little Marie-Rose.

Jack turned to wave to the crowd, to see that there was no one there, then looked back at the tent, it to was gone, and so were the people, as he walked towards them he felt like running, only to feel like he was being pulled the opposite direction, to hear, "Jack, wake up, Jack its me, Ingrid, as Jack opened his eyes, to see her pulling on him to say, "Have you been out this whole time, you know a lot has happen, the whole world is abuzz of the news" she said as she got up, to unfold the panels to show the hidden TV, she turned it on, to see that the news reported, that Russia, was behind the plot to end all the violence, and that your actions were the key to their master plan, which they have now allowed for the first time since the cold war, UN inspectors into the sacred compound, she turned to say, "You're a hero, as she went up and bent over and kissed him on the lips, to break away to say it's all over the world, what's wrong, are you alright?"

"Yeah, I'm fine" said Jack thinking about he had a sister.

"Come on you can tell me, I'll keep it a secret, you were dreaming about that Queen Ana, she too has flown in, to thank you, do you know what this means?"

Jack shrugged his shoulders, "No", in response.

"It literally means that all the colonies that broke away from Mother Russia are now free, including us, and allow us to finally be part of the UN, to receive its aid, and be free."

Jack was still non-responsive as all he wanted to do was go back to sleep, for her to hang on him.

"I thought that you were excited, that's why I came here, to help you, you know with what you said earlier?"

Jack said sleepily, to say, "What are you saying, what did I do?"

"Were the ones who called you, to erase the terror that was of Mother Russia, and expose the terror?"

"Now that is done, I'm done here?"

"No, don't miss understand me, we our government allowed you in, to show face with the U S, in an agreement, so that at some point we could be eligible for an allegiance, but really we still were still under Russia rein, and for some they said it would take an act of god, to accomplish, well your that act of God, and the Premier of Russia Vladimir Ecklon has made notice that your actions would be held in high esteem, and that rogue agents will be caught and prosecuted, in addition, he has asked if you will come back to Mother Russia, to the palace for him to show his appreciation to you for you acts of heroism, so what should I tell them."

"I don't know yet, I'm just enjoying the time off, I don't know what I will do, I'm really not ready to go back into Russia yet.

"Shall I tell them that?"

"No I'd appreciate if you stay out of my business, now can you leave me", just then the door opened, to see Porter John, who asked, "Ingrid, please leave him alone", she left frustrated, and closed the door, for Jack, to say, "Aah, peace and quiet," he pulls out his phone, to see all the messages he missed, as he opened them up, ten were from the Premier Ecklon himself, in one he expressed how sorry he was for believing Jack did something wrong, which actually was a blessing, if it were twenty years earlier, well then we would be at war, but with time, forgiveness is paramount, and he thanked him for getting his wife back safe and sound, and for the destruction of the nuclear plant below Moscow, which he had no idea, and for wiping out the terrorist group, please respond.

Jack deleted those files, to see somewhat negative to good comments from, the President of United States, calling Jack's actions as reckless, wild and unthinkable, and is questioning if he made the right decision, to elect him a Super spy, overall just disgusted by him.

Jack deleted that one, then the most resounding endorsement came from the Chief of the International Council for Worldwide Corruption, which he said, "This is a major breakthrough towards World peace, and the adaptation of the World's council, the last player was Old Russia from truly joining, and now that they have, is a victory for all of us, thank you, see you on Friday."

Jack erased all those, to see that his family even texted, one by each of them, beginning with Sara, who said, "The news here is vague, but, nice job, so have you married Queen Ana, of Latvia yet?", also I'm pregnant again, this time it's a boy, his name will be Jack Junior, Cash of course, listen everything here is fine, it's a fortress here, we are being well taken care of, and now with this latest event, security has tighten up, were all on lock down." "Whenever you get back Mobile wants to claim you as there own and put on a huge parade and show, and if you want bring home another wife or two, I love you, Bye". Message saved.

Next message, it was from Maria, who said, "At the end of the month is my three days with you. When will you be home?", next was Alexandra, who said "Hi, I hope your O Kay?", then there was Alba, who said "Hi", that was it, then Jack scrolled down to see new one from Doctor Elizabeth Snyder, he opened it to read "Jack, I have read about your exploits in foreign lands, and think that's so brave, that you have stole my heart, I'd love to see you when you get back, and Yes I know about your other wives, but your like no other man I have ever met, call me soon."

Next was the newest wave of wives especially that of Tia, who smartly wrote, "That was the bravest thing I'd ever seen, and hope to see you back here safe and sound, I have a surprise for you."

"Interesting, could it be a baby?" thought Jack.

Next was Isabella, she said, "I made the right decision on marrying my hero, your like no man I have ever known, your right Daddy, wanted to take back Maria, but she told him No, and felt better protected, with you, and she is pregnant, actually, to be truthful, its all going around, Sara, and well the others, I need to go, they say we can only text this short, we don't want you to be found, take care, love you bye."

Next was Melanie, who said, "Your big news here in NOLA, and our sorority has tripled awaiting your return, there are fifty two beautiful girls waiting your arrival, and we have since partnered up NOLA U sisters, to form one big alliance, and they two, claim you, and their the same, I gotta go, love you."

Next up was, India, who said, "My dad says, he is scared of you, you are by far the most dangerous man in the world, the baby and I are fine, and have the best people helping out, thank you I love you, bye."

Next up was Model Samantha White who said, "My life is so wonderful, I've buckled down, and am doing well, and I have a surprise for you, take care, love you, bye, Next up was Lindsay, who said, "I think your just swell, I have a surprise for you, I love you, bye. The last two, and countless others, was Cara, and Christine, who said, "It was riveting to see what you did, as it a real eye opener to what you really do, both of us are fine, but we both fear our safety, and would like to go home, we have been in talks with Sara, and she will be up here later, is there any way we can see you soon?, bye, from the sisters.

"Weird", thought Jack.

The next one was from Jim, Jack opened it up, to read "Boss, its not like me to say anything to you, but I must say, from what we all saw was quite remarkable, and you have all of our staff's total support, It wasn't like you never had it our support, however, we were asked to help you, it wasn't up for vote, we were assigned, but not anymore, were all here for you, we are here at the hanger waiting for your return, and we pledge support to you, here and from now on."

Jack erased it, to think to himself, "So that bastard, was the one, the one who could not be trusted, oh well, I could care less if they support me or not, the only one I really can trust is Mitzi, woman are more trustful, than any guy, maybe it's time to retire those guys."

Jack saw the rest as some junk, except for one from Blythe, which he opened it to see, "I'm sorry, if you think I am something that I'm not, all I ever wanted to be is a spy, and thank you for inviting me to the council, this will give me a shot, also I will show you how appreciated I am."

Jack deleted that message, closed up his phone, to look at his watch, and gets up, goes to the door, and opens it to see Porter John, and allows him pass, Jack made his way to the grand entrance, as all was quiet, he made his way, down the stairs, to go the other way, down a huge wing, that said, "Library", so Jack tried each door, till he found pay dirt. The library opened up to some historical volumes, magazines and the countries history, to hear, "Go ahead, and pull out any book you like?"

Jack turned to see it was the Queen Mary, who closed the door, to add, "Don't worry, those books are collecting dust, nobody ever reads them anyway, but If you would like to read about our history, have Ingrid, take you out to the churches, and all around the city, I'd also let you know, the administration has approved, the adoption to royalty, and your next in line, for the kingdom, had you thought about marrying my sister?"

"Perhaps, I have a couple of days before I go to the council, so I will consider courting her, if she is still interested?"

"Interested, yes she is, I'll call her and she should be in tonight" as she exited the room, without Jack responding, the door closed, as Jack held an oversized book, to see the door, he slid open the pocket door, to see a huge billiards table, whereas, Jack sets the book down, and goes over and racks up the set of balls, then, taking the white ball, he goes to the other side, sets the ball down, Jack chooses a heavy stick, sets up to take a break only to see Ingrid, he stops to stand back up, for Jack, to say, "Now what?"

"Wow, what has got into you, you seem annoyed by my presence" said a very confused Ingrid.

"No, not really, what do you want?"

"The Queen, has asked me, to show you around the city, its historical sites, and the city at night, so what do you say?"

"Sure, let's go" said Jack.

"I can wait till you're through."

"I haven't even started" said Jack eyeing the balls, and then back at Ingrid.

"Not from where I'm at." she said with her arms crossed, flirting with him., as Jack puts the stick away, picks up the book to hear, "Why don't you bring that, we could use it as a reference point."

Jack shows her the book, for her, to say, "Oh not that book, that's probably an heirloom, you better put that away."

Jack went back into the library, replaced the book on the shelf, and exit's the room, to see Ingrid, step in next to him, to say, "Do you want to drive?"

"Sure, I'll drive, let's go, you know it seems a bit quiet here."

"Yes, after the circumstance and pomp, it dies down, to normal business, and all is quiet, but overall, the Royalty is still an integral part of the country's wealth and power, although as most Royalty has stepped away from the political processes, the social aspect is what fuels the countries riches, and trade agreements with other countries, especially now that our country is totally free, as this spring will be our first democratic election for Prime Minister, and as we speak, the royal guards, will be training a new force, to control our borders with the Ukraine, we have the super dam, that we built, then of course, the defectors from Russia and the river Dvina which is contaminated."

"What do you mean contaminated?"

"Well simply that, as it starts in Russia and picks up the metals from the over used lands of the Soviet Union, leached into the water supply and well by the time it reaches us, its undrinkable."

Jack led Ingrid, into the car barn of the royal house, to his car, "Open" he said, as he went to her door, and opened it up for her, to allow her in, then closes the door, he gets in behind the wheel, the car starts, and out it went, down the sweeping driveway, thinking if it weren't for Ingrid, he would go home, then thought about the conference, as he slowed at the gate, as it was opened for him, he drove through, to see the middle of the village, as he drove through to hear, "This village was built on top of a clean reservoir, you already saw, which is clean water, comes from a spring, along that mountain, the village is called the King's village, its design is to support all functions for the King, alright slow" she said. Jack came to a near stop at the T in the road.

On the left is the conifer forest, which is still on the King's land, and the road up to the spring, and the royal horses, on the right is the road to Minsk, on the right is the remainder of the battlement from WW2, do you want to see it?"

"Sure let's go" said Jack driving the super car, with Ingrid next to him.

"Take the road to the right, were going to the mines", the car, zip downward, on a well-traveled road, he kept his pace good, as on his display sensed a large grouping of men, behind him on a road, further south of his position, as he made it across a wooden bridge, he came to a stop, to say, "Which way?" he looked at her who held a gun on him, to say, "We can wait, they will be here shortly."

Jack held his hands up, to look over at the display, which displayed sleep or ejection?"

Jack thought about sleep, and in that instance he saw the smoke come out, and enter her nose and she went out and then retracted back. As a huge truck came and parked right in front of him, as troops with guns came to him, they were ordering him out, as the apparent leader, yelled, then they opened fire on him, as Jack employed defensive measures, as rounds bounced off the car, it went backwards, to give him some room and employed guns and took out the troops, all that was left was the leader, as he saw a barrel come out, for he immediately, dropped his weapon, to raise his hands, as Jack stepped out, to pull his weapon, Jack spoke Russian, to tell the guy to kneel, and place his hands above his head and interlock his fingers, as Jack made it to him. Jack zip tied his wrists, Jack pulled up on his wrists, and drug him around, to say "Open trunk", it opened, as Jack heaved up the man, to use his weapon, to strike his head, thus knocking his out. He threw his lifeless body into the trunk. Jack zip tied his ankles, then closed the trunk, to look at the large truck in front of him, he went around, and along the way drug off the dead bodies, as he jumped up into the truck's cab, looking it over, he took out his phone, to punch in the serial number, it displayed the vehicle as Jack asked how you start it, it showed him the sequence. Jack had the truck running and he drove it over under some trees, he parked it, looking over he saw the two dead Russian terrorists, so he took off his gloves, and tried a pair of them on, they felt warm, one of the guy's reached out, as Jack opened the door, and they both fell out, the guy was on top of Jack throwing punches, that was till Jack kneed him in the groin, and threw him off.

Jack stood to see the man winching, so Jack turned his back, and went back towards the car, to hear a gun fire, he turned, to feel it, hit his back. Jack turned to see the guy, as he drew his weapon, and shot at his gun hand, then one to his knee. Jack went back over to the guy, who spoke Russian as Jack understood it, to say,

"You know me as the preserver of life, yet you shoot me in the back, why?"

"You weak agent and soon Varfolomey himself will end your life."

"Really, how about I send him a message?"

The guy looked up at Jack, who went back to his car, opened the door, and pulled a rope from his back pack, then went back over to the guy who was bleeding, and double zip tied his ankles, as he saw the guy's hand was to mutilated to zip tie it. Jack tied off the rope, to the guy's ankle, and undid it, then went back to his car, started it up, and made a left turn, to park it to get out.

Jack tied one end to the other end of the bumper, as the guy came alive with information, about where Varfolomey was and who to get in touch with him.

Jack went back to him, to look at the failing guy trying to untie the rope, to say, "From this day forward, I want the whole world to know my name and if that doesn't put fear into their hearts well you'll be the example, for I am the Parthian Stranger."

Jack jumped back into his car and sped off, there was a little bump, but after that it was smooth sailing, as Jack saw the guy stand up in his rear view mirror, with the rope in hand to say, "I really liked that rope."

Jack placed his car in stealth mode, the car sensed he was hot, and cooled his seat to near freezing, in addition, it sent out a signal to Jim, that Jack was shot, as Jack had his phone in the dash board to hear, "Incoming call from Jim, ignore or answer?"

"Answer, "Yeah Jack this is Jim, how bad are you?"

"Not bad a scratch or two get the plane ready, I'd like to fly out of here" said Jack.

There was silence on the other end of the line then Lisa came on to say, "Jack, were tracking you now, what you encountered, was a group of hold outs, and they were heading towards a last strong hold, any idea where it's at?"

Jack used his laptop to punch in the voice recording, to say, "Here is what I have, and this man in the trunk, are you saying, I need to turn back?"

"No, come to our location, and we will fix you up, I have a gift for you, see you soon."

Jack looked at his laptop, to hear, "Jack its Jim, sorry about that, our intelligence is that Queen Ana, is coming back to Minsk to see you specifically, we have agents in place, as Mitzi is controlling their activities, and Clarance told us some time ago, he is heading towards St Petersburg, as all the terrorist cells are fleeing Russia, a countrywide lookout for those who defied the name will be shot on sight, lastly the wife of the Premier would like an audience with you when you can...., she left all that info for us."

Jack clicked off Jim, to see that the city was visible, as the car raced on, at a hundred and fifty or so miles per hour, the car calculated, every turn, as it entered the Airport on the outskirts, the only light on as the darkness set in, was where he was heading, the car turned in, and parked as the door went down, Jack had the door open, as Jim, was at the trunk, assisted by the strike team, Jack kind a of tired, and up the ramp to see Mark and Mike swing in to help hoist Jack up the ramp, then to the room, the door was open, he past by Blythe, who looked out of it, to step in, to see the council for Spy Club, Lisa and Erica, flanked by Trixie and Mitzi, in the corner always on the phone was Tami, as Jack undressed, Trixie escorted the high ranking women out, as Mitzi, helped Jack undress, and start a shower for him, Jack set his gun on the charger, then stepped into the shower, as the indentation, from the bullet wound held the bullet, and Mitzi pulled it out, washed it, then let Jack finish the shower, then dry off, he stepped out, to slip into a pair of new white underwear, to the bed, where he lied down, only to hear the two women arguing over him, Erica was ready to go to Switzerland, whereas Lisa wanted him to stay in Minsk one more day, besides the King and Queen of Ukraine, was coming in for a meeting with him, as Mitzi put a patch on his back, she finished it up, to place a special skin bandage over it, to say, "There all finished, now let's get you dressed."

Jack rolled over on his side, to see the two women to think, "I feel so controlled", then looked over at Tami who smiled back at him, to hear, "Alright here's what we know, the man you captured is Fyodor, a former KGB terrorist, who works with Varfolomey, they have a fortress on the outskirts of Saint Petersburg, and our sources tell us that he plans on taking Queen Ana, tonight at the ball, that's why we need you to be there, all three countries have pledged us some troops, along the Russian border, although their firepower was destroyed by you in shooting down their helicopters, were placing a destroyer at your command, and Jim will sync it up to your phone, so when you need it the arming mechanisms will be in your hands, here is 20,000 dollars of euro's for use as you see fit, I'll need your credit cards, here are your two new ones, with the update from the UN contribution, and payment for participating in the three week required attendance."

Lisa stepped back and closed the door, to say as for Blythe, we can't get her off the protocol list so you'll have a week of her, then Trixie, then Jill, lastly, the girl in your passenger seat., well she is a former KGB operative, with ties to Varfolomey, we will try to pump her for information, about his whereabouts?"

"After that I can come back?" asked Jack getting dressed, as he saw all the girls look at one another, then Lisa said "Yes, Jack, then, Jim and the strike team will escort you to Switzerland, and the rest of us will go home."

"Fine, I wish I could have gotten a meal before I leave?"

"Normally, we would but you have an hour for you formal ball, you don't want the Queen to be waiting, and believe me you'll get fed" said Lisa, smiling.

Mitzi added, "The King John and his staff, contacted us, to ask us what all your favorite foods were, so expect a feast", as Mitzi came in to give him a big hug and kiss, the door was open, to see Blythe was gone, for Jack to say, "What happen to her?"

"Oh let's say she's on assignment" said Lisa, to add, "She isn't you worry anymore, her days of being pampered are over."

Jack stopped to see that his white box was gone, so he went to the armory cage to see Brian was ready, as he presented the box to him, he pulled out the gun, to feel a pull, to hear, "I changed out, the surface guards, they just came in by jet, there a magnet, you'll find out in the field their use, in addition we updated your backpack, with another rope, and some night vision goggles, I see your wearing your new jacket, plastic explosives along the bottom, with zip ties, and a thief's pick tools, opposite your heart pocket, where a magnet is sewn in and in the back, another magnet, which should have been in the other jacket."

"Great, so I'll definitely will be shot."

"No it's a deflector, just like the plate in back, so if you're ever shot from the rear again, the bullet will be drawn up, then away like a ricochet."

"Alright, hey do you have anymore of those protein bars?" asked Jack.

"Yeah how many you want?"

"Two, please" said Jack kiddingly.

"You don't have to say please to me, there yours exclusively" and hands them to Jack, who places them in his pocket to hear, "Inside, place them inside, there is two slots for them" as Jack looked inside, to say, "So there is, now I've got two more, hey where are you at with that rifle I found?"

"Well I cleaned it" said Brian.

"Great let me have it, I could use it on this trip" Jack looked at him, as he lowered his head, to say, "Well I would, but."

"But what, what's wrong with it?"

"The firing pin broke off in the chamber, and jammed the firing mechanism."

"Let me see it, I'll fix it" said Jack.

"Well I would" said Brian.

"What's the hold up, Jack you need to get going that girl is going to wake up" said Jim.

"Listen I don't know what's going on here, but I want that rifle back" said Jack as he stormed off, mad.

"Well about that, it's not Brian's fault, it was me, I had it sent out to our lab to fit it with a special stock" said Jim, watching Jack raise his hand, he turned to look at Jim, to say, "When will it be back, I need one now."

"I have this one", said Casey.

Jack yelled, "Load the sniper case on board."

"Yes sir", said Casey, as Jack and Jim, saw the crew finishing washing the car, Jack saw Jill and Gia, to say to Jim, "How are they getting along with the others?"

"Just like one of the guys".

Jack just looked at him, for Jim to rethink what he said, to say,

"That's not what I meant; they are as protected as Mitzi and Trixie are, as all the girls are yours."

"No you're wrong, there not mine and they will never be." said Jack as Jim held his arm he said, "Can we have a moment to talk?"

"Sure what do you have in mind" said Jack, following Jim back into the flight cabin, for Jack to step in, Jim closed the door, to say, "What the hell is going on with you?"

Jack looked at him face to face to say, "What do you mean Jim?"

"With us, what is going on?"

"Nothing, you do your job and I try to do mine, and all around us, is I guess figure themselves out for themselves" said Jack.

"That's not it, cut the bullshit, and tell me what I've done to fracture our relationship, as he looked at Jack. Jack took a deep breath, then said, "Alright, let's dance, first off, you're selfish, and I can't trust you."

"That was the Jim you use to know, I've changed, ever since that rescue, that changed it all for me, and that's why I called you, I had a realization, why I'm here, and my purpose for life."

"That's a nice story can I go now?"

"Are we cool now" asked Jim both looked over at Bill, for Jack to say, "Not really, I don't know, maybe next time you decide to drug me, you'll let me know?"

Said Jack, opening the door.

"You still hold that against me?"

"Yep."

"Will you ever forgive me?"

"Does it matter to you that much?" asked Jack, ready to leave.

"Yeah, I'm trying here, so what do you say?" pleaded Jim.

"Cut the crap, Jim, what do you want?" wait, are you up for a review, and if they ask me about your performance?"

"No, no that ain't it."

"Go fuck yourself, you ripe bastard", Jack laughed as he walked out saying, "You kill me Jim", as Jim closed the door to hear, "You know you are a ripe bastard" said Bill the pilot.

"Shut the fuck up".

Jack made it to the end of the plane to the ramp, to see Casey, and the rest of the strike force assemble. Jack saw the two girls, to smile at them, then walk over to his car, he got in, to see a huge black square suit case in the back seat, for Jack, to say, "What the hell, is that the sniper rifle, oh well, Jack hit the display, as the car started, the hanger door went up, and the car took off.

The strike team disbursed as the door went back down, only to see Jim on the top of the ramp, only to see Casey, who stopped to look up at him, to say, "You want something?"

"Just checking to see what you guy's been doing?"

Casey walked on, for Jim to hear, "You better lay off."

Jim turned to see Mitzi, who said, "Come in, we need to talk."

Mitzi led Jim into Jack's room, to close the door, to say, "What is going on here, I'm not here to babysit you, and your way out of line, I'm off to the hospital, and come back to all this division, let me make this perfectly clear to you, from this day forward, we only work for one person, regardless of what you think, and if I ever hear you complain or disrespect him again."

"It wasn't like that" said Jim.

"So what you're playing a cop out there?"

"No, it isn't like that."

"You know if it weren't for me, you would have been gone long ago?"

"What are you talking about, I'm the gadgets guy?"

"True, why do you think, you're here and not behind some desk, at Quantico?"

"It's my plane?"

"No that ain't it, it was because of your passion, for having you in the field, but Jim this is a privilege, just like all those people on the strike force, would love to be out in the field each one of them would give their lives to protect him, and I have a list of about four hundred more candidates ready to jump on board."

Jim looked at her to realize his days were numbered, to sit on the bed to say, "So that is what Jesse is doing here?"

"Yep, he is another, younger version of you, if it were for Jack alone you would be gone, but I trust that you would look after him, when I'm not here, is that still true?"

"Yes, that's all I want, to be here to support him."

"Then go back into the cockpit and take the first shift, and monitor his progress" said a confident Mitzi, smiling.

She opened the door for him, to allow him to pass, and then closed the door.

Jack drove to the gates of the palace, as Ingrid woke up, as she felt for her hidden gun, by placing her hand down on her leg, then smiled over at Jack, but did a double take, to look at him, as she went over the sequence, in her mind to say, but out loud, "But how, where did we go?"

"Just for a drive, and you fell asleep" said Jack smiling.

"What about the troops?"

"Oh that was a misunderstanding; they went onto the coal mines and up to crow's valley."

She looked at him, strangely, as the gates opened; Jack drove up the curvy road, and into the parking garage. As he came to a stop, she quickly exited, as Jack got out, to see her flee, he thought about that sniper rifle, and got out, to his rear seat, to touch the zipper, he peeled it back quickly, to see hands and feet, then a face appeared, whereas Jack said, "Well you're a pleasant surprise, I haven't seen you since the limo drive, how are you Michelle?"

"Here to protect you long distance, can you give me a moment?"

"Absolutely, take as long as you like", said Jack as he backed out, and allowed the door to close.

Jack walked the car parking garage to see a few men, appear, with guns drawn, and then several more, appeared, Jack stopped in his tracks, to hear, Varfolomey sends his regards, and sent us to finish the job Fyodor, started."

Jack was ready, he zip his jacket down, and pull his gun, but one by one, each man fell, and before either him or the man talking, six of his comrades were on the floor, bleeding from their heads, the man looked around, at the sight, to look back at Jack, who held his gun out and pointed at him, but at that instant the man was speaking something, he stopped, spun around, and fell down, he was dead, as Jack turned to see Michelle in a military stance, with the rifle still in the ready position, as he waved her off, as he holstered and went in, and Jack went through the door, then it closed itself.

Jack ran across the courtyard to the entrance, where the Queen of Belarus stood, she stepped out, to see him and say, "You're a bad, bad boy, now run up stairs and get ready for dinner" she said with a smile.

Jack past her, and a flood of emotions overcame him, as he took the stairs two at a time, with visions of past years that surrounded him, he felt like he was nine years old, remembering that he just beat up Jeremy for kissing Margaret, or was it Elizabeth, oh who cares he probably deserved it, some day Jeremy I'll get my revenge."

Jack reached the door, but before he touched the lever, he stopped, to capture the moment. He realized he had done this before, but where, when, and some day recapture this" Jack thought. Jack opened the door, pushed it open, and stepped in, then closed the door.

Down below in the canyon, along the raging river, and the coal mines around them, two squads dressed in all black running at breakneck speed, darting in and out of the dark shadows, each had their missions in their minds, with the philosophy of the Marines Forced Recon; swift, silent and deadly. But they were under strict orders to observe and report, and silent in their execution.

The team leader was Captain Paul Clark, and his group, and the group from Lisa's team, of cleanup men, ready for action, each wore an ear piece, and only one spoke it was Paul.

The road they were traveling, the road to the fortress, as all the roads led to the fortress on the mountain. Seen in the distance it was stationed on the three corners of Belarus, Latvia, and Russia. It was an ancient castle ruins of the past and a labyrinth of caves and tunnels as they were told.

Paul, led the two groups, along the valley of the famed black crows that guarded it were true to their meaning, and the silence of the night came alive, with the first wave of the attack of the crows, gun fire thundered throughout the valley as it echoed through, and out, then it went silent, as the men seeked cover, to see the huge black cloud, of birds were gaining strength, and coming in for the attack, as the men were scattering, into the caves.

Jack stood at the top of the stairwell, looking down, to see that the guest were filing in, it appeared to be a small gathering, he adjusted his suit jacket of his tuxedo, he took each step one at a time, till he saw an object of delight, it was Queen Ana, of Latvia, she was dressed smartly, beside her was another couple who wore an air of distinction. Jack went to her in a slow distinct walk, only to see the snob Blythe, but she seemed confused, so he approached the group, where the man said in his richly accented voice, "So you're the famed Super Spy, your building quite a reputation."

"How so?" inquired Jack, still smiling at Queen Ana.

"Well, from what I heard, you took on the, the whole of Russia, and sleighed the fame Army."

"That's only rumors, what I did was save the Premier's wife from evil hands" said Jack confidently.

"That part of your reputation, is no rumor, I'm sure every woman out there would love to have you rescue them, you're a modern day knight" said the man.

"Just doing my job."

"Yes but doing it well", said the gentleman, then leans in to say, "Your quite a hero, and so humble about it."

"Thank you "said Jack looking at the man only to hear, "Jack have you met the King and Queen of the Ukraine, King Josef, and his beautiful wife Isabella?"

Jack bows to them, as they hold out there hands to grasp his to say, "Rise, you don't have to show me courtesy, it is us that are in awe of you and to be in your presence is our honor."

"Thank you" said Jack, as he let them pass, only to have Queen Ana, lean into him, to say, "I got a rather interesting call from my sister, and she told me that you would consider, me as a wife, is this true?"

"Depends on what that entails?"

"Well first off a title, of high lord, an endowment, and the ability to be my husband, any other questions?"

"How are you to be single now?"

"Well about that, my last three husbands were all killed."

"You said it in such a way that it was delightful for you" said Jack very suspicious.

"Well not really, Richard, my first was my childhood love, he drove off a cliff, but they ruled it to be an accident."

"Sorry to hear about that."

"Me too, he was my truest love, then there was Henry, the people didn't like him, so he was exiled, poisoned, then past after a long battle, then there was Frank, now he was as handsome as you are, yet he was a player."

"I'm listening", said Jack looking at her plunging neckline.

"My eyes are up here" she said noticing him looking at her assets.

"So why do you want me, that is to marry?"

"Because you're a protector, a bad boy if you please."

"Well sorry to tell you this, I'm already married, in the general sense" said Jack.

"I know silly, you're married to fifteen women."

"Fourteen now" said Jack.

"I'm sorry what happen?"

"One past on, sadly."

She touched his shoulder, to say, "Everyone knows all about you, all you have to do is type your name on the web, and it tells you all about that person" said the Queen smartly.

Jack just looked at her, to say, "What about forsake all for the Queen?"

"Well that surely doesn't apply to you, besides where I come from, most men like you, easily have ten or so wives and mistress's see I know all about how you men need it, and I'm alright with it."

"Really, I would think most women want a single man to themselves?"

"Where did you read that? Said the Queen, but added, "You see Mister Jack Cash, it's my country, and I make up the rules, and if you agree to marry me, I will reward you a palace twice the size of this place, and financially you will be taken care of for the rest of your life."

"And in return?"

"You'll agree to be my husband."

"Jack, Ana, will you come in for dinner", said King John.

Jack looks at her, for her to giggle to say, "Well what do you think?"

"Perhaps" said Jack as she threw herself onto him, to kiss him on the cheek, to whisper, "You won't have to change a thing, I'll make all the arrangements", she slid along as Jack held her hand, she held onto his hand, they walked in together, she was smiling, as her sister was equally smiling, then it was the King, doing the same, as they found there seat, at the side of the Queen, who sat across from her sister, as Jack took the seat next to Queen Ana, next to him, was Blythe, a thorn in his side, across from them was Ingrid, she kept, her head down, as Jack knew she knew, he knew about her involvement, in the assassination plan, on the other end was the King and Queen, first course was served, it was a fresh green salad, Jack slid his watch along the plate only to hear, "Don't worry, it's not poisoned, you're not my husband yet."

She picks up his plate and trades his with hers, in front of him was four single serving dressings, he chose the clear one, and lightly drizzled it on, he slowly ate, while the two girls conversed, next was the soup course, it tasted like broccoli and cheese, next was an appetizer plate of sliced meats and cheeses, with crackers, and a lump of fish eggs, as Queen Ana, leaned over to him to say, "That was harvested this morning, from one of my factories, it's called the royal caviar, packaged for those that can afford it, ten thousand dollars a tablespoon, I know you have to go to Switzerland in a couple of days, I've already shipped a case to you, there, as one of the many presents you'll be getting."

"This place you live, may I come visit?"

"Those were the words, I so long to hear, of course you can."

Jack took his spoon, and scooped up, half of the eggs, to place it on the cheese, and layered some meat on it, but used a knife and fork to take a small bite.

"You're also a gentleman" said the Queen, whispering to him, as he looked back up, from his phone, he ate slowly.

As the conversation was still in high gear, their plates were taken, and an instant aroma, of fresh BBQ could be smelled, as a heaping plate of pork ribs, were placed, in front of him, Jack hesitated, only to hear from King John, "Go ahead Jack, pick them up, we contacted your secretary, and she told us that you loved pork ribs, and a raspberry chipotle sauce, it was the least we could do, thanks for all the coffee, and the coffee maker."

Jack just looked at him, to say, "Your welcome."

He kept it to a minimum, what he said, he was the guest, he ate slowly with the ribs, as the two King's ate like it was their last supper.

"Jack I just got word that a flock of quail, have landed on our north forty, would you like to take an evening ride?" said King John proudly.

"Yes, that would be fine" said Jack in between bites.

"Alright, we will leave, after supper, would your friend like to come?"

Jack looks over at Blythe, who had become an embarrassment to him, as she had her mouth full of ribs, to shake her head yes, for Jack to say, "I think she wants' to go."

"Fine, then we will all go, even the ladies, take your time eating" said the King., as he waved his hands, off the plate, to receive the plate of vegetables, as a hand went to pick up Jack's, when accidently Jack had his hand on the plate, the hand went away, but the vegetable plate, was set in front of him, instantly he saw the artichoke, he turned his head backwards to see the butler, who said, "Yes sir?"

"Could I have melted butter and catsup, please?"

The King over heard that to say, "Yes, that sounds good, bring it out to all."

Jack finished his ribs, as the plate left, the melted butter, and catsup, was in front of him, the King watched as Jack ate the artichoke, down to the heart, and then added the catsup, and the heart in slices, Jack tried the roasted corn, and long green beans."

Lastly as the plates left, was the dessert round, a smartly cut piece of royal pie, to Jack, it tasted like a cross from apricot and a peach pie, it was good with cinnamon and nutmeg, a fresh cup of coffee, and a slice of lemon, in a huge mug, placed where the pie used to be.

Jack drank it down, it was refreshing, and he looked around to see everyone else was drinking his drink.

The King stood, as did everyone, to hear, "Come men lets retire to the study and smoke a cigar."

Jack set down his drink, to catch up to the King, and King Josef was behind him.

Queen Ana, saw Blythe, as Queen, Isabella, said, "Go upstairs dear, I'll have Ingrid show you where to change, so dearly sister what did he say?"

"Perhaps" she responded in a favorable tone.

"Excellent, and of the arrangements?" as Blythe overheard her talking to say, "He isn't that great" walking around like she was drugged or something.

"Ingrid pulls her out of the room, as the two Queens looked at her.

"Are you crazy, she will have your head cut off, you need to keep this on the down low, for our plan to work, you won't make it through the night" said Ingrid.

"What are you talking about" said a bitter Blythe.

"When you told me, that your career as a spy has been stalled, well Russia will take you, all you have to do, is keep quiet and get into the UN council, and there you will meet with Alexander."

"You promised that nothing would happen to Jack, that was our deal right?"

"Absolutely" said Ingrid, escorting her to Blythe's assigned room. Ingrid closes the door for her, only to see that the hallway was empty, Ingrid went down to Jack's room, opened the door, to see Porter John standing at the door, to say, "State your business?"

"Why are you inside the room?" asked the curious Ingrid.

"Because I asked him in" said a half dressed Jack wearing his regular pants bottom, his chest exposed, Ingrid was ready to take him, but instead the Porter pushed her out.

In a tree one hundred forty yards away, sat Michelle, with her eye on the scope, and seeing the whole interruption, she took a picture from her scope, and sent it back to Lisa. To say to herself, "If you get in Jack's way I'll kill you".

CH 11

Midnight games

The moon was full, and another hundred of the countries riders were assembled, as Jack stepped out after choosing his rifle of choice, from the pack of men, three distinct groups the King John's men, King Josef's men, then a group of the suppose best were in the middle for Jack, from the ladies Jack choose by name as the next Queen of Belarus. Off to the right were a smaller group, as one called the ferrymen, or as Jack said, "The thugs", they carried a small club.

Jack mounted the white stallion, thinking if it were the middle ages, he could be a knight, instead of the rifle; he could pull a huge sword. The ride started off to the north, as the riders all fell into a column, as the Kings rode together, then Jack, behind him was the two Queens, or sisters, then the two women.

Jack pulled out his phone, as he dimmed it, to inferred red, he saw that he had forty five new messages, he hit the urgent one, as he switched it to text, instead of voice, it was Mitzi, who said Agent Michelle, is on the ground watching your back, as we feel, Blythe has turned, to the Russian side, does she have authorization to kill her?"

Jack sent, "No", then texted to Michelle, "Men left behind are ferrymen, watch them, and leave the two girls alone".

Jack saw the text come back, "Confirmed".

Jack continued to ride, alongside but at a distance from the men, who didn't even look at Jack, as he looked at his messages, one was from Sara, he read it, as she said, "Are you married yet, that Queen Ana is sure pretty."

Jack saved the message, then closed up the phone, to hear someone coming close, he put his phone away, as the trees were behind them, to the open plains, as a man spoke in perfect English, "Mister Cash, I'm your runner", as he caught up to him, stride with stride, he added, "Were the ferrymen, we will get anything you shall desire?"

Jack looked at him, to say, "What do you mean?"

"Well sir, if you want a tent, shelter, you name it we will bring it out, set it up, and so forth."

"Interesting, what else do you do?"

"That's it, if and when you shoot a bird, it will be one of my groups that will run it in and take it to the chef, for you honor."

"How many birds will be out here?"

"Oh about a thousand?, who really knows?"

"What, really" said Jack surprised.

"Oh yes, this is called the spring migration, from Italy, the quail likes the cooler condition, you know this is their breeding grounds, they come early this year, maybe in your honor."

"Why's that?"

"One it's been warmer, and two the black birds have been out crowing giving the indication of some sort of change."

"Nah, I'm fine, but thanks for the information."

"Alright sir" said the man.

Jack kept the separation from him and the group, as the hills turned into valleys, and then back up, as they got onto a higher level, easily covering five miles, in the distance, a huge castle was visible, as Jack caught up with the two Kings, who were talking, they came to a stop, for the King John to say, "Hold up Jack, over this ridge, is the targets, allow the men, to go ahead."

"Yes sir, who's castle is that" points Jack, as King John, says, "Oh that's abandoned after World War One, a nuclear bomb was dropped in that valley below, and contaminated the water supply, and poisoned the famed Black birds, now it's called radiation valley, for some reason the birds have been agitated, they may affect, our night, however they are still twenty miles to our west, look above."

Jack saw the huge creatures, for him to get back on his phone, to text Lisa asking if there are troops in the valley?"

"Yes" was her reply.

"Evacuate… immediately, and have radiation suits ready for them, there in danger", Jack sent the text.

He waited the response, "Confirmed."

"Jack get ready" said King John.

Jack put his phone away, to pull his rifle, just as the noise of men screams and shrill, and in that instant, a sea of birds took flight, King John, was slaughtering them, with each shot, as did King Josef, while Jack hit several, as the sky was filled with thousands, it ended as fast as it started, as the ferrymen, raced behind and around them to collect the fallen birds.

Jack turned to see the Queens, all three have assembled on the hill, while Blythe and Ingrid, seemed buddy, buddy.

Jack saw the ferryman get every bird shot, to hear "Go another round gentlemen?" said King John.

"Yes I fancy a bit more" said King Josef.

Meanwhile Jack was reloading his rifle for twelve shots. Thinking about his gun, would be another fifteen shots. While all the men collected the birds to say, "Thirty six collected and accounted for".

"Round up the men for another go around" said King John, to add, "Then it will be the ladies turn".

Jack waited on the west ridge, while King John, was to the north, followed by King Josef to the south, "Interesting strategy" thought Jack, as he waited, then the noise began, and the birds took off, all above them, Jack aimed fired, all until his twelve shots were through, and the flock landed.

Men were on the ground around them collecting another thirty six. King John past by Jack to say, "Lets allow the Queens to shoot."

Jack followed them, down into the valley, then back up, where all five women were as each man passed their rifle to the equal opposite, Jack gave his to Queen Ana, already reloaded and ready to go, Jack caught on to what was going on, so he went west, and Queen Ana followed, next to them was Queen Isabella, and King Josef.

King John and Queen Mary stayed where she was at, while Blythe and Ingrid, accompanied two men to the east, while King John pulled out his sword, to yell, "Are you ready on the left, ready on the right" as all used their hand as a gesture, the King lowered his sword, instantly the Quail appeared like out at a target practice range at low level, in a pattern above or beside the horses head, till all were through, each placed their rifles upward. The men scurried over the field, collecting all the birds, to hear "Reload, ready" said King John, as he looked over at Blythe, who wasn't playing any longer, so the King took his horse to her to say, "Where is your rifle?"

"That man has it" she said as she pointed to the man on the ground.

"Are you finished firing?" said the King angrily.

She looked up at him to say, in a rather disrespectful tone, "I'm done killing innocent birds."

"James give her, her rifle back" said King John, and rode off.

"Here Miss, you must make the attempt to fire at them."

"I don't want to."

"You have to; it is the King's order."

James leans in to say, "You lucky you're an American, tied to Jack, if you were one of us, you'd be dead, here take it and play along, aim over them, but remember, if the King wants it, you shall do it, or else he will have your head cut off.

Blythe nodded, then took up her position, and did what she was told, out of respect, as the birds were up flying she hit true all twelve shots. Men in front of her collected all twelve of her birds, as James came closer to say, "There that wasn't so bad, was it."

"I didn't like it, but I didn't want to lose my head either."

"That's not the point, these birds are the royals birds exclusively, now that it over, they can go breed, in specially nests, down in that valley, it happens every year it's a tradition, and tomorrow marks the royal feast of birds, to begin the start of spring."

"Oh so its tradition then" said Blythe.

"Absolutely, that's why we are all here, however they came two weeks earlier than expected, maybe because Jack Cash is among us all."

"Yeah maybe." she said, as she turned to catch up with the others.

Jack was riding next to Queen Ana, third in line, as she talked and laughed, as Jack talked with her, for Jack she was a lot older than Sara and Maria, she was a bonafide Queen, with immense power, she mentioned her country was in the Winter Olympics in Vancouver British Columbia, in North America, the same time he was going into the UN Council, so he declined her offer to accompany her there, but said right after the Council, they would have a proper courtship.

Joy and happiness filled the air. As she let out the sounds of vocal speech.

Jack was concentrating on tonight's sleep, and if he could recreate his childhood memories, all the while agreeing with Queen Ana, who might be a good allied, besides he kind of like that whole idea of royalty and what it means, especially when, you get waited on at any request, not to mention a palace of his own, especially if it's a gift, I may move all the wives there. He thinks, as the ride came to an end, everyone dismounted together, for the King to say, "Tomorrow will be a royal feast, in honor of my new son, Jack Cash."

Three cheers went up for Jack, then stepped in, to the palace, as the King's went there way, and Jack was going up to his room to retire, when he heard his name, he turned to see it was the Queen, who said, "Where do you think you're going, without saying good night to me, properly?"

Jack turned to face her; she placed his head in her hands to say,

"For you to agree to marry me, you will receive gifts of unbelievable amounts."

"The first being a child?" asked Jack.

"No silly, I can't have any?"

"Well that changes everything" said Jack pulling away from her.

"Wait", she said, to add, "What I lack in one area, I'll gladly make up in another?"

"That's all perfectly well, but I want children, and lots of them" said Jack walking away.

Porter John opened Jack's room, to say, "Are you expecting any guests later?"

"No, not that I'm aware of, but who knows what could happen in the middle of the night" said Jack.

"Then sleep peacefully, you won't be disturbed."

Jack went in, undressed, in the foyer, and took his gun, to the night stand next to his bed, and slipped into the softest thread count he has ever felt, and fell fast asleep.

Jack thought he was dreaming, but could sense a presence above him; he opened his eyes to see it was the tiny Michelle, dressed in all black, smiling to say, "I have news for you?"

"And the phone doesn't work?" said Jack sitting up to look at her, her natural Chinese descent was coming through, as she continued to straddle him, she was a trained cold hearted killer, to say, "This morning we took Blythe into custody, for meeting with a unknown man, she is a beyond a doubt a double agent."

Jack just looked at her, as she continued, she looked at him to say, "But you knew?" to add, "How did you know?"

"I asked Queen Ana, to help me out, so we planted a counter spy for her to meet with, and I imagine the Queen will tell me everything, but nice try, wait can you do me a favor?"

"Anything, you name it?" said Michelle.

"Strip and hop into the bed with me?"

She looked at him, then began to pull off her black knit sweater, and then her black pants, then looking at him, her bra, to show her small yet firm breasts to him, then she stepped out of her panties, picking all of them up she placed them on the other side of the bed and slid in next to him, for him to say, "Now pretend your asleep, face the other way", she did what she was told, as Jack stood up, he pulled the covers back to admire the view, only to hear, voices, as a secret passageway opened and for Jack to quickly pulled the covers up, as he stood there in the nude, for the Queen Mary to admire, Queen Ana, looked down then up to his eyes, for Queen Ana, to say, "I thought about what you told me."

"Can't you see I have company" said Jack showing the head of Michelle.

"So what, we all have our lovers" said the young Queen Mary, passing Jack, to pull the covers back, as Michelle rolled onto her back, and smiled.

"Nice choice she is pretty, I gather she was the one in the tree last night, one from the spy club, I have to admit, and beautiful women follow you everywhere, some not as smart as that other one."

"Her name is Michelle" said Jack.

"I can see that, you're right, your assistant Blythe has taken a better offer, she is suppose to meet with Alexander of Russia, at the Summit, where he will give her Varfolomey exact instructions, and lead us to our countries fortune, you know when you first told me of this man, Jack, I had doubt's if you could do anything for me, but now, I see how you work, care if another joins your play?" said the Queen Mary, beginning to undress.

"She is actually only a decoy" said Jack looking back at Michelle, who stood up, to say, "I don't mind, if you don't mind" said a smiling Michelle. Jack watched as both Queens, stripped out of their full length dresses, to their under garments, as Queen Mary giggled, as she pulled the sheet from Jack, as the two sisters went at it.

Back at the United Nations, in Geneva, the men and women of the world council, assembled for a meeting, "Order please" said the man at the head of the semi round table, to add, "This is the final day we have to work out the unified deal, that allows the top three agents into any country they so choose to work, now with a raise of hands, all were raised, to say, "That concludes all 206 nations have made into law one of the three chosen agents, will be allowed unlimited access and support, and will be taken from the twelve we have invited here on Friday, from the 356 that qualify, let's talk about some sort of qualifier, to whittle down to the top twelve any to oppose or show concerns please add any additional comments, Ali, from Iran go ahead?"

Ali spoke in his native tongue and was translated, for the head of the UN council, John-Philip, from France, to say, "Do they have to notify us if an invasion is eminent?"

"A direct call to you, from us at the UN, will be your notification, any action or force against them will result in a full scale retaliation, consider who we choose, will be a representative of the UN itself, acting on behalf of all the countries, with the emphasis on peace, and to neutralize any terrorism in their way", to add, "Next please, go ahead Omar, from Dubai?"

"We still are short the funds for our annual dues of ten million dollars, will you accept a barter, say an acre of oil wells?"

"You and your country must take it up with the UN Bank; they may hold a special session, to help you and all others falling behind or just below the amount needed to stay a voting member." "Next please, yes, Rashid, from the Saudi Arabia."

In his native tongue he said, "If an agent comes into my country, will they abide by our local customs and traditions?"

"If need be, they are considered a guest, who is attempting to stop any violence, especially with your country and the pirates, after this summit, we will send an agent down there", he adds, next please" looking around the room, he sees a small man get up, to say, "When can we invite one of our spies to this council?"

"As of right now, Mustapha from Beirut, there is a change in place, to allow two or more to this qualifier, we have put in place, but until your country shows world interest, and support, you won't be considered, as of today, your still in what we consider dangerous status, too many terrorist have known ties to Beirut, but we may send someone in their to assess the situation, and once they give the O Kay, then we will consider it, next please, yes Omary of Libya."

"We are of a great people and need a protected drinking supply, when can we have an agent available to assess our situation?"

"For Libya, a UN team will be touching down, to assess your situation, and if need be, a super agent will be called in, next please, yes Yaswir, from Israel, Jordan and Turkey, what is your question?"

"May we request an agent, even if he is not the top three?"

"Yes, actually any of the twelve, represented spies can be contacted, as in the case of our Russian friend Vladimir Ecklon, who's wife was kidnapped by the former KGB operative Varfolomey, and he asked for Jack Cash to go get her, as we monitored the assault on Jack Cash, we were unsure if it was a set up, then an action occurred that will forever change the Russian landscape, Jack Cash, uncovered a building plant of unknown bombs, and blew it up."

"That's not what happen, we had an earth quake."

"Yeah one that measured 10.2 on the scale and killed a half of million people."

"That number was incorrect, it was only hundred of thousands only, were still sifting through the rubble." said the Russian President." trying not to take any responsibility.

"That goes to show you, if you request a foreigner, and he uncovers something like an illegal ammunition dump or weapons of mass destruction, they have the complete authority to call us in, or solve it themselves, it will be up to them, any retaliation towards that agent will be met with first a disbarment from the council, then any food or financial aid cut off, and lastly shut down, air or water traffic to them, till the matter is resolved, all we want is peace, and we will go to great length's to preserve that, and the last question, yes Karim, from Iraq, go ahead?"

He spoke in broken English, but said, "When will the war be over, in our country?"

"If you like it could be tomorrow, granted that you prove to us that you provide a democracy style to your people, and you and your force can stop the violence and rampant terrorism?"

Karim held his head down, with not a response, so the John-Philip said, "Were looking into sending a spy in to track the terrorist and ending the unnecessary fighting, but after years of CIA led operations and support to terrorist, has officially ended, the CIA of the world, will only work in their countries, leaving the world to deal with its own issues, namely us the UN., now lets talk about this world qualifier, I just received a report, on how we should go by and allow every country in the UN to send two or more agents, to this summit, they will arrive, on Friday, and be there by 3pm sharp, anyone late will be barred, we will have temporarily housing available for them, be it a man or a women, oh yes from this point forward we are going to be training women, in addition we will have twelve professional spies, they will compete with, so send us only your finest, the meeting is adjourned.

The men all left, except the voting council, of the UN, sat the US President George White the 3rd. The Russian President Vladimir Ecklon, and the British PM Kurt Lockwood, rounding out the six are Chinese PM Tan Ming, and Japanese PM Akowa-Ulie, and finally the French PM Jean-Luc Pierre, as John-Philip, took a pedestal near the six he begins,

"Starting on Friday and lasting three weeks, twelve of the top 356 agents in the world, will be here, training, in the art of espionage, intelligence, counter terrorism, bomb building, and ethics, along the three weeks, there will be tests. Each of those tests will be recorded and sent off to each of you for evaluation, then you will vote for the agent you would like to be on top, in addition we here at the UN will rank the agents in all areas, and come up with our choice, and the top two that is selected from the panel will make it, then, a final vote of seven, will place the first, second and third. The top three will work specifically for the UN." "Any questions?"

The President of the US wrote, "Jack must lose this."

As the British PM Kurt Lock wood said, "If my agent gets top three what's his status with in our country?"

"I don't follow what you're asking?"

"Well you said he would be a property of the UN, is he still able to work for us?"

"Yes I see now, your question, you're asking, if a British, or American, or a Russian, were to win this competition, then yes, they may live within their countries, and provide service for your respected countries, but I doubt you'll see them, as they will be all over the world, and then some."

President of the US spoke, "What if he rejects the offer?"

"I'm sure they won't do that, as it will be serving the entire World, and keeping World peace, now granted he may have multiple people working for him, and that will be how they carry out our will."

The President of the US wrote, "Jack must win this competition."

The President of the UN John-Philip said, "Then we will go down the list till we get at least the three we need, lest not forget the treaty and ratification we all made to the UN charter, we are electing to place three of the top super spies in place to oversee an advance into any country and protection of peace, at what cost, most of the twelve have real world experience, take for instance Jack Cash, the American, and former German spy, he was the one who led to the destruction of the Berlin wall, and the break up of the mighty Soviet Union." as the President of Russia looked hard at John-Philip, in a manner like he had no idea. as he continued, "For some of you many of these spies are just that, but are more than spies they are the futures super agents, and the top three will have connections to all the security and military forces at their disposal, even though we know the US provides Jack Cash and Benjamin Hiltz each a 28 ship support, and the state of the art in technology, like the super gun, excuse me the signature gun, only two in the whole world, besides that, the agent who chooses this assignment will be known, then on following Monday, who you can vote for, as some may not have the means, nor the education for that title, but we shall see over this weekend.

The President of the US raised his hand.

"Go ahead, sir."

"You know about the stuff our agents have, can them come as they are?"

"No, no weapons, nor devices are they allowed to carry, all the clothes will be provided by the UN, any trackers and ear pieces will be confiscated, to include their phones."

"What about a phone book" said the President of the US sarcastically?

The others all laughed to hear, "This design is to place everyone on an equal playing surface, they will get a uniform, wrist watch, and additional gifts, and they will be paid a million a day, plus expenses, I've sent the packages out to the respectful organizations, detailing our intentions."

"What if an international crisis occurs will they be able to get away?"

"Perhaps, Mister President of the United States, but seeing that you have the largest country in the world, I'm sure you have other agent's that can handle them."

"Yes, but not in a diplomatic way that it would, I was skeptical with sending my top two agents I have, when someone wants' us, it seems were the first on everyone's list to call."

"That is true Mister President, but rest assured, if you need either one of your top two agents, you shall have them" said John-Philip angrily.

The President was ready to go, as the session came to a close, he stepped out, and into the hallway, and down to his suite, and on his phone, to the Vice President, telling her to come here and watch over the training, and question everything, especially, the actions, and she agreed to come, as he called down to Air force one, to say, "Get ready, were leaving", then looked around to say to his staff, "Pack up were leaving, as the President exited the room, out steps the President of Russia, who stopped his momentum, to say, "I'm sorry for the mix up, over the taking of my wife."

"I'm sorry too that my report says that you were building weapons for mass destruction."

"I had no idea, you must believe me?" said the President of Russia.

"With the same belief you shared with my agent who risked his life for what, if it weren't for him, I'd have declared war on you myself, you know its ironic really, the same agent that broke up the Soviet Union in 1991, is the same guy who takes out the entire KGB underground police, with one bomb, well placed."

"It was an earth quake."

"Call it what you like, but if something were to happen to any of my agents or personnel, you will be hearing from me", said the President of our United States, on his way out.

President Ecklon of Russia looked down at the paper, that he wrote 28 war ships, a complete battle group, the size of which, could wipe out Japan, he thought to himself, "Wow".

Jack laid between two hot women, the young and very flexible Michelle, and then the older more mature and firm Ana, each had their own characteristics that made Jack a happy man, his mind was on their naked bodies, as he was a bit overwhelmed by each of their eagerness to sleep with him, and each for totally different reasons.

Ana was first to speak, by saying, "See Jack we could do this all the time, what do you say, are you game, as for Michelle she went with the flow.

Jack was enjoying the moment, and both was nice for him, and it seemed the same having a Queen and a spy club member, "I guess it's all in the mind", he rose and went into the shower, he came out to see the room empty, Michelle and her clothes were gone, and Queen Ana, and herself and clothes equally gone, his watch said it was Thursday, and one day left before leaving."

Jack dressed, in his outfit, holster and gun, he zipped up, then went out for the last time, thinking, "He didn't dream about his childhood anymore, what a shame."

Down the stairs he went to see a huge carriage and a team of four horses, along with a man dressed in all red, he looked like a colonial soldier, to run across Queen Mary, who smiled and said "Come here son."

It was that voice, that tone and its meaning that brought him back to his childhood as he ran towards her arms, she whispered in his ear, "I heard, why I wasn't invited".

Jack broke the embrace, to realize it was in the present, and greed had overcome her thoughts, for Jack to say "It just happened, nothing more."

"Call it as you like, come were going in the carriage, all six of us."

Jack thought about his car, then thought he would move it later, to step out with the underdressed King and Queen, similar to Jack, and the new brightly glowing Ana, who got what she was looking for, to whisper, "Does that mean were going together?"

"Yes, I do think it does" said Jack.

"Fabulous, I can't wait till later, do you mind if my sister joins us?"

"Do I have a choice?"

"No, but I thought I would ask?"

"Then no, I don't care, more the merrier."

"I'll let her know the good news."

Jack stepped out, with the two Kings, followed by the three Queens, laughing and giggling. This time with a whole lot of guards in red, as Jack saw the numbers of guards triple, then he saw one of the ferrymen, then it clicked, they were the ones in the field, unlike those who were guests and gave gifts.

Jack took the stairs up, to the second level, where the chairs were all lined in red velvet, lined up in the middle, and in a step down fashion, a porter was there to lead Jack to the first level chair, next to Queen Ana, who he helped to her seat, then he stepped up into his chair, as she leaned into him to say, "Where's your mistress?"

"Oh probably in some tree somewhere" said Jack.

King Josef, followed by Queen Isabella, up to their seats, finally it was the older King John and the young Queen Mary. As everyone took their seats, the horses took off, Ana, took hold of Jack's hand, her hands felt soft, as she removed her white gloves, Jack looked down to see her hands and at her very pretty face, thinking that Sara wants this to happen, so if she is cool with it well let's see what happens" he thinks.

The carriage made it down to the end of the road, at the massive gates, guards were all over the streets, as the horses pulled straight south through the start of the village, as people lined the way, as the Queens waved, music played, and announcement made that the visiting Queens, and a special guest and new favorite son, Jack Cash.

To Jack, it was easily 1000 plus people, in addition to the banners that signified the royal spring festival.

In the middle, the carriage came to a stop, Queen Ana held Jack back, to allow King John and Queen Mary to go first, as they passed, then it was King Josef and Queen Isabella, and then it was Queen Ana and followed by Jack. Into a hall of the royals, was a open and again the elevated seats above the dance floor held six high backed red velvet chairs, along a huge table, the King and Queen of Belarus, in the middle, next to the King, was King Josef of the Ukraine, his young wife next to the Queen Ana, and next to her was Queen Isabella, on the other side, was the place for Jack. The program was printed, and Jack picked up his copy, where it said the festivities will start with the dance of the forbidden lovers, two female dancers danced to live music, heavy drum beats, it was kinda of cool, so much so, he pulled out his phone, and began to tape the event.

Jack looked up to see Michelle, across from him along the wall, she smiled back at him.

After the dancers was a traditional folk dance, was somewhat of a polka, with an interesting varied musical rhythm's, Jack was toe tapping to it, when his phone rang, although it was on vibrate, it was on an international line, he viewed who it was, it was the Premier's wife Victoria, who called to say, "Thank you, what you don't know was Vladimir was held by terrorist, and traded my life for his, all for 100 million dollars, well that Man didn't do a thing, except ask you to save me, well I owe you my life, as for Varfolomey was taking me out to the Ural's to sell me off to the sex traders, and he wasn't going to return me, now however he is on the run, and in hiding, but my husband knows where he is at, if you get to the council early, you'll have a chance to get it out of him, take care of yourself, you're an angel among men."

Jack closed up the phone, as he thought about the dilemma, what to do with Blythe, do I take her to the council or substitute her with the faithful Michelle, Jack was torn by which one to bring, and what the quarters would be set up." he thinks. Several hours had passed, and it was the feast time, all that food and the courses, Jack was filing up fast, but the next four hours, gave him time to snack, rather than straight in shovel.

Evening was on, as the lights filled the great hall, Jack's mind was thinking about ducking out, but that all changed, as the crowd went to the sides, and the dance floor opened up, then the band moved forward, and visible, as the call out for the royal's dance, first up, was the King and Queen of Belarus, to a waltz, that lasted a long seven minutes. Next up was the King and Queen of the Ukraine; it was like watching a father and daughter, dancing close to close, as there song ended. Everyone stood up and clapped, and then it was Queen Ana, on the dance floor, as she called out to Jack to wave him down, Jack gets up with ear piece in place, and his phone set to waltz.

He set his frame, and she slipped in naturally, the music started, and he was off, swinging his arms, and his feet were light, and graceful, as he did a perfect waltz, as it ended, the audience went wild, with clapping and whistling, Jack and Ana bowed to the crowd, then he let her go, but she held on to him to say, "Now we have the walking waltz."

Instantly Jack pulled his phone, to type the Belarus walking waltz, it came up, as the other Royals took their position, as Jack held a lower hold, stiff frame, the music began, Jack and Ana did it flawlessly, it was the two other Kings and Queen that were stumbling, the traditional dance. The music lasted a good fourteen minutes, as he was sweating up a storm, it was hard work, till it finally died down, as they left the floor, tables were put back on and it became a beer festival, huge steins of beer, were delivered to the Royal's table first, four mugs of different beers, with each group of brewers were together. Jack tried the darkest one first, it tasted good, he set it aside, next was a bitter one, yet everyone else seemed to like it, next was a caramel crème, too sweet, and lastly a bitter, so he went back to the dark one. Then it was announced for the finalist for Mister Jack cash's choices for Princess, as the following ladies appeared, first it was Natasha Loata, from the north, who seemed to look a lot like Austin. Daria, Trinuska from the east. A tall 5-10 beauty, an Olympian, training to ski cross country, and the biathlon. Next up was Lena, a wide as tall beautiful woman, with a remembering smile. Next was an earlier dance partner, Emily, a dark haired lady, who was polite and well reserved. Next was Nina, a polish girl, from along the border, a real beautiful girl. Next up was Julia, a super sexy and beautiful golden haired lady with an amazing smile. Next was Anastasia, a tall mean looking Russian lady, who has all the pedigree of her famous sister, Victoria, which she leaned into Jack to whisper, "I want to give you a present later, from what you did for my sister, Victoria, she told me how you rescued her, amazing, truly amazing." Next up was an auburn hair charmer, with a cute smile and perfect teeth, she no doubt was breed for royalty, her name was Brigitte, earlier King John mentioned his huge dairy farm, and that her family runs it for the King, and she is the chosen one. Next up was a real gem, she was tall as she was wide, and well built for lots of children, for she was Alexandra, large features, from her face, to her breasts, to her hips, and her hands were huge, she was without question nearly a giant. Next was clearly the best, her name was Bianca, a smartly looking dark haired lady with a spectacular smile, and piercing eyes. Jack was growing tired of this parade, as he let others go by, until he raised his hand up at Tatiana, a dark haired Lady, short hair, "Gypsy" spoke Ingrid, as Jack ended the parade, as he turns to the King to say, "Shall I choose one now?"

"You may choose one, or all its up to you, you may have as many wives as you so choose, but beware son, you must support all of them as one?","Can you do that?"

Jack had a smile on his face, thinking, about the eleven that was to the side, but before he spoke the King said, "Before you choose, ask them if they would share you with the others."

Jack thought about that for a moment, as he knew he had Anastasia, as she smiled at him, as did all the others, in that instant he knew he had to have Natasha, and went over to her, to say, "Will you accept me, and be my Princess?"

A bigger smile formed on her mouth, as her eyes were wide, to say, "Yes, of course, and with that she leaned into him, and kissed him on the cheek, to hear her say, "You can choose whoever, they will all accept your choices?"

Jack whispers, "How about Julia, can you accept her?"

"Yes, she is my friend?"

"Who else is your friend?"

"Lena, Daria, Emily, Brigitte and Bianca.

She stepped back, for Jack to really decide, and thought about the two Russian ladies, and of the Polish one, the wild card was the gypsy, to say, "Next I choose, Bianca." She comes to him, and kisses him on the cheek, for Jack to say, "Will you choose me, and Natasha together?" she leaned back, smiled to say, "Yes, of course, if you so shall want it." She stepped back for Jack, to pause as everyone was waiting for the next choices, for Jack to say, "Emily, will you accept this arrangement."

"Yes", she said firmly.

It was getting harder for Jack to decide as the remaining ladies were all smiles, waiting to hear their names to be called, but for Jack he was thinking of other things, he had three, all were together, and they seemed fine, in his mind, he let go of Nina, and Tatiana, as she reminded him of his former partner, he thought of the DOD, and the processing, then in the crowd, he saw his chamber maid, Nadia, she wore a smile, but was she available, as he turned to King John, to whisper, "Is this all I have to choose from, or may I choose another?"

King John smiled, to say, "You may choose from anyone in my kingdom, these ladies are from the best privileges afforded to them, who you shall choose son?"

Jack thought of that luxurious bath, and how she held him, and of her smell, to say, "Next I choose, Julia." She was extremely excited, as she stepped in and gave him a kiss; her smile was infectious, for Jack to say, "Will you accept me and my other choices, to join our family?"

"Yes, of course, as she went to Natasha, and embraced her, as a division was forming, from Jack's selections. Of those left he only saw, five with four solid, as he looked at them, they were all smiles back, his next choice, was simple, he said, "Next I ask, Brigitte." She came out to him, kissed him on both cheeks, to say, "Yes, and whisper, "Thank you, to continue the life of privilege."

Jack just looked at her, to think maybe that was a wrong choice, so from the rich to the Queen's attendant, Jack said, "Next I'd like Nadia." As all was silent, as on the line, there was no one of that name or distinction, but someone said, "Excuse me, as she made herself known, a girl, of the working class, but her beauty was very evident, and for others it was evident from her long graceful neck, and sculptured face, she was a seriously looking specimen, she came out to the floor, in front of Jack as he said, "Will you accept me and of the others?" The others appeared to snub her, as she looked over at the King, who knew not of her, as she was like other young girls, a bit of a unknown, worker in the palace, for her to say, 'Yes, if the Queen, and King should allow?"

King John nodded, yes, to say, "Yes, you are here in my kingdom, if you can share, with the others, then I shall allow it."

"Then yes, I will" she went up, and kissed Jack on the cheek", for Jack to whisper, "Will you be in my bath tonight?"

She lowered her eyes to say, "No, sorry, you made me a princess, I'm no longer a worker?", she left to join the others, as Jack was now rethinking what he was doing, as all he was thinking was like what Anastasia said to him, as his mind was going crazy, with what he was doing, and put that out of his mind, and went for who was good to look at, to say, "Next Daria", who seemed relieved, as she came and gave him a hug and kiss, to whisper, "I'll make you feel that you made the right choice?" Jack just looked at her as she strolled by, to see the two Russian women, to say, "next up is Alexandra, ", she came up to him to say, "Take me to the conference with you, I'll be an asset for you.", she went to the others, and then Jack said, "Lastly I choose, Anastasia."

She came up to him, to say, "Wise choice, thank you".

All the new princesses were whisked away, as Jack sat back down by the King, to say, "What have I just done?"

"Nothing that was the choosing round?"

"What do you mean?"

"Well now is the courtship phase, as you narrow it down to just one, and then we will have a royal wedding."

"What about Queen Ana?"

"No worries, she is from Latvia, the ladies you choose now, were the future queens of Belarus, if I were to pass, and then you would, assume the throne, and a princess, to rule?"

206

"What if the Queen is left?" asked Jack.

"Oh you can't marry her, she isn't of blood, she will go back to Latvia, that would be unless she was to have a son, and then the son she bore, would be next in line behind you."

Jack said, "What of my choices when will I get to see them again?"

"Oh, you won't, there off to the next phase, of being a princess, except for those going to the Olympics, as for the first time we are allowed to go as our own country, so says the UN."

The evening was wrapping up, the King and Queen of Belarus were standing, as the crowd acknowledged their departure, as Jack fell in behind them, to hear, "Oh you don't have to go."

"I'm a bit tired" said Jack now fully rested up.

"I think I'd like to go as well" said Queen Ana.

Leaving behind King and Queen of the Ukraine, as the four went into the carriage, as the cool night gave way to the cold air, they took a seat on the inside level. Queen Ana nestled by Jack, to say, "Are you planning on leaving tomorrow morning?"

"Yeah I think so."

"Can you wait till I get back?" she asks.

"What does that mean?"

"Well, I want to give you a gift to remember me."

"Alright, so what does that mean?"

"Well it means, I'm flying home tonight, and I'll see you in the morning, perhaps wake you up one last time, if you're not leaving too early?"

"I'll wait, but I am sorry to hear you have to go."

"That's alright we will have plenty of time, after the council to see each other."

"You mean start the courtship" asks Jack.

"Yes, that too, I'm also being flying off to Canada, for the Olympics, which lasts about three weeks, I wish you could come with me, I'm going to miss you."

"And I will miss you too", said Jack as the two kissed. They continued that till the carriage came to a complete stop, Jack looked out the window to see her helicopter, as she waved him goodbye.

Jack sat watching it start, then lift off, towards the city, till it was out of sight.

Jack stepped out of the carriage, to see the guards, then went in, up the stairs, and down to the single porter, who greeted him, then opened the door for him, Jack stepped in, to see the door close., he quickly undressed, as he laid his clothes out, and set his gun and holster by the bed, he pulled the covers back, and slipped in, as he put his head to the pillow, he went to sleep.

Jack felt a soft hand on his back, as he was getting a back massage, he was waking up, to another night of not a dream about being royalty, as her warm hands spread the oil, and worked it in, she was in a kneel position, this time she used her elbows, and really dug in good, she was a master, he could feel her skin against him, whenever she changed positions, until she said, "Roll over I want to do your front", that voice, was different than Ana's, he turned to see it was her sister Mary, in the nude, being bad, Jack said, "Are you crazy, what are you doing?"

"It's not what I'm doing, looks like you found yourself a place to put it, and it feels so good." As she was grinding against him.

She said as she grinded upon him, as her breasts were bouncing up and down.

"What about your sister?"

"She already knows, I told her."

"What about King John?"

"Why can he have his secret mistress's and I can't enjoy life and its pleasures?"

"Because you're sacred to him."

"What's sacred to you, I knew the moment I saw you, I wanted you, besides John is impeded, and I need someone who is live, so that I can get pregnant and have a son, so can you make sure you deposit it into me" as she continued to grind on him, and much to her surprise she said, "Your much thicker than John, do you work this thing out, how did it get so big?"

"Nah" said Jack, wondering, what to do, either to enjoy it or throw her out, he looked over at the time it said 0200 AM, she seemed pleasant, her breasts were nice, but little did she know, he was in it for the long run, and as she reached her very first orgasm, she went crazy as Jack tried to keep her mouth shut, as she fell back, Jack changed positions, and mounted her, with long plunging strokes, getting her to another orgasm, this time he used a pillow, to muffle her sounds, he spun her over, and on her knees, and drove it in, he was really going at it now, till she collapsed a final time, from exhaustion, he was still inside of her as she was out, he pulled out, but now he had another problem, he was rock solid, it hurt to contain it, as he began to dress her, in her evening wear, then carried her to his empty tub, and laid her down, to sleep, taking the comforter, he threw it over her, he turned to assess the situation, it was 0400 or there about, and a massive problem to deal with, he took off his pants to let it swing freely, he went to his phone, and scrolled down to Michelle, and dialed her up, it went to voice mail, then thought about a cold shower, and went into the auxiliary bathroom, and started the standup shower, stepped into near freezing cold water, he washed up, and yet it was still as hard as it was, only difference now was it too was cold, to the point he began to shiver, he stopped that dried off, and went back into the bed, and fell fast asleep.

Meanwhile his phone vibrated, on the end table. Jack was sleeping, when he heard the door, and some voices, he turned to see it was 0600, and there was Queen Ana, back from her trip, carrying a animal container of sorts, she dropped everything, and ran to him, they kissed, for her to feel how excited he was to see her, and for her to say, "Let me help you out there, as she pulled the covers back to see how large it was, she said, "I don't remember it being that big" she said pointing down at it."

Jack was undoing her dress from behind as she was being reserved, looking at that purple creature bobbing up and down, but her excitement swelled, and minus the dress, and under garments, she allowed Jack in, he filled her up, and she was way excited, and it was the same old thing he pleased her, with no end results, and with each orgasm, she too was fading, till she too was near exhaustion, and still Jack was stuck, he couldn't release.

He stepped away from the exhausted Queen, to see his phone humming, he went to it to see it was Michelle, he answered it to hear, "Thank god, you answered I was worried, you needed me, and I wasn't there, how can I help you?"

"Well its delicate, I need for you to come here, and then you'll see what I need." said Jack.

"Sure I owe you I'll be there in fifteen minutes." she said.

Meanwhile Jack covered up the very tired Queen Ana, thinking "Where are all the chamber maids when you need them?"

Looking around the room, thinking, "What about a cold bath", so he went over to the Queen of Belarus, uncovered her, and picked her up and carried her over to the bed next to her sister, and then covered her up. He went to the bath and turned on the cold water, he filled it up three quarters of the way, then eased in, it was cold, his mind was elsewhere, yet it was still the same, it was no use, then he thought about the ice machine in the kitchen, only to hear a noise on the balcony, and to the door was Michelle dressed in black, she opened the unlocked door, and stepped in to see him, and went to him, to see it, and say, "Wow that's big, what happen?"

"It gets like this sometimes."

"I see your predicament; you're in cold water now?'

"Its mild, I'll drain it, if you."

"Your not putting that thing into me like that, no disrespect" she said looking at it in amazement, contemplating it, for Jack to say, "Can you go down stairs and into the kitchen, find the ice machine and bring up a couple of pails of ice?"

"What part are you looking at, I can barely carry a rifle, let alone two buckets of ice" said Michelle.

"Bring what you can, or..."

"I get it", she said as she went past the small crate, to hear a loud pitch scream, which she jumped back to say, "What do have in there a tiger?"

"I don't know, a woman your size carried it in."

"Yeah, right."

Jack thought to himself, "She is sure cocky to him, and then thought what if either of them wake up with both of them in bed together.

Jack waited then finally, she returned with two buckets of ice, which she set them down, then one at a time, dumped them on his throbbing member, the ice from the second bucket fell away as it was cresting out, for her to say, "Looks like a huge cucumber."

"Thanks, now I need you to carry the Queen of Belarus to another room, is the Porter still outside?"

"Yeah, he was the one who helped me carry the ice up" said Michelle.

"Good, tell him, I'd like breakfast in bed, and have him leave, and then you find a room to put her in."

Jack was concentrating on not thinking he was cold, while Michelle went to the door, to say, "Sir, my master would like you to go down stairs and bring him up some breakfast?"

"Don't worry I can call it in" as he spoke on a walkie talkie, to say, "There it's done, was there something else miss?"

"Well actually, can you just leave for five minutes" she said nicely.

"Listen, I can't leave this post or the King will cut off my head."

"Alright then we have to get rough about this."

"What do you really want?" he said to her amusement.

She just looked at him, thinking, but before she could speak, he said, "Is it the Queen, I know she is in there, something wrong?"

"Well she is kind of out of it?"

He barged past her, to see the larger box, and went past it to see Jack and say "Hi"; Jack waved his hand up to him. then the large man picked up Queen Mary, and carried her out.

Michelle closed the door. Then came back past the box to hear that scream again, and jump back, over to Jack to say, "Is it working?"

"Nah, it's still the same."

"What can I do anything?" she said with a smile."

"Now that's better, I don't feel that threaten now."

"Looks like you're in so much pain, can I touch it?"

Jack stood, to feel her small hand on it, it was still the same, except colder."

"Let's say we try to warm that up" as she led him to the bed, she knelt over and Jack pulled down her pants, and in it went.

CH 12

King's Review

The next hour was over, as Jack subsided, and forgot all about that as he was back in his childhood, and his mother, came in and said,"Gunther, who is in that bed of yours?"

As he used his foot, he pushed her out, to the floor, Gunther smiled, with his accomplishment, as Michelle wasn't so happy, as she dove at Jack and the two went off the other side, he had her in a sleeper hold, as she dug into his side, the more Jack pulled onto her neck, the more she dug into his side, till finally he let go, and Michelle, stood up to exclaim, "Look its gone down."

A smiled formed on Jack's face, as Michelle jumped into Jack's arms, in celebration, only to hear, the Porter, announce, "If all's up, the King would like to see Miser Cash, please."

Jack dressed, and was armed, and ready, as he made his way down the grand staircase, to the bottom, where King John, stood, to say, "My boy, I want to show you my city before you go, come, a car awaits."

Jack followed the King, to a slick black limousine, no sign of Ingrid, or Blythe, as he got in, as he instantly got flashbacks, of his first ride, and of his very first mission with the SIT girls, Magdalena and Michelle. The car drove, a short distance to stop, they exited, to see a pasture of many black and white cows, for King John to say, "This is the royal herd of dairy cows, the cows are milked twice a day, and delivered to that factory", he pointed to say, "Shall we see the operation?"

"Lead the way, I guess I have time?" Jack looked at his watch, to see it was early, and check in time was by 3 pm, so they got back in and went down to the operation, Jack got out, and was led in, by Royal guards, were everywhere, for the King to say, "Everywhere, each step is protected, and what we don't use, is sold to other kingdoms, and from now on, you my son, will be getting unlimited, of everything, on a pallet, sent to you every week for the rest of your life., how does that sound son,?" as they put on, a sterile uniform, and hat and mask and booties, as they went in with the workers, to see mozzarella being made, and other cheeses, for the King to say, "This is our largest commodity, cheese, fresh, to aged, in underground we have places we age them, do you want to see that?"

Jack opened his hand to motion led the way. The next huge room over was the cream separator, as pipes, went to all sort of different places, candy, Ice cream, etc... As Jack stopped to see ice cream vats for the King to say, "What flavor do you like?"

Jack was careful on what he said, as he remembered what Ingrid said, "Careful what you say, for you will get in unlimited quanties?"

"I don't know, I don't really eat ice cream, what is the Royal variety?"

"It is a blend of fresh strawberries, we only pick wild alpine, and vanilla bean, as we grow our own orchids, for this process, with bits of walnuts mixed in, shall we sample some?"

"Sure,"

With that, they went into the ice cream section where, production was at a all time high, as they both went to the tasting table, and before Jack was literarily hundred of samples, with a spoon in each, from chocolates to vanilla's to different names, as one even had apple, he tried that one which was pretty good, he thought, to hear, "Those apples come from your orchard, it's a blend of several."

As Jack said, "What do they do with the seeds?"

The King looks around to say, "I don't know?", when a manager, spoke up to say, "Your highness, the seeds we save as every part is sacred, why do you ask?"

Jack spoke up, to say, "Can we grow, more trees?"

"Yes sir, I mean your highness", as he looked at Jack and at the King, who looked up at the manager, who further said, "I will take what we have to the green houses to have them start up the royal apple trees, for Jack to say, "I really like this one."

That's all it took, as the King, tried his, and said, "Yes, this shall be King Jack's ice cream." Then Jack tried another combination.

But kept it to himself, as the King moved on from the tasting room, to the actual production of the milk cows, being rubbed down, bathed, in some sort of oil, and fed a rye mixture, for the King to say, "That is what makes our milk taste so good." To add, "A happy cow means good milk production." Just then an older gentleman and his son came to greet the King, to say, "Your highness, to say, "Thank you for choosing Brigitte, she will make an excellent Queen."

Jack looks at the pair, to think what do they mean, an excellent Queen, the last two barely had any stamina, and Jack thought, "He could hardly wait his encounter with any of the ones he met", Jack would have to ask the King what it takes to be a good Queen?

Jack followed the King out, and past the Brunelli family, so said the sign, as they walked in, and out, and into the car, for the King had, a pint of ice cream, and a spoon, he pulled out of his coat, to offer it up to Jack, who shook his head No, as the car drove, up a hill over a bridge, to the first building, that was well protected, they got out, to unmarked building, as they were let in, and it became apparent, it was an armory, or so it seemed, it was a gun and rifle factory, everything imaginable, as it was all laid out for the King's approval, and on the end, was a hunting rifle, that bore the name of Jack Cash, as the King hands it to Jack to say, "Here Son, this is for you, a custom made 30-30, just like the one you shot in the field."

"Thank you, father", said Jack respectfully.

Taking the gun, he felt the grip, all custom crafted, it was a well built rifle, Jack set it down, as it was whisked away, and placed in custom carry case. As the King and Jack watched the array of hand guns, laid out, and this time Jack chose which one he wanted, he chose a heavy .45 cal, and in that instance, his name was carved on it, or so said engraved on it, and given back to Jack.

Meanwhile back on the prop plane, sat Bill, he buckled himself in, to look over the pre-flight, checks to hear, "Whoa, hold your horses, he isn't even on board" said Jim, looking over at the new pilot who said, and "I thought we were flying out this morning, for Geneva?"

"It doesn't work like that, just because we say were going out this morning, may mean tonight or even tomorrow, we work on Jack's schedule."

"Alright, so what shall I do until then?"

"Sit and wait, till orders come down, our last reports was Jack was seen spotted with the King of Belarus, going place to place, so I imagine, when that is through, he will be heading this way."

"Alright I get cha, can I ask you something?"

"Sure, what do you got?" said Jim.

"What do you think if I invited Jack over for dinner when we get back?"

Jim looked at Bill weirdly, to say, "What like a date?"

"Nah, not like that the Misses, wants to meet him?"

"How did she find out who you fly for?"

"I guess I told her, I was going to be assigned, for an important man."

"I wouldn't call Jack important per say?"

"Are you crazy, its all over the World what he has done, and my last transmission, was from here, so she put two and two together, so what do you think?"

"I don't know, but I do know you're on radio silence until we get to the UN, you might have given away his position."

"I hadn't thought about that, so I say oops again."

"What do you mean oops again" said Jim, looking over at Bill, to say, "Remember that hot landing I did?"

"Yeah, that was some pretty impressive flying."

"Well when you were outside I was on the sat phone to her?"

"Did you have the scrambler on?"

Bill looked over at Jim, who was motioning for it, as he showed him the side button, and then flip it on.

"Oh" said Bill.

"Nah, I think you need to keep that request under wraps, till after the UN, when the dusts settle."

Back in Belarus, in the King's village, it was the grand tour of the glass blowing shop, where the peddler, wanted to give Jack an elaborate fountain, but Jack said, "Can you present to me, at the wedding?"

"Yes, Jack, will do."

"Next was the pottery barn, where huge pots, were made, King John said, "Our workers grow vegetables out of them, on their balconies." There were royal plates, done in blue with the crest, as the merchant was ready to box some up for him as he explained the 46 day process, to make porcelain. They left to see the next building over was the royal beer factory, as King John, said "What beer did you like last night?"

Jack was careful to respond, as he went the safest route, "They were all equally fantastic."

"Fine then you shall have a pallet each."

Jack saw the huge pallet, to say, "Alright, I really enjoyed the darker over all else."

"Fine, two pallets, one dark and one mixed."

Jack held his tongue as it was no use, the King was going to give him, whatever he wanted, as another short walk, as Jack looked at his watch, for the King to say, "My son, the flight is two hours, even in your prop plane, relax, I want you to see a performance." The King led Jack in, to a sole seat next to the King, in a very deluxe red felted chair, in the center, he waited for the King to sit, then Jack sat, as a woman came out to announce, "Springtime in the King's village." And with that, the curtain went up, and instantly, there was all kinds of performers, trees in the background, and then the singing began, some famed, opera star, Eleanor Vitol-Sky. She was by far outstanding at holding the notes, and then an Italian famous Tenor, Benjamin Waite, was her partner, as the two played out a scene, as the princess was chosen to be the next Queen, and all came out to rejoice, or so said his phone, as he was recording the whole performance. It ended quickly, as Jack waited for the King to do something, he didn't so Jack stood and clapped loudly, much to the surprise of King John, and he then got up and followed suit, an clapped, as Jack whistled, they bowed, as the curtain went down. Jack stopped the over celebration as he looked at the King, who smiled, to say, "Come Son, there is more, King Richard, of Latvia, introduced this next thing that brought us out of the middle ages and into the present, as the King showed Jack, the lake, to say, "It goes down 200 feet, and holds enough water, to last forever, at the top, is a hydroelectrically generator, that powers all of the village, and some of Minsk, they will be paying us, forever, a left turn walking the King said, "This is King's street, on the left are offices, on the right is the business owners, they live up stairs and work below, even the Guards live here with their wives, children."

"Speaking of wives, when do I get to see mine?"

"That's just it; you won't not until the courtship, where you will choose one lady to be Queen."

"I thought you said I could have multiple wives?"

"Nah, what I was referring to was the amount of mistress's you can have."

"Aright, so where are the Mistress's?"

"That's just it, after, you decide on the Queen, the rest make up her helpers, and if she were to past, then the next one would be chosen."

"Ah I see now, so where are you at?"

"Unfortunately, the last one, I didn't know, the rules, and chose three, the first one died of an overdose, and the second she went over the cliff."

"Tragic, are you aware of the circumstances?"

"No, but it became apparent who would be the winner, so that's how I'm stuck, but lets talk about you, it was a good choice my son, by selecting who you did, the diversity will keep them all guessing, especially the two Russian ladies, both extremely loyal, and extremely trust worthy, those were an excellent choice, the only wild card, was the peasant girl, our chamber maid, how did you know of her?"

"She came to me for a relaxing bath."

"Really tell me more?" said the King enthusiastically.

"Not much to tell, she washed my back, then my front, and put me to bed, and I went to sleep."

"Really." They both saw a cheese shop, and Jack held the door open for the King, as he went in, and for Jack to see one of his choices, behind the counter was Brigitte, a huge smile on her face, as she called out, "Mamma, its King John, and Jack."

With in moments she was gone, for an older lady, who said, "This one was aged 90 days, care to sample, as she cut a piece for the King, then Jack, out of the corner of his eye, he saw, Brigitte, spying on him.

The King spread his hands out, to say, "What would you like to take my son?"

Jack saw that their was each a sample laid out, and then cut some to put on a wafer, to taste. Jack closed his eyes to savor it.

Back at the hanger, there was a knock, Casey, opened it up to say, "Yes, what can we do for you?"

"We have a delivery to Jack Cash, courtesy of King John of Belarus, will you sign here." Casey did so, to swing the door open, to see a tall cargo truck, waiting to back up, so he hit the hanger door, for Bill to say, "I guess were close to leaving?"

Jim got up to say, "What the hell?" and went back, to the ramp, to say, "Clark, Casey", and stood there, to see the pallet, on the ramp gate go down, and wheeled to the ramp, as they went like clockwork. With Jim having his hands in the air, he said, "Who signed for all of this?"

Casey stood with his hands out, as the truck, lifted the gate up, and quickly sped off.

Casey lowered the hanger door, as Jim looked over the cargo, to say, "Now what?", easily seeing the ten foot high, by 6x6 wasn't going to fit, both Clark and Casey were stumped as well. Next was Bill on the end, to say, "You better lock that up, or...."

"No, no one will touch this do I make myself perfectly clear?" said an angrily Jim, to add, "Find a way to get it all on, and wrap it up?"

Jim calmed down as him and Bill made it back, to the flight cabin, for Bill to say, "One time our CO got a horse for a gift."

"Enough Bill your not helping out here."

"I was just saying".....

Back at the cheese shop, Jack was in heaven, as he literally said, "I'll take the whole thing." The tour was lasting well into the noon, and the cheese did do some of the work, thinking back at the beer, only to get into the car, as it was following them as the King said, "Yes you are now running out of time." To the last place, it was a castle of sorts, as Jack exited, though a rather large wooden door, into the main field where the royal guards were fighting as if it was back in the middle ages, and off to his left, was a giant, an impressive man, who the King said, "He is the brother of your Porter, his name is Ivan, he used one whack, and literarily, knocked down two people, he is fierce."

He was summoned to the King, for an audience, then he was the most soft spoken a gentle Giant, his hands were huge, everything was enormous, as the King joked, tell him, "Ivan, how much food you consume everyday?"

"Four chickens, twenty biscuits, gravy, and two pounds of beans, I like BBQ", he said in his best polite English, but Jack could see the Giant's hands trembling, as he couldn't stand still, for the King to say, "Is everything all set?"

"Yes, ready" said the Giant.

"Son, care to see our fortune?" said the King, as Jack followed, inside, through a secret passage, and down old steps, past the rushing water, of the spring, an above, to a door, it opened, to show an immaculate room, easily 100x100, with support pillars, and immaculate painted floor, where tables were all laid out from diamonds, rubies, sapphires, and turquoise, and over in a case, was the crown jewels, as the King said, "This dates back to the days of Charlemagne, we Bella-Russians rode with the famed King, and many generations ago my great father was presented this, I hope you'll keep it in the family?"

"Yes, its magnificent", said Jack looking around at all the wealth, but Jack thought, "Where is the money or gold, as that is what he collects," as the King said, "Wait there is more," as they were led to a highly secure door, it opened and the radiance was immense bricks of silver, platinum, and in the back gold for the King to say, "We have a private mine, we are mining this out, what do you think?"

"Impressive, can we go see the mine?"

"Not now were running late, care to see what's behind that door?"

Jack nodded with anticipation, as the door was opened, and he saw literally pallets on pallets of 1000 dollar bills, for Jack to say, "You print your own money too?"

"No, this is the results of our trade agreement with the government, one billion dollars a month, and over there is your share half of all of this, what do you think?" Jack was stunned, as he went back to steady himself, thinking of the briefcases, as the cave kept going back further, as he turned to say, "So from this day forward, I'll receive 500 million a month?"

"No, that number is not right, as the King turned, to some weird looking guard, to say, "The number is closer to 1.6 billion, go ahead take some for the trip, how shall we mail it to you?"

Jack was now beginning to realize how monumental the, mistake he made, he was clearly overwhelmed, as he heard,

"From this day forward, your whole life will change, and at the center of this change, You'll have a Queen to sit beside you and rule over this very free land, and all thanks to you". Jack touched a stack, literarily 100 thousand dollars, and carried it out, to pass by the King to say, "Thank you."

"You don't have to thank me, it is only fair, so I sent a pallet on as your team should receive it anytime, allow me to show you the upstairs rooms, and then the Royal stables."

Back at the hanger, another horn blew, just as Black ops had just finished all the beer, when another knock on the door, this time it was Clark, who answered it, saw the truck, quickly signed off on the ticket, to yell, "More incoming."

The hanger door went up, and the truck pulled in, as a guy went to the switch to set the door back down, as then the cargo door went up, as the team was eagerly awaiting what was next, as instantly the whole bay, smelled of cheese, each looking at the other, but the pallet, was smaller, as Clark, yelled, "Jim we need your help?"

Both Jim, Brian and Bill, saw all the cheese, Jim, saw that the troops section was where they stored all the beer, for Jim to get an idea, "Break that pallet in-half, and store against Jack's cabin, as the Black ops team did that onto see another one, of equal size or smaller, for Jim, to think this out, and then he saw the pallet, and motioned for Brian to roll it out, and that pallet, took its place, for one of them to say, "who is in charge?

Jim stepped forward, to say, "I am, what do you have?"

"This next pallet is for your eyes only?"

Jim stepped off the plane to see what was going on, for the guy to say, "They must be blindfolded, before we proceed."

Jim shook his head, to say, "You heard the man, scarf over your eyes, all of you, you too Brian, have Bill stay in the cockpit."

Once everyone was secure, the pallet was wheeled out, to the edge, as Jim, was beside himself, as he said 'How much?"

"Ssh, quiet please, you sign?"

Jim's hands were shaking, as he saw the bottom figure, 1.6 billion of dollars, as he leaned up against, it for them to say, "Are you going to take it?"

Jim, put his hands up in the air, to say, "How, I got to fly out, in an hour, to add, "Will there be anymore gifts?"

"Yes, but at a later date, according to your planes configuration, you should be able to get everything in."

In that instance, Jim knew what he needed to do, the crane, system, to see the other man smile, to say, "I knew you would figure it out, hint it weighs what his car weigh's."

Jim was moving fast, as he chained it down, then using a horseshoe clamp, he controlled the gantry crane out, it lifted, and slowly at a time, until it cleared the roof, and then was walked to the ceiling, able to have the car still come in, as he secured the sides, and to the rear, he used a reverse tarp, to hid it as he used strapping tape with his two helpers to conceal it, and just like that they were gone and Jim was smiling when he said, "Take off your scarf's.

Meanwhile back at the royal guard's house, Jack saw that the lookout could see his palace and that of the King's. Next was the royal stables where Jack got to say good bye to his new stallion, Parthian Stranger, and they were off, out side to the car, where the King said, "I hope I haven't kept you waiting too long?"

"Nope, and if it were up to me, I'd stay here for the rest of my life."

"Sorry Son, it doesn't work like that, you have to wait till my passing, before you can move in, and however, your princess's will occupy the palace till its ready for the wedding."

Jack got in with the King, as the car took off, back to the King's palace, for which he said, "I have but one last surprise." The car pulled up and they both got out seeing Michelle carried the box, thinking would it fit into the trunk or not, she too was walking funny, from the two attempts to warm him up, it was no use, the car opened, and Michelle placed the box in the trunk, the big cat was asleep. Jack set his gifts in, and closed the trunk, and slid in carefully, as Michelle did the same, he was ready to get out of there, as he pulled out, and there was King John, standing in the way, arms crossed, not looking well.

Jack stopped the car, and turned it off and got out, he knew it was happening; it was time for a showdown.

"My boy, where are you going, without saying goodbye to me and my wife, come in we need to talk."

Jack slowly went out of the garage, while Michelle went to touch the radio, and instantly she went to sleep.

Inside the house was a little different, down at the table was Queen Mary, looking so ever refreshed, she stood, then embraced Jack with a hug and a kiss on the cheek, to say, "Thanks for a wonderful night, I had to take some speed to wake up, you wore me out."

"Now Jack, we have one last present for you, come with us" said King John, as he led them out, this time, it was to the west, where the land had many trees, a single path opened up, thank god he tied it to his leg, or he would not have survived, actually he thought it was going down, some.

They entered the forest, he was thinking, "No backup, where is Michelle?", he went to his phone, to view the inside of his car, only to see Michelle was sleeping, as some video replayed it, then he went on, across the bridge, to a huge building, up some stairs, looking out, thinking at any time he was going to be ambushed, and ready to pull his gun, then up the stairs he went, to a clearing, where the royal guards, were, easily outnumbering him one hundred to one, when the trumpet blew, as the doors open, from the writing on the sign it meant execution, then he stepped in, to see the guillotine, in all its glory, there he stood, by himself, instantly he went soft, much to his relief, he was scared out of his life, waiting for them to rush him, when the King said something, and a huge wall turned, and spun, to show two women, naked, apparently beaten, one had an excellent physique, he recognized her as Blythe, and next to her, her pretty face, showed a broken nose, both her breasts were slashed, her lower body mutilated, she was dripping blood.

The King spoke, "This two women were plotting against you my son, one is a respected member of the parliament, and the other a so-called spy, who stole my ring, which she still wears, normally, under this circumstance, we would turn her over to the cities police, to send back to the United States, but after our conference with the UN, they told us if their was any doubt of treason, against any agent of the UN, the punishment maybe dealt with at our digression, like the Americans have given you the ability to kill for no particular reason, well my present to you, is to give both of these women, our justice, and lets begin."

Jack wanted to show pity on Blythe, but she had crossed the line, "What a shame?" he thought, a specimen of near flawless beauty, and as she was cut loose, she fought, until a blow from Ivan now the executioner, who held a huge mallet, she was bleeding, from the head, her pretty face, was slightly crushed in, as he changed to a huge axe, the guards placed her hand on the block, then in one swing, it popped off, for the King to pick up.

"This was barbaric, Blythe was dying, as the executioner, pulled her by the hair, under the edge and the King positioned himself, at the lever, to say "Jack my son, come over here and I will allow you to do it."

Jack wandered, slowly over, and took the position, where the King was; Jack forgave her, and all of her misgivings and secret dealings, and pulled the lever.

Blythe's head popped off, and into a basket, her blood drained out. All was quiet, when Ivan the executioner, picked up her lifeless body, and carried it out. The King was playing with her left hand, and twisted his ring off, then discarded her hand. Jack looked up, as the executioner came back in, and cut down, Ingrid, she was half dead, and disgraced, nothing had to be said, Jack knew this was the old way to kill someone, who wronged the Royals, even for himself, who felt maybe he should confess, or never come back here again, as the executioner, pulled her over, to the guillotine, and inserted her hands, and locked them down, Jack knelt down, to look at her, she opened her mouth, to show him, that her tongue was cut out, Jack went back as other were laughing, Jack stood up to hear silence, as he stood, he released the lever, it went down, and pop, off went her head, that moment he would cherish, it was real, hardcore, and it was something he had never seen before, or maybe ever will, the total loss of power to do anything.

"Come my son, it is done, I hope you like our present to you?"

"Yes, thank you, I didn't know what to do with those traitors."

"My men told me of your encounter with the terrorist, and how Ingrid led you down there, we want to assure you that your next visit, we will be better prepared to handle those who want to kill you, and have your palace ready, so lets walk together, I want to let you know, I've had our financial team, assess our assets, and you are the primary beneficiary, as you know by now, my wife is unfertile, yet she is a wonderful companion, I hope at some point, you'll take care of her, till she dies."

"Absolutely."

"I knew I could trust you to do that, Jack you're an honorable man, and we welcome you into our family, and are delighted that your considering to marry our Ana, she is a dynamic women, too bad, she is as infertile as her sister, too bad, there both so young, at least there won't be no reservations on unlimited sex, so Son how was she?"

"What?" asked Jack?

"I know all about it, she asked me, I told her, if I had a mistress, then she could take a lover, if only if it was discreet."

"So you set me up?"

"Yes, Son, that's what fathers do" said the King.

That resonated with Jack, as his own father once said that to him. Jack tried to savor that moment to hear one more, "Son, I will always be here for you, for any reason, as for your future wealth, well lets say, a trust fund is set up in your name, and you'll have access to it, as well from now on, I'd like one of the royal guards to accompany you to the council, as we know you have a slot available?"

Jack thinks to himself, "Who knows all of this, so who gets to come, I like the Porter, I think his name was John."

"Do I get to choose" said Jack, as the King had a firm grip around his neck as the two walked together.

"Sure who do you have in mind?"

"My porter his name is John."

"I know his name, he is very trusted, but I can't allow him to go, he is the Queen's bodyguard, anyone else?"

"Yeah, how about Ivan the Giant?"

"Good choice, yes I will allow Ivan to go with you."

"That suits me well" said Jack.

"Yes, Ivan came to us, as a lad, to help defend off our lands from the Pols, he was a warrior, now he teaches combat to our guard and others, he will keep you safe, while you are there without your weapons, his one punch will do what that mallet did, he is fierce."

The two made it back to the parking garage and the car that was off, for the King to say, "Don't be a stranger around here; we shall see you next at the wedding?"

"I hope so "said Jack, as he hugged the King, which took him by surprised, and returned the favor. They broke the embrace, to shake hands, as the metal door slid open, Jack waved to him, as he drove by, then took a right instead of a left, and down the driveway to the royals guard, where one man stood, cleaned up, dressed in royal red outfit, Jack stopped, got out, and to the other side, where he lifted up Michelle and placed her back into the suitcase, and zipped it up.

The Giant got in, the car shifted for his weight, and then Jack slid in, and off they went.

Jack noticed the turn off, as Ivan kept quiet, holding his bag, on his lap. The seat was all the way back. Jack was driving, and exited at the airport's cargo entrance, a gate guard, stopped him, but was waved on, Jack saw the hanger, that was open, as his earlier call gave them a heads up, he was about to be there, as he pulled in, it was all hands on deck.

Jack and Ivan exited as the doors swung open, on the ramp stood Lisa, to say, "Sorry about Blythe?"

"She got what was coming to her, there was nothing we could do?" said Jack.

"Looks like you have some large help."

"He is my bodyguard for the council?"

"So you plan on making no changes for the three weeks, come on in lets talk."

CH 13

Meeting of the Spies

Two members of the strike team jumped back to the sound of a screech, for Lisa said, "What do you have there?"

"It's a gift from a Queen, don't fret I'll have Ivan get it", Jack turned to see that he had the bag, from the back seat, to say "Ivan put that down gently, and bring the box, in please."

He nods as others watch him, as he pulls the box up all they could see was the large eyes, and it appeared to look like a lynx. Ivan ducked as he climbed up and into the cargo bay. As did Jack to say, "Hey Jim what's up with the pallet in the middle of the bay, bout took my head off, as Jack saw the cellophane wrapped, beer, stacked up, and the smell of cheese was intoxicating, he stopped at what appeared to be a box of things, to see Mitzi who embraced him, to say, "Thanks for that heads up, half of those men had forty percent radiation poisoning, you saved their lives.", to lead Jack in to the room, and as Lisa steps in shuts the door.

"Several things for you, Clarance reported to Mitzi that he has followed Varfolomey to a castle in Polatsk, north of the King's land, although there is radiation everywhere, is waiting till you get back from the council." said Lisa.

"Both Mike and Mark is in the flight cabin, securing some ground travel" said Mitzi.

"Like what, I'll just drive the car in."

"Sorry you can't do that, it's too hilly, with fierce ravines." said Lisa.

"Then I will drop in."

"And your way out?"

"Simple, just yank me up afterwards."

"No I don't like that" said Lisa.

"I agree, with you Lisa, just you by yourself, no, you'll jump with the strike team, and travel with you as your eyes and ears" said Mitzi.

"I agree with that" said Lisa, to add, "Listen to your ground officer."

Jack had his back to them to say, "You're making me out to be some coward, why don't you let me go now, and skip this council all together" said Jack taking a cup of coffee, with a wedge of lemon.

"You simply can't, your obligated to attend, as asked by the UN, besides after the council, things may change" said Lisa.

"How so" asked Jack.

"Well each year, they have this meeting, to update and determine each spies ranking."

"What's my ranking?"

"As of now, your number twelve, but all that could change, based on who accompanies you to this conference."

"How so?"

"Well, most of the spies have a reputation, and they tend to bring an up incomer, and it will define you to bring the next great spy, that's why we had who we had."

"Alright, put down Michelle, Trixie, and Jill, down and I'll stick to the plan, but I need to decide what to do with Ivan, and my new pet."

"Well I'm sure you can get an exemption, and for the pet, I'll watch her" said Mitzi.

"How do you know it's a girl?"

"What woman wouldn't give you a girl?"

"Good point" said Jack.

Over the intercom, was announced, Lisa all is accounted for including the two wanderers, shall we take off?"

"Yes, we need to go" she yelled.

"Next I need you to reassure Jim you think you have faith in his backup abilities" said Lisa.

"As far as I'm concern, Jim can have this job for as long as he wants it, I don't know where the idea, that came from, I trust him, if he is honest with me in the future and not lie to me, I know he was just acting on orders he received."

"Your right Jack, we thought you needed sleep, it was Erica and I idea."

"Well that should all change, now that Mitzi's here."

"That's true, she is your ground support, as the plane moved, Jack sat next to Mitzi, and Lisa took the seat, as the plane taxied out, then, picked up speed, and it shuddered, inching up and lifted off as the wings went back and forth.

Jack lay back, as both Mitzi and Lisa told him how it was going to go at the retreat.

Outside the door sat Ivan, the Giant, next to him sat the very small Michelle, Brian, was in his cage cleaning her sniper rifle, the strike team, were securing the gear, and sat back as Casey, was loading the air suit and canister with Morris and Bauer, Jill was up in the galley, and Gia, Art and Brooks, were cleaning the used field equipment.

Mark and Mike sat in the flight cabin, on the communications gear, working the communications board.

Inside Jack's cabin, Lisa said "During your time in there, you may not need the strike team, what would you say, If I took them to two weeks of team training, to train with the Rangers."

"Sure, actually, they can stay in the US; all I need is a plane to drop me in, after this council."

"I hear what you're saying, but everyone around you is your support team."

"Well give them time off, let them go see their families, I'm sure you need some rest away from me" he said to Mitzi.

"Never, I'm here to the very end."

"And look what happen to you, you nearly died, really, take the time off, and take everyone with you, so I need to leave everything behind, that's fine, I'll leave the gun with Brian, and my phone with Tami, and my watch with Jim, what about my wallet?"

"I'll hold onto that" said Mitzi.

Jack hands it to her, as she pulls out his ID card, and hands it back to him. he sees the clothes neatly folded up, that Mitzi got up and hands it to him, for Jack to say to Mitzi, can you have the team come in to include Brian and Jim."

Mitzi left the room, for Lisa to say "I believe each Sunday is the transfer day, and the last Sunday is graduation day, and that will be when each girl will be traded out, and anything you need will be traded out, all I can say is keep your eyes open, ears listening and your mouth shut."

There was a knock on the door, "Come in", said Jack.

One by One they came in, to file in, along the door, they stood, as Jack saw, Mitzi, Trixie, Mark, Mike, Jared, Roxy, Jesse, Brian, Tami and Jim. Jack began, to say, "A lot of speculation, on what is going on, and from what I know is nothing, were all in foreign territory, so what I'd like for you to do, is go take a break, take a three weeks vacation.

They all looked at each other, then Jim spoke up, to say "Jack, a moment, of your time."

Jack looks at him, and then says, "Alright" as he sees, Mark, Mike, Jesse, and Brian, Jared, Roxy and Trixie leave.

"I know we haven't seen eye to eye lately, but this is serious, this is where we draw the line in the sand."

"If you want to go, there's the door" said Jack.

"No that's what this is about" said Jim. to add, "A while back I was tasked to guard another spy, and he was pulled in every direction, then he told me and several of the team to leave and go on the vacation, and I heard he was killed, this is not about, us, our lives, or some vacation we need, our job or mission in life is to support your every need, to allow you to go do what you do." He continued by saying, "And this whole thing with the UN, is only the tip of the ice berg, a spy that is invited to be part of the council is a very high honor, and while you may not be wandering the country side, we will be there when you go in and any transfers and when you get out and where ever else you need to go."

Jack looked up at him to see his face, to say, "Are we cool?"

"Yeah, you're right, what was I thinking, we will just let it ride."

"That's what I'd like to hear; now I need, to land this plane," said Jim.

Jack watched him go, and saw only Lisa and Mitzi to say, "Alright what do you have for me?"

Jack I just got a call from the President of the UN, about your request for another room, and it was approved", said Lisa getting off the phone, to say, according to my GPS, we should be landing soon."

"Really, was it because were heading downward", said Jack jokingly.

Jack finished changing, by removing his holster, and gun. He paused at the wrist watch, to feel the plane drop down suddenly, but the room was unaffected as the lower supports adjusted to the elevation shift. And just like that they were on the ground and taxing, the plane went into a huge hanger, and found there place next to Air force One, they shut down, and dropped the ramp, the strike team with weapons drawn, surrounded the perimeter, to announce all clear."

Mitzi opened the door, for Jack, who stepped out, he saw Jim to say, "Take care of the plane and all my stuff."

Jim pulled out and shook Jack's hand, to allow him to pass", to say, "Thanks my friend", passes him to see Tami, who kept to herself, she smiles to hand him the address book, and he hands her his phone.

He sees Ivan dressed in all red, and next to him was Michelle, to say, "Ready to go?"

Jack led the three out, past the car, to see Brian, to say, "I want that rifle, before I get back?"

"It will be" said Brian.

Jack stepped down, on the ramp, to see a UN representative from the UN, to say "Do you have any weapons on you?"

Jack looked at Brian, to pull off his jacket, and then pull out two knives from his pants, and gives them all to him. For Jack, to say, "Nah, just me."

"Great, so come with me; are these two guests?"

"Yes."

"Is this your wife?"

Jack looked at him as they walked, to say, "What does it matter?"

"Well a wife is treated with dignity, whereas, like your huge friend will be lumped together with the support personal."

"Then she is my wife."

"What is her name?"

"Michelle Cash" he said with confidence, and then looked northward to see more planes, to say, "How big is this place?"

"The largest in the world at 50 football fields, that can store a complete air force, over three hundred jets from all over the world, and fifty large planes like yours." they stopped. The UN guide says, "Alright mister Cash, through this door, is for you, the next door, are for your wife, and the last door on the end is for your support guy, good luck".

Jack opened the door, only to hear, "Shouldn't you kiss your wife goodbye" said Michelle waiting.

Jack turned to bend down, as she grabbed his neck and kissed him, they broke apart to say, "Well I guess I'll see you later?"

"I hope so."

Just then as it seems the guy with the watch box appeared, he goes to Jack's wrist, set's the pin, and then unfastens the watch, he takes it and walks the other direction, just as the doors slid open.

Jack stepped into a room, and the door closed shut, a bright light was on, to hear over the speaker, undress completely, then standing with your arms apart, on the foot marks."

Jack waited, then heard, "There is a locker behind the mirror, where your new clothing is at."

Jack opened the mirror to see, shoes, socks, pants, t-shirt and a short sleeved shirt, he dressed, to hear, "Now pick up your wallet only, which I can see is on the ground, and take the door on the left."

Jack did so, and stepped into the hallway, then to the door, where he set down his exposed wallet, for a older woman, to say, "Take out your ID and any credit cards, then slid your wallet into the evidence bag" he did as he was told, to hear, "Did you leave your phone in your clothing?"

"No, just a phone book."

"We will get that to you; in addition we will dry clean your clothes."

"Don't bother, their waterproof, and steam proof, just be careful" said Jack liking his position.

"Spies, their deadly" she said to another, to add, "That's why we older girls work here, young girls wouldn't have a chance." she scanned, Jack's ID, to gather info, and print out a UN badge, then she scanned, his two credit cards, only to see the lines going way past one billion dollars, she ran over to pull the plug.

"Something wrong?" asked Jack.

"Nah, then whispered, this is one of those trick cards that acquires information then blow up our machine, just issue him a one hundred million dollar line, I'll need to get some lead sleeves."

Jack watched them scramble and thought, "I hope this gets better, and its nice being a spy, wonder how Michelle is making out, not to mention, Ivan the Giant."

"Sir here you go" said the older woman.

Jack takes the two cards to hear, "The black one is your assign credit limit, and the blue one is your per diem card, use it at the commissary, shopping mall and food court."

"Where is all that?" asked Jack, putting everything in his pocket, and went out of the door. He looked back at the door he went through, was it the same he entered, he continued west, down a set of stairs, to a left turn, where windows showed a view of the lake below, he followed it down a set of stirs, to the west, then to a tee, left was to the UN and right was to the defense squadron. Jack went to the left, following the bank of windows and the lake below, he went down another flight, to a guard station, where his pass let him go, into a huge open bay, behind him he heard, "You can tell when the super spies are here."

"Haws that?"

"All the pretty girls, the hottest models, Queens and princess's, these are the rich of the riches" said the UN representative.

Jack continued on, seeing Ivan and Michelle, sitting together, dressed in matching clothing, a light blue, to say, "What are you waiting on?"

"It's suppose to be a debriefing, but were close to lunch, so they asked us to wait here, what about you?" asked Michelle.

"I don't know" said Jack.

Back in the hanger, Lisa and Mitzi were talking in the flight cabin, to hear, "Lisa Curtis, this is the President."

"Who is going to answer that?" said Bill.

"I will", said Jim, "Yes Mister President this Is Jim."

"Yeah, Jim, I was told you just landed, may I have a word with Jack Cash?"

"Sorry Mister President, he already went in."

"I told Miss Curtis, I wanted to talk with him, before he went in."

"I don't know where she is at, what message can I pass on to him."

"That I would like to talk with him."

"Will do, I'll go get him" said Jim, who went to the door to hear, "Can you do that?" asked Lisa.

"To bail you out of this mess, It will be my pleasure" said Jim getting up, and passing them, down the ramp, to see Casey, to say, "Round up the strike team, and lets get filled up, and begin to clean out the back, some of you go in and clean out the armory", Jim was on a mission, as he hit the middle door, walking, he remembered that place somewhat, as the spouse door, the least of all resistance, he went through to hear, "Remove your clothing?"

"Visitor, for Jack Cash, passes a message, where can I find him it's an emergency."

"Lower level, place the ID badge around your neck, you have five minutes, Jim."

Jim smiled for the camera, as the door buzzed open, he was on the move, down the double stairs, to the left, to the security guards, to hear, "Wait", over to Jack, to say, as the two guards grabbed him.

"Leave him alone growled an enormous voice", said Ivan getting up.

"Alright, sit down Ivan, let Jim go", the guards released, to hear, "The President wishes to talk with you."

"Well lets go" said Jack as Jim lead the way, Jack was right behind him, up the stairs, to a sign that said, Exit to the hanger, through the squadron, Jim walked with purpose, and like he knew the place well. They popped out into the fighter wing, high performance jets, as Jim was trotting with Jack, they turned the corner, to see Air Force one, Jim went to the platform, waited till Jack got on, up it went, to awaiting platform, and two secret service guys, waved them in, and escorted them into a conference room, where the doors closed. Jack looked over at the bottled water, on Ice, and went to it, when the door slid open, and the President motioned for Jim to leave, he went where the President came from.

Jack was thinking which one, to reach out and hear, "Take one, the President won't mind."

Jack grabbed one, turned to see President George White, who came to him and embraced him, to say, "You're doing one heck of a job, I wish, my staff had the same enthusiasm as you do, so do you have everything you need?"

"The water" said Jack.

"Sure take the whole thing I don't care, listen your doing such a good job, that I feel they the UN will make you one of its top agent."

"You sound somewhat disappointed by that?"

"No not really, I just hate losing you."

"You won't, I'm moving to Washington D C after all this."

"Really I wasn't aware of that, I was under the impression, you had enough, and you like to retire."

"Nah, I was disappointed in who Lisa sent me, for a partner."

"It doesn't have to be like that, you have the authority to hire who ever you want and make as your partner, actually, your never been assigned to go anywhere, you just do it, and uncover, that terrorist cell, and along the way, your reputation is making terrorist flee, and your up coming marriage to the Queen of Latvia is all the buzz, not to mention, Queen Ana, has just signed a 250 oil rig deal for our country, thanks to you."

"Thanks, you can always call me" said Jack.

"Nah, I really can't, but I know you have your heart into whatever you do, and when you're in Washington DC come to the White House, in the meantime, I'll coordinate with Jim, about a home for you and your family and the Queen, thanks for putting my mind at rest."

"Not a problem, my plan after this, Jack stops as he looks at the Commander in Chief, putting his finger to his lips.

"Alright, after this program I'll be in Washington DC and thanks for the water" said Jack on his way out, as the door slid open, and Jack walked out, as Jim walked in to see the President, to hear, "So how is it going, any problems with Jack?"

"Nah, he is on course, and were fine, except...."

"Except what Jim?"

"Can you take Miss Curtis home with you?"

"I thought she went home with your Jet, and Erica?"

"She would be better than her."

"Well I had no idea, she was hanging around, come lets go visit her."

Jim was at the door, as the President went out, and took the platform down with the secret service, across the concrete, to the ramp of the plane, to say, "Really Jim you need a more modern plane."

"Nah, I love this type besides I need a slower one for lift offs and pick ups."

"I'd love to see your training session" said the President.

"Anytime after we get back", as Jim hit the ramp first to announce, when, the President, to say, "Hush, I want to surprise them", the President entered first, to the different smells, he remarked, and ducked his head, to say, "What gives, it smells of beer and cheese, and what is above my head?"

"All gifts from the King of Belarus" said Jim.

the strike team were washing the car, they dropped what they were doing, as they all came to a stand still, as he past, he saw Ramon, to say, "Son grab your gear", Ramon got up and went back, he saw Trixie in the galley with Jill, to say, "Hi", Trixie stopped in her tracks, as he popped his head into the flight cabin, to say, "What are you watching?"

Both Mark and Mike turned in their chairs to see, and then got up, to say, "How may we help you, Sir?"

"Which one of you guys was the one who went to the brothel?"

"It was me, sir, said Mike."

"Ah Mike, do you know how much it costed the government, for wanting to be an agent?"

Mike was hesitant to speak,

The President got into his face, to say, "One point six million, do you still want to be an agent?"

"Yes sir."

"Your lucky to have made it out, did you know that fortress is where the Marine held out during the invasion of the Bay of Pigs?"

"No I didn't."

"If I ever hear subordination like that again, I'll have you shot myself, your aware, Jack Cash is my representative, and where ever he goes he is treated as if it were me, so next time I hear about someone taking his name that isn't him, well it will be their death, where is the trouble maker?"

Both scared men look at the President, who says, "I'm talking about Miss Curtis" said a somewhat displeased President.

"She, maybe is in Jack's cabin?" said Jim, as he banged on the door.

"Do you have a key?"

"No Mister President, usually when Jack isn't here it's used for storage."

"Get this keyed up, if Jack is here, he can dead bolt it, but all others its off limits."

"Yes sir" said Jim.

Jim continued to knock, as the President stepped back to see the door open, inward, Jim, stood back, to allow the President to go first to hear, "Your too soft on Jack, you need to keep a leash on him, to be successful." He entered as Lisa turned holding a cup of coffee, stirring it, she passed by the President, to sit down, as Mitzi froze, to point to her, Lisa saw the President to stand, he stepped in, and slid the door shut, to say, "You stay right there Mitzi, so what are you doing in my super spies room, wow what's in that box?'

"It's a present from the Queen" said Mitzi, defiant.

"I believe, I instructed you to go home, after the Belarus capture, why are you still here, Miss Curtis?"

"We have an agent in the field."

"Who is that?"

"Clarance."

"We know about him, AWAX is tracking him, we just dropped him a ground force team, with delta force members, so how does he figure in why you need to be here, in my opinion, your bossing Jack around, not to mention, your drinking his coffee, to me that seems like if you were on Air Force One, you would be in my room, drinking my coffee, perhaps watching my TV."

"No sir" said Lisa, defending herself.

"Then why are you in here, look at the bed, I doubt Jack had slept in it, he just left the palace, yes we track his every move, and we know about that agent who flipped, it was the Rangers that caught her, and allowed a CIA operative to give her to you, I know all about your spy club, and that is fine, but if I hear about anymore defective agents it will be your last move, you know what, your through, grab your stuff, and get on Air Force One, your going back with us."

They watch her pull some stuff from the cabinets, then open the door, and walk out.

"I hope that isn't you in that bed?"

"No sir, I'm here looking after his pet."

"Let's see it" said the President who lifted it up to set it on the cabinet, to look at the beautiful hissing cat, to say, "That looks like a lynx, do you see its eyes?"

"Yeah, she doesn't like men, I've had her out."

"Really, what do you feed it?"

"A pound of beef and bones."

"Where did you get that?"

"It came from the Queen, why do you ask."

"Well if you plan on being here for three weeks, that's a lot of beef, how about I take her with us, and I will have our vet, give it a complete exam and shots, and quarantine."

"You're the boss."

"I am, but were talking about Jack's pet, what do you think?"

He said respectfully, to add, "You know him better than anyone and your back in command, which is where I like it."

"Thank you sir, I try, I'd say go ahead and take her it will be one less thing we have to worry about here."

"I will, and where is the beef?"

"Locked up in the cage."

"Hold on, said the President, as he went out, to see the secret service had doubled, and escorted Lisa and Ramon out., to see the armory cage, and a man at the new freezer, looking at the royal beef, to hear, "Soldier, begin to unload that beef, and have your team carry them over to Air Force One."

"Yes Mister President" said Brian.

Jack finished harassing the older secretaries, in the intake room, as he was going back to the food court that was open for business, all kinds of different people filled the food court, and a lot of them were pretty girls so he thought, but he had a very faithful Michelle, Jack stood in line as with others, until a guy with a clip board came up to him, to say, "Mister Cash, this is not your area, please follow me, and your party.

Jack, Michelle, and Ivan, went through a secured door, to a whole new surroundings, warm and tinted lights, past a few rooms, to the entrance, to say, "This is your mess, you can eat anytime, there is a chef on hand 24/7, to include room service. After lunch we will all meet in room one, at 3 pm, Michelle led the group in, to the front of the line, to see the hand written menu board, to hear, "These are all on the special's including the regular menu" he said pointing to the huge menu book."

Michelle was undecided, as Jack said, "I'll have turkey club, on whole wheat, and the works on it."

"I'll have what he is having" said Ivan totally out of place, Jack led Ivan down to the salad station, grabbed a bowl, and took everything in small amounts, so did Ivan, where this was new to him. Behind them was still Michelle, undecided; at the end was a big woman, who said, "Swipe your blue card."

"I'll pay for my team."

"Doesn't work like that sir, everyone pays for themselves, except for room service, she said in a negative sort of way. Jack walked around her, and took his platter, a mile high packed sandwich, complete with an array of sauces, in little cups, a sliced pickle and chips, to the drink station, where as he took four glasses, and filled up two with chocolate milk, and the other whole milk, Ivan did the same, they past several top spies, to sit in a booth. Ivan took the seat across from Jack, literally taking up the whole space, Jack watched as he took his time, tasting each different dressing, then laughing to say, "Just pour it over, like this" Jack shows him what to do, next to them was over ten different kinds of condiments, he grabbed a herb only shaker, for his salad, which, he added Balsamic vinegar. Jack cut this huge sandwich in half, when Michelle finally showed up, with a small bowl of soup and a small salad, and a diet pop, for Jack, to say, "That was it?"

"Yeah, so many choices, I don't how you do it?"

"It's easy, just order what you want, the trick is knowing what you like, look around, there is a diverse of people in here, and if they don't have what your looking for, well next time they will."

Michelle slid in next to him, while others were looking at her, as Jack watched them, thinking, "Spies which one is the best?"

Back in the hanger, the strike team and the rest of the support team was escorted to the Squadron's mess and convenience area, where rooms were provided, and unlimited food was available. The strike team did everything together, as Casey was the clear leader, with Paul said, "Hey Casey looks like you have an admirer."

Casey looked over his shoulder to see the guy, to say, "Nah he's not my type."

They all laughed, as he came over, to say, "Hello, I'm Gregory and I'm with the UN advisors, what do you guy's do?"

They all look at Casey to answer, he looks back to say, "Were on a peacekeeping mission."

"Ooh undercover, that's cool, is this whole team?" he said looking at Jill, who was quiet, and eating her food.

"Yeah, this us, we do everything as a team."

"Cool, cool, say how you like would to do some UN training, were going out in the field, to set markers and we could sure use some help?"

"How long do you think it will take?"

"Oh with your help two hours top" said Gregory. Smiling.

"I don't know, Greg, let me ask the team, with a show of hands, who wants to get some exercise?"

Everyone raised their hands, for Casey, to say, "Looks like you have some volunteers."

"Meet me here in an hour."

"Will do" said Casey, as he dialed up Jim to wait then say, "The team is busy the next three hours, if you need us just call."

"Well, I just got news that there is a field exercise on Monday and it would be nice to have you out there to give him support."

"Were way ahead of you."

"What do you mean?" asked Jim.

"We were asked to assist the UN to go out there and set up markers."

"This is excellent, you go and get close to them and maybe will be able to support Jack on the ground." Said Jim.

Casey closed up his phone to say, "Looks like were in, finish up, sounds like Jim has got an idea for us."

The team waited till everyone was done, then walked back together, in a tight formation, with Casey calling the cadence, to the ramp of the plane. They broke apart to go up inside, to see that the car, was under a heavy blanket, sown to the deck, for Casey to hand Jim a sandwich, to say, "If you ever want to go we can watch the plane."

In between bites, Jim said, "Who was he?"

"How do you know it was a guy?"

"All the advisors are men and the women are on the inside."

"Oh, nice to know" said Casey.

As Jim led them over to the cage to say, "Brian lets see that homing beacon."

"How do you know what it is, their going to do?"

"This isn't my first rodeo, Casey, this first challenge according to my inside source, told me, that they are going to be dropped from an airplane and glide back to home base, with this device, someone has to climb the highest tree, and affix it to the top."

"I get it, you want us to attach that, at the drop zone closest to the base, and somehow get on that team that watches over them."

"Precisely" said Jim.

"Will do, anything else?"

"Yeah, afterwards you're going to have to get it back."

"No problem, consider it done."

Gregory stood by the conference room, waiting for the others to come back, only to hear, "Do you think your plan will work?"

"Yeah, it's in the bag, and wait till you see the other one; she is hotter than the one I like."

In the background, was the cadence of Casey's voice, till they saw them, and the guy stepped in the door, and then reemerge with armful of markers on a cart. Casey stopped the formation right by them, as the other guy had his thumbs up, to his friend. Both girls were in the middle, as Casey said, "At ease", then everyone listened.

"This is what were going to do, I have a hummer outside, were going to load up, then, at each point, I'll drop off a few, there are nine of us, for three area's, that means three per zone, is it all right If I divide your troops up?"

"Go ahead" said Casey.

'Alright, I'd like you, Casey, Myself, and Paul, as team leaders, he looked at Tony, then at Spancer, to say, you can have Jill and Gia, and I'll have, Morris and Bauer, Jonny, you can have Art and Brooks, that leaves you two, Gia with Jonny, and I'll have Jill.

As they moved the stuff, Gregory asked Casey, "Why do you have girls on your team?"

"Because they deserve to be here.."

All the gear was loaded, as Casey realized, Morris had volunteered to climb to the top, so to gain control he said, "I'll drive."

"Alright, I'll sit shotgun." said Gregory.

Casey took off, as Greg led him over the runways, to the trails, and then drove three miles, to a clearing. To stop., they all got out, for Greg to say, "In each drop zone, we need to place these markers, in each of these circles, my team will start here, and the next place, drop off Jonny, and then, bring the hummer back, to pick us up, and we should be done in two hours."

Jill and Bauer worked together to off load the supplies, and see the hummer take off.

Tony handed the device to Bauer, because from what was evident this would be the closet area to the base.

Jill knew her job, was to distract Greg, while Bauer went into the woods, while Greg set the stakes, with Jill's help, Morris was off, he was a good climber, in his own right, with his gloves on, he was like a monkey in the tree.

Jill purposely, kept knocking over the marker, to Greg's frustration, her young girlish, behavior was testing him, as so she thought, and he actually loved the attention. Morris reached the near top, using a telescopic baton, to go the extra twenty feet, he could see for miles, and the lake below, the huge complex, and something else, Greg was behind Jill, Morris raced to get down as fast as he could, retracting the baton, he made later use on Greg.

Jill kept her slow pace, as they acted like to love birds, she gushed over him, and he was touching her. He showed her how to swing the sledgehammer that was till Morris showed back up, to say, "Hey what's going on here?"

"Are you alright mate?"

"Yeah, sure, just had a case of something that went right through me."

"I hope you buried it."

"I did indeed do that."

The hummer came back as they had finished, and picked them up, as Casey drove he noticed Greg looking back to see Jill, several times, till they got to Jonny's group, and picked them up, Morris gave Tony his baton back., then to the last drop zone, that Paul and Bauer had done, and were waiting, for Greg to announce "Stop here, my team and I will check out this trail, Jonny and your team the other."

Behind Greg was Jill and Morris, across the road was Tony and Gia, as Casey drove off, down the road, he came to a immediate stop, thinking, "Something fishy is going on here", as he tracked Gregory, he heard Morris yell, as Gregory was on top of Jill forcing himself on her, she fought back, using her nails across his face, as she was holding her own, when all of a sudden, Greg was quickly off of her, as he was kicked, Casey helped Jill up, to see the man on his knees, to hear Casey say, "What is going on here?"

"She attacked me; I was trying to get up?"

"Where is Morris?"

"He fell in some hole, I turned to see her attack me."

"Jill go check on Morris, as for you I don't believe a word of it."

"How can you say that?"

"Because I know her, and you're not her type."

"What type is that?"

"Who cares, she isn't yours to play around with."

"Then who is she?"

"For your purpose, she is married" said Casey.

"She had no ring on."

"Enough of that, as the bigger Tony came through the bushes like a buffalo, with the baton out, to say, "The other one is tied up, he tried to make a play for Gia."

Greg looked up to say, "So what?"

Tony couldn't control his anger, yet it was Morris and Bauer that got there to help out, holding Tony back, to hear from Greg, "Let him go let's say we fight over her."

"Fight over who" said the defiant Jill, with her arms crossed.

"For your honor."

"Your too late, it was already won."

"What by that lug, you can do much better than him."

"How is Morris?"

"He is up, now; I think he led us here."

"Tell them how you kissed me" said Greg as the men let Tony alone and draw their own knives.

"Wait, don't you want to hear the true story?"

"Tony, take Jill and the rest of the team back to the hummer, were done here.

Casey waited for them to leave, to hear, "How did you get that guy to back down?"

"It was easy, I out rank him."

"So you're her husband."

"Shut up, your lucky were not carrying, I'd shoot you myself, but I think, your gonna suffer a lot more, when Jill's husband hears how you tackled her, and forced yourself on her."

"Wait, are you gonna leave me out here?"

"Sure why not, what do you have that I need?"

"The codes to get back in."

Casey continued to walk, to hear, "I know about your device."

Casey stopped to see the guy, behind him, to say, "So what, are you talking about?"

"I know how she kept me busy, while Morris went into the bushes."

"So now your blackmailing me to get a ride back, well your right, get in, but come closer first, as Casey kicked the guy in the groin, sending him down, he bent over him, to say, "You really want to know who her husband is?"

Gregory nodded his head as he wept.

"His name is Jack Cash, super spy."

Greg wet his pants to say, "I didn't know he was here?"

"That's why were here, we work for him, and he is a phone call away, you know he has the License to kill anyone he wants for no apparent reason, so if you plan on telling someone then be prepared to feel his wrath, said Casey.

The End.